Fresh Starts

Bree's Story
Second Chances; Volume Three

A Companion to the Sweet Montana Bride Series

KIMBERLY KREY

KIMBERLY KREY

Fresh Starts

Bree's Story
Second Chances; Volume Three

A Companion to the Sweet Montana Bride Series

Alasha,

with so much

thanks,

Kimberly Krey

KIMBERLY KREY

Second Chances Series:
by KIMBERLY KREY

Rough Edges

Allie's Story

Mending Hearts

Logan's Story

Fresh Starts

Bree's Story

See Amazon.com for availability

DEDICATION

To my Boston Boo:
There's so much to love about you!
Your compassionate heart, your easy manner,
and your quick humor to name a few. But I'd
like to give particular notice to that inquisitive
mind of yours. That thirst for knowledge will
be like a good friend to you. Always nurture it,
and enjoy the gifts that it brings.

ACKNOWLEDGMENTS

Immeasurable gratitude goes to my hubby and kids. We've been weathering some unexpected storms, but we've been strengthened because of them and blessed along the way. Love you guys with every piece of my soul!

Jamie, thanks for getting me back on track and for not letting me let go.

To my Writing Group of Joy and Awesomeness: Continued gratitude for each one of you! Thanks for the reads, feedback, support, and for the many unforgettable (and slightly wild) times. I love you all so deeply.
Suzie: keep up the good fight! You are one of the loveliest, most courageous warriors I know.

To Margie Lawson, thank you for the amazing week of learning and fun in your Immersion Master Class. What a gift that was; can't wait to do it again!

Further acknowledgements: Edits by Donna Nolan, at Always ~~Write~~ Right Proofreading and Copyediting

CHAPTER ONE

Bree spun full-circle as she looked over her now vacant home. Blank walls and empty spaces that – to anyone else – would look like just another house on the street. For Bree it was different.

In the kitchen, she saw little Sophie proudly making her very first pizza. She envisioned Carter in the front room, dancing his heart out to his favorite tunes.

Her chest rose as she considered all she'd accomplished in the six years since her divorce. Running a successful daycare business from home was at the top of her list. Second only to an achievement that had taken nearly five years to master: fear-free living. Would all of it be lost to her now?

Her brother's footsteps sounded down the hall. "You about ready to go?"

Bree gulped, trapped in the mental mud of her mind. The part that held memories of her terrorized years. "Almost."

If the clock Mom gave her were still on the shelf, Bree

would hear it in the quiet moment. The absence of it held a significance all its own. One she wouldn't focus on then.

"Come here, sis." Braden draped an arm around her shoulder, pulling her in for a sideways hug.

Bree hugged him back and stepped away before she could cry, squeezing her eyes shut to trap the tears. Tears from leaving the home she loved. Leaving the only sibling she had. Leaving her very own kids.

"I wish there was a better way to ensure your safety."

His words were laced with a sense of burden that put a rock in Bree's gut.

"We just don't know what Carl Ronsberg is capable of." He glared down at the floor. "Or maybe we do."

Or maybe we do... Four words. Four words that – when used separately – were as harmless as a stray kitten. But when used with that name they were enough to shoot ice through her spine. Carl Ronsberg – the stalker she'd help put behind bars. The stalker who'd be out in just fourteen days.

Haunting images soaked into her mind like a crimson stain, spreading to her blood in a wicked flash. "Yeah." It came out in a whisper. She cleared her throat, put strength into her next words. "I still can't believe you bought that orchard house. I, I can't..." She shook her head, awed by Braden's plan to get her safely out of Montana before Ronsberg was free. A plan that would let them test the stalker-infested waters while she stayed in a place off the Oregon Coast. A home Braden purchased just after the scumbag was sentenced five years ago. "I really appreciate you letting me live there for..." she couldn't get herself to say the better part of a year. "For a while. I know it's a sacrifice."

"Hey, I wouldn't have bought the place if it wasn't a good investment. This won't put me out a bit." The expression on his face changed, a pained look she'd seen before. A look that pulled at her far-too-close-to-the-surface emotions.

"Mom and Dad might not have been around at the time," he said, "but I'm positive they're the ones who led me to that orchard."

The truth of his words swelled in her chest. She pulled in a breath of promise. "I'm sure they were too." Whether in her home state of Montana, or the soon-to-be safe house in Oregon, they would always be with her.

"Should we clear out? Your new tenants will be here first thing in the morning." He glanced down at his watch. Dad's old watch. "And it'll be officially tomorrow morning in just twenty minutes."

"It's that late?" Bree asked. "Think the kids are still up?"

Braden chuckled. "With Jillian and Paige to keep them company? My guess is yes."

She didn't mind the idea of her kids being up so late. Not if it was with Braden's darling stepdaughters. And not if it meant she'd get to see their faces when she got home.

Braden pulled open the front door and held it for her.

Bree flicked the lights out, forcing herself not to look back.

The door closed. "You'll be back in nine months," Braden said.

What he didn't say was the part that usually followed: *if all goes well. You'll be back in nine months if all goes well.* Two-hundred-seventy days.

"I know." She had to practically shove the words off her tongue, but at least they went. She gripped the stair rail, the pulse in her palm hammering against the cool steel. "It's more than that. It's leaving the kids. It's living in fear. It's knowing that that creep is ruling my life again."

Braden stopped halfway down the steps, spun back to look at her, his jaw clenched so tight it had to hurt. "Trust me, Bree. If I could take this guy out in his sleep and get away with it... there'd be no stopping me."

More burden. More rocks filling Bree's middle. "I know." This time she stopped there. If she said any more it would force her into a full-on freak-out, and she could not let that happen in front of Braden.

She focused on the steps as she lowered herself from one to the next. Beneath the streetlamp stood Braden's truck. Taped-up boxes filled the flatbed, seeming to weigh it down the way she had him.

The air was soured with unspoken words. Words that would rile and rage and rob her of all things good. Words that − if she chose to speak them− would give new life to the small, tormented girl inside her, the girl that came to life the day Carl Ronsberg singled her out. Sure, she'd learned to bury that little girl long ago, giving life to the confident, semi-adjusted woman she'd become. Still a different version of who she might have been, but adjusted just the same.

"I meant to tell you," Braden said, opening the passenger door for her. "I might have found someone to help care for the orchard while you're there. So you won't have to do it all on your own."

A distraction. One point for Braden. "That's good."

He closed her door, circled around the truck, and climbed in behind the wheel. "He grew up on an orchard his father owns not far from here, so he's got plenty of experience."

Whoa. "Did you say *he?*"

"Yes…" He dragged out the word while giving her his take-it-down-a-notch look. "It's not like you'll be sharing your bed. He'll stay in the guesthouse."

"How old is he? What does he do? What kind of guy can just put his life on hold and move to some orchard in an entirely different state?"

The look was still glued on Braden's face. "Take a breath, Bree. He's about your age. Never been married. Kind of between jobs –"

"He's *thirty-two* and he's never been married?"

When her brother tipped his head, Bree bit back her words. Braden hadn't married until he was in his thirties. She grasped for something else. "Does he have any children?"

"No. And can we save the twenty dozen questions for later? We don't even know if it's a sure thing." He fired up the truck, began backing out of the drive.

Sure. She could do that. Forget that this news filled her with enough angry heat to launch a hot air balloon across Glacier National Park. "I just don't feel like spending my *sentence to misery* with some jobless, lifeless louse. I'd rather do the work myself and be left alone." She felt a hint of relief once that was out, but guilt was quick to snatch it away.

Braden put on the brakes, the rear of his truck halfway into the quiet street. "You know, Bree, you're going to have to learn to trust people somehow. They're not all Carl Ronsbergs, you know?"

Oh, she knew. But she also knew there were all types out there: Ronsbergs, and those who *created* the likes of Ronsberg. She had to watch out for both. She shrugged, done with the argument for now. "I just figured it would be a woman, that's all."

He sighed. A heavy-laden sound. "Probably because old Ms. Clemmins has run the place all this time."

Bree managed a stiff nod. "Yeah, that's probably why."

She vowed to let that be the closing words on their discussion, but as Braden cranked the wheel and pulled onto the street, the topic pinged and ponged in her head faster than Braden's rhythmic tap on the wheel.

Yet one particular question bounced higher than all the rest. One that made thoughts of her stalker fade faster than the house in the distance. Just who was this guy Braden had in mind?

CHAPTER TWO

Greyson shook his head as he walked down the far aisle of his father's orchard. He reached for a nearby branch, pressed a thumb into the nearest peach. "Too soft." He stepped along, doing the same with every peach on the limb. "Lazy kid."

Todd should have picked at least half of them by now. Not only would the batch bruise during picking and packing, they'd get bugs if they ripened even one more day. Already he was losing daylight. The sun, hidden behind a band of clouds, was setting at an alarming rate.

He blew out a burdened breath, wanting to shout Todd's name to the evening sky. Dad was getting too old to take care of the orchard himself, and Greyson had already put his life on hold long enough. If Todd couldn't prove to be of more help, they'd be forced to hire someone.

The low rumble of an engine purred in the distance, the sound telling Greyson just what he needed to know: Todd was home. He glanced back in time to see his brother kill the engine and climb off the bike. After prying off his Mohawk helmet, Todd yanked his fingers through his scruffy hair. In their youth, it was often said that the two looked alike. Couple of blond-haired boys that sprouted taller than most kids by middle school. That had changed by now. While Greyson's hair had shifted into a sandy color of blond, his brother's had gone nearly black.

Todd caught eyes with him across the stretch of land. As much as Greyson wanted to chew him out, he almost hoped the kid would go inside. Of course, Todd wouldn't be Todd if he did what Greyson wanted.

"What's up?" his brother asked as he neared.

Greyson focused on his posture, shifting to his eyes once he was close by. Still sober. Good. Now he could lay into him. "Do you remember what I told you about harvesting?"

Todd squinted as he eyed the orchard at Greyson's back. "You told me a million things about harvesting, Grey, so I'm not sure."

"There was one thing that I said you needed to remember above all else. One. Thing. Do you not remember what that was?"

And there went the shrug. Todd's stupid lazy shrug. "Don't let them get too ripe," he said in his equally annoying slur.

"Do you realize," Greyson said, jabbing a thumb over

his shoulder, "that we're losing money right now? There are peaches on those trees we could have already sold. *Should* have already sold. Peaches that we'll no longer be able to sell because they're too ripe."

"Then we'll just eat them." Todd glared at him after saying it, folding his arms across his chest.

Bait. Stupid bait that Greyson would not even sniff at. There was no point in telling him that they couldn't possibly eat that many peaches in time. The only way they'd see a good use was to stick a sign out front and let the locals take home bushels for a reduced price.

"Grab a bucket," he said, leaning down to secure the handle of one himself. "We're going to fill these things tonight and set up the stand. We'll leave the money box out and let folks serve themselves."

Todd chuckled. "Dad still does that? Wow, he's just asking for robbery, isn't he?"

"No, he already did that by allowing you to come help out. He'll make half what this batch is worth. All because you just couldn't stay on top of it."

"It's just that last row," Todd growled, his face pinched in anger. "I got all the rest and I've been busting my butt to stay on top of it. Besides, you haven't even been around. You leave for weeks at a time, and even when you're here you're at your place more often than not. You think you know everything that goes on while you're gone. Truth is you don't have a clue."

Greyson didn't reply, only secured another wicker basket and headed back down the aisle. He hoped what

Todd said was true. Prayed that if he checked the other aisles, he'd find only solid peaches at his fingers. He started to pick, irritated with how gentle he was forced to handle the fruit, and realized something was missing: Todd. "Freakin' creep," he muttered. "Thanks a lot."

The sky grew darker as Greyson collected one bushel after the next. How much leniency do you give a recovering alcoholic? Could someone answer him that? Greyson couldn't help but feel that his younger brother was capable of giving a whole lot more. Then again, why should Todd step up when he had an older brother who'd pick up the slack? It was enough to make him want to back off completely and start construction before schedule on his up-and-coming training center there in Montana. Better yet, he could jet back to Washington and run the existing center himself. Forget about the fact that his father was too old to run things on his own. And that Todd was too self-centered to give more.

In the fleeting moment of delusion, Greyson set his mind to it. He would call his business partner, take the lead in management once more, and go back to work.

Yet as he creaked his way up the old, wooden deck, pulled open the near-weightless screen door, Greyson released a labored sigh. *If only I could.*

"Hey there, big guy," his dad said as he entered. "Where you headed? I was just about to join you out there."

Greyson looked over his shoulder, eyeing the darkening sky beyond the dusty mesh screen. "I already finished up, pop. You go on back to your show."

He'd been fastening one of the buttons on his coat, yet at Greyson's words, Lloyd's shoulders dropped. "You're already done?"

Greyson gave him a single nod, opening the coat closet at his side.

"Well there goes that," Lloyd said. "And I had so much to tell you, too."

"What about?"

Lloyd shrugged out of his gray, corduroy coat, the pale color matching his eyes. "Had a visit with Braden Fox the day before yesterday."

Greyson nodded. "Oh yeah? What's he up to?"

Lloyd waved a cupped hand toward the kitchen. "Let's sit down to a cup of joe, shall we?"

Irritated heat flared in his chest. His patience had been tested enough for one day. He wanted nothing more than to go home to a warm shower and a soft bed.

A wave of guilt struck him as he watched his dad pull two mugs from the rack, a rather pleased expression on his face.

"No coffee for me, pop, thanks," he said, taking a seat just the same.

His dad left the mug in place and shrugged. "Perhaps your brother will want some."

Greyson rolled his eyes at the mere mention. "So what did Braden Fox have to say?"

His father grabbed the coffee pot and poured while he spoke, steam rising to veil his face. "Turns out the guy bought an orchard a while back. It's on the west coast someplace. Oregon, I think. Anyway, he's had the tenant of the place taking care of it until now, along with some hired help during harvest and whatnot." His dad set the pot back into place and fished through the drawer for a spoon. "When he stopped by the other night looking for you, Braden told me they're switching tenants and he could use some help. There's a home on the property, you see. But also a guesthouse out back."

Greyson's gears began to turn. Working to guess at his father's plan. He was most likely thinking about sending Todd to help. And while Greyson liked the idea of getting rid of the guy for a while, he knew it wouldn't be right to let him go on his own just yet. Especially when a good guy like Braden Fox was depending on him. Not to mention the delicate issue of his brother's sobriety. His father had gone on talking, and Greyson tuned back into his words.

"...said I thought you'd be perfect for the job, but I told him I'd check and see if you agree." He broke off there, looking at him expectantly.

"Wait, did you say he's interested in me or Todd?" Not that it mattered; neither one of them could do it.

"You, of course," Lloyd said.

"*Me?* I'm running one training center and prepping to build another."

"Yes," his dad agreed. "But you've done a hell of a job delegating so you can step away from time to time."

His father's counter brought Greyson to the real root of his concern. "Well I've got to help keep this orchard going too. Didn't you see what happened out there? There's no way I could –"

"That's the other thing I've been meaning to talk to you about," Lloyd said. He shuffled his way over to the table. Metal shrieked against tile as he tugged out an old chair and lowered himself onto it while balancing his cup.

Greyson's shoulders squared in preparation.

"I appreciate everything you do for me, Grey. I really do. But I think – now that Todd is home – he should have a shot at doing things on his own."

Metal screeched along the floor once more as Greyson shot to a stand. The sound was sharp and angry, matching the words on his tongue. "I've been *trying* to give him a shot, Dad, trust me. Todd's just too..." he struggled for the right word. *Lazy? Selfish? Idiotic?* "Too immature to take it seriously. I *want* to go back to work, but the truth is, this entire orchard would fall apart without me." Greyson knew he should be watching his voice, but he couldn't help it. He'd been holding back for far too long. "How irresponsible would it be for me to leave, knowing how much you'd struggle?"

"Now hold up there, son. It's not like I've got one foot in the grave. I have plenty of seasons left in me, and I'm perfectly capable of managing my own kids."

The stern look on his father's face had Greyson choking back his next words. A kinder, gentler version came out instead. "How do you know he'll be able to do it?"

Lloyd rapped a knuckle on the table and puffed his

cheeks with a pent up breath. "Treat a man like he's doomed to fail and he's likely to prove you right. But show a little faith in him... and he just might take on the world." He took a sip of his coffee, cradling the mug in his palms and sighed. "I guess what I'm saying is we should give him a chance. Maybe — when you're not here to pick up the slack — he'll take the responsibility himself. It might be just what he needs."

Greyson knew his silence would be mistaken as consent, but in this circumstance, he stood no chance at changing Lloyd's mind. Todd was the only one capable of that. And he'd do it by letting him down in a big way. The last thing Greyson wanted to do was sit around and watch.

Trouble was, Dad's analogy had him thinking about his business partner, Johnny Mac. Greyson had spent plenty of time getting him set up to run the training center in Washington. If Greyson showed up now, Johnny's ego would be crushed. Irony was, Greyson's purpose in leaving the guy in charge was to let him see just what he was capable of. All so that Greyson could come back and minimize Todd's duties in the process.

Still, there was one thing that seemed horribly out of place. Why would Braden want him — out of everyone — to run that orchard?

"I'm not going to tell you what to do," his father continued. "But, taking this job on the coast — a lovely orchard to care for all your own — might be a good way to ease back into the protection business, versus that training end of things. If that's what you'd like to do, that is.

"*Protection*? How do you mean? I thought it was an orchard job."

Lloyd tipped his head back and chuckled. "Heavens no, son. You've got too much to offer this world than to go wasting away doing nothing more than caring for fruit. I know that, and Braden does too. It's why he thought of you for this position. He's sending his sister out there. She needs some sort of safe haven for a time. He'd like you to offer protection while you're there."

Whoa. Bree? Bree Fox? The now-divorced brunette who'd never given him the time of day? His chest seemed to swell with the steam he saw rising from his father's mug. A tingling, prickling steam that gave life to the old feelings lingering there. Bree had captured Greyson's attention clear back in grade school. And as much as he'd like to say otherwise, she'd kept his attention throughout their school years. There'd been something about her; while most girls seemed caught up in the social scene, Bree Fox had her nose in the books like she'd find her life's breath in the pages.

"I remember catching word of some troubles she'd had," Greyson said. "Something regarding a stalker. 'Course that can't be the issue she's facing now. Not after all this time."

"Not sure." His father dug a hand into the front pocket of his flannel shirt and pulled out a square of paper. Braden's name was scrawled along the top in his pop's thin, squiggly script, a phone number penciled beneath it. "Call him. He'll give you all the details." He took on an expression that Mom used to wear in moments of concern. A look he hadn't assumed until after her death. "Consider it, son. Please."

Greyson thumbed the corner of the small slip, back and then forth. "I have a question," he mumbled, thinking back on something his father had said. "If Braden came by a few days ago, why are you only telling me about it now?"

Lloyd took a long sip from his mug, lifting one crooked finger while he gulped it down. His eyes settled on Greyson as he uttered just one, single word. "Timing."

CHAPTER THREE

"I don't understand why we have to count the marbles." Carter's grumbled words caused Bree to furrow her brow. She repositioned herself at the foot of the bed, waiting until he pulled his gaze from the empty jar.

"No, buddy, you don't *have* to do it if you don't want to. But we won't see each other for thirty whole days. I just thought it would be fun to keep track of each day as it goes by." Bree paused there to compose herself, knowing that the first month would only be the beginning. Multiply that by a total of nine months and she'd be away from Carter and Sophie for nearly three hundred days. Of course it was less when she counted the times she'd be back to visit.

Sophie, nestled into the bed next to Carter, shook the plastic container of marbles, her brown eyes set on the colorful sight. "It's a countdown, Carter," she explained. "Like for Christmas. We move the beads from this container to that jar."

Bree had been tracking a mental countdown since Carl

Ronsberg had been sentenced five years ago. Counting down the years, months, and days until his release. She liked the idea of a new countdown. One that didn't induce waves of panic.

Ten days until Ronsberg was out.

One day until she said goodbye to the kids.

Thirty days until she saw them again.

Bree sighed. "It's just a way to keep track of the days that pass until we get to spend a little time together." Little was right. A three-day weekend to be exact. A stabbing pain sank into her chest. It felt as if someone had placed her heart in that small jar before crushing the glass around it. Sharp, cutting shards doing their worst. Leaving the house had been difficult, but it was nothing compared to leaving the kids.

A list of questions collected in her mind, a growing pile of worries and doubts. Would she really be able to last — being away all that time? If Ronsberg showed no signs of pursuing her, would she feel good about moving back? Could she ever have a normal life again?

Carter's small fingers curled around the miniature jar. He twisted the lid off, sniffed at the empty space within, and closed it back up. "I guess I'll do it," he finally said.

Bree forced a smile. "Good. Now you two go to sleep. Daddy will be here in the morning to get you." She leaned in, pressed a kiss to Carter's warm face, and pulled the blanket up to his chin.

"Oh," she said, realizing he still held the jar. "Do you want me to put that up here?" She patted the nightstand.

Carter shook his head, and Bree rushed in to kiss his forehead next. "Love you, Carter boo."

"Does Daddy even know where Uncle B lives?" Sophie asked. "I've never seen him come here."

"Of course he does," Bree said. "I grew up in this house, remember?" She bent down, kissing Sophie's doughy cheeks.

"I'll be the one to count the beads," Sophie whispered. "When you're nine years old, you're really good at stuff like that."

New splinters burrowed around her heart. How she would miss Sophie's lists of what nine-year-olds could do. "What about Carter?" she asked, rubbing her nose as she sniffed. "What are seven-year-olds good at?"

Sophie's thin brows scrunched. "Hmm. Seven-year-olds are good at opening and closing the lid."

A small chuckle escaped Bree's tightened lips. She ran a hand along the silky sides of her face, adoration tugging at her emotions. "Okay. But promise me something, will you?"

Sophie's brown curls bobbed as she nodded.

"Promise me you'll let Carter put some beads in too, if he'd like. You might need to take turns, you know?"

A pout, and a loud puff of air came before the answer. "Okay."

"Okay. Night, Sophie bear. Love you." Bree shot to her feet, the tears threatening to spill before she could escape the nightlight's glow. The hot pain spread to her stomach as she left. A sick pit of missing and wishing. Wishing their circumstance could change.

She'd barely made it to the deck out back when Braden called from behind.

"I uh, wanted to talk to you," he said, closing the patio door. Crickets chirped beneath the starlit sky. A horse neighed in the distance. And Bree wiped a fresh onslaught of tears from her cheeks.

"I just wanted to let you know that the guy I wanted to get – the one I hoped would join you out there in Oregon – said yes."

Wow. It just kept getting worse, didn't it? Bree's dreaded sentence-away-from-all-she-held-dear was bound to be even more hellish than she imagined. She spun away from Braden, covered her mouth, and stifled a sob. But it snuck out as she replied.

"That's great." An odd laugh snuck up her throat. Not a *ha-ha* sort of a laugh. A tear-soaked, manic-sounding laugh Bree barely recognized as her own.

"Yeah," Braden said. "It really *is* great." But his tone was cautious. Leading.

More laughter bubbled up and burst from her lips as she nodded. Big huge nods toward the dark night. "It's wonderful. The fact that you managed to find some homeless, unloved stranger for me to care for while I'm gone. I can't think of anything better."

Braden's hand cupped around her arm. "Hey, this isn't a joke, Bree. I thought long and hard about who would be best for this – "

"Did you?" It came out in an ugly mocking tone that

even she despised.

"Yes, as a matter of fact, I did. I wanted this guy from *day one* and the fact that we actually got him feels like nothing less than the hand of fate."

Her temper had reached its peak, but her curiosity had too. "Who? Who is it, Braden? Go ahead and spit it out. I'm waiting." She tapped her toe to prove that point.

"It's Greyson Law."

An image of the handsome-and-he-knows-it high school football star turned bodyguard broke into her mind like an uninvited guest. *"Greyson Law?"* Her arms dropped to her sides. She spun to face him. "Are you kidding? Greyson Law is the guy you hired to stay out there with me?" New things were happening to her insides. Dizzy, spinny, funny things making her legs feel like part of the deck at her sock-covered feet.

"Yep. He actually said yes, if you can believe it."

"Are you sure you have the right brother? Todd – his younger brother is the unemployed one. Are you talking about that one?"

"I'd never trust that guy to watch after ..." He paused, cleared his throat and ran a hand over the back of his neck. "I'm not just having him take care of the orchard. He's also going to make sure you're safe. And I trust Greyson to do that. He's been in the protection business for years. Beyond that, I spent a good deal of time with him during my senior year, came to know him fairly well in the years that followed. That's a quality man right there. Solid."

The new information spun in her head. *Braden asked Greyson Law to move to Oregon for nine months?*

And he'd said yes?

The idea was too much to take in. Her vision blurred as she considered. The dark land and hazy sky merging into one twisting mass of grey and black. She didn't like guys like Greyson. Not back in high school. Not after she'd graduated. And certainly not now. The last thing she wanted was some loud meathead asking her to hit the bar with him on weekends and weekdays alike. Heaven only knew what guys like him did in their spare time. She, for one, didn't want to find out.

"I don't understand why you think so highly of him," she finally said. "I mean, isn't there any possible thing I can say to get you to just ... call him off?"

"Call him off?" Braden's face scrunched up. "You make it sound like he's some bulldog I unleashed on you."

"Well you just said that he'll be watching after me, so in a way it feels like that. All I'm going to want is to be alone with my miserable self. I don't want to worry about things like hosting and being social and ..." *Polite.* She didn't say that one aloud, but she felt it. "I hate the idea of having to worry about him."

Braden scoffed, walked over to the porch light and flicked the thing on. "Did you say worry?" He scratched along his jaw as he looked at her. "The worry is *not* having him there. This guy is good. He has just shy of ten years experience as a personal bodyguard. His training agency has been featured in newspapers and magazines across the globe."

Her brother had made it sound like he was some sort of celebrity. It'd been like that in school too. By the time Greyson had reached his senior year the entire student body practically worshiped him. She, on the other hand, did not.

"I just don't understand why. I mean, if he's as great as you say, why would he take time out of his life to look after some woman and a bunch of fruit?"

"Well that's where fate steps in, isn't it? Something happened that brought him back home not too long ago – after he'd lived out of state and country half of his adult life. And while I'm not sure about what the encounter was, I know it was meant to bring him home for this exact reason – so he could watch over you."

It took everything in Bree not to roll her eyes. Ever since Braden got married he had this whole new outlook. This "it was meant to be" type of approach. Of course, considering the shift in his life, she could see why he believed his path was carved out in the stars. In the last two years he'd gone from single bachelor to husband of one of the greatest women Bree knew. He'd also taken on the role of stepfather to two teenage girls and father to a sweet baby boy. If there were such a thing as fate – it had been good to him, and she was glad.

"It's going to be alright, Bree." The surety in his tone made her wince. Braden was certain all would go well. That this plan – this arrangement he'd set up years ago – would keep her and the kids safe. And while she was grateful for all the work and preparation he'd put into it, she couldn't see things from his perspective no matter how hard she tried.

The months ahead would strip her of her kids. And from the only family she knew. Fate — if such a thing existed at all — was about to deal her one mighty blow.

CHAPTER FOUR

Greyson tugged at the zipper on his suitcase, satisfied he had everything he needed. It felt strange, packing jeans and T's instead of suits and ties. Also strange was the duration of the job. Nine months. Nine whole months of being away, isolated from loved ones – something *this* particular client wasn't used to. Of course, he'd bring her back a handful of times within that time frame, when her kids had breaks from school, but that alone presented a unique set of difficulties in itself.

No, this definitely wasn't his typical job. Wasn't his typical client either. Bree Fox had never been typical in any sense of the word. She was exceptional. And capable of speeding Greyson's pulse each time he thought of her.

"Get a grip," he mumbled to himself. He couldn't afford to be distracted. Not with the kind of psycho that had been after her for so many years. Greyson walked over to his desk, lowered himself beside the work lamp, and flipped through his papers beneath the amber glow.

It wasn't often Greyson had a particular predator to watch out for. A profile, yes. He'd studied profiles for years. Types who were likely to target prominent clients within each profession. In his personal time, Greyson studied those who had accomplished the Godforsaken act they'd obsessed over for years. Yet with all of that knowledge stacked on the mental shelves in Greyson's mind, the file Braden had on this guy was chilling.

Dark shadows fell across the pages as he flipped from one to the next. Photocopies of cryptic notes, strange photos and threatening emails. He'd heard that stalkers — the few that got prison time over their offense — often spent their days fixed on the object of their obsession, and with this case it seemed all the more likely.

The thought caused a collective tightening throughout his body — throat, chest, and fists all at once. It'd been a while since he'd pounded that punching bag in the garage. He wouldn't mind paying it a visit then. To the tune of Carl Ronsberg's face.

Braden insisted that having Greyson there was just a precaution. Yet Greyson mused that if he had a sister of his own he'd make sure she had nothing less. The plan was to monitor Ronsberg's behavior — with Bree at a safe distance — and get an idea of what his intentions might be. If, after the allotted time, Carl hadn't been caught looming around her Montana property, or the few others they'd be tracking, Bree would move back with the hopes of living a normal life. Greyson only hoped that was possible.

He nodded with that thought, stretching his arms over his head. Braden Fox was a great guy. And kinder than most of the guys from the varsity team. In fact, Braden had shown Greyson a particular kindness at one point, a heroic one, really – something he'd never forget. It was the same reason he was compelled to take a more modest salary for the job when Braden asked what he deemed a good sum.

His thoughts were interrupted when a buzz came from his phone. He glanced down, saw that it was Braden calling, and brought it to his ear.

"What's up, Braden?"

"Hey, Greyson. Not a whole lot. Just touching base with you on a few things. Bree's all packed up. She'll be headed out first thing in the morning. She has plans to trade in her car like you suggested. It's all been arranged. The dealer's just down the street from the hotel." His words were firm, his voice tight.

Greyson was glad they'd taken his advice. This way, no one from back home would know what car she drove; it'd give her a little added safety once the guy was out and asking around. Of course, Greyson had offered to drive Bree out to Oregon himself, but Braden hadn't gone for it. Wanted Bree to have more independence once she was there.

"There was one thing I wanted to... I don't know, warn you about, I guess."

Greyson straightened up, his eyes darting to the files on the desk. "Go ahead."

"Well, Bree... I mean, you know her from school,

right?"

Greyson let the dead air linger while he weighed his words. Just how honest should he be? "I can't say I did know her too well," he admitted.

"Yeah," Braden said. "You along with 90 percent of the school. That's how Bree is. I guess I just want to make sure that you don't take anything personally. You know, if she seems standoffish or whatnot."

Nervous energy flittered over his skin, reminding him of how awkward he'd been around her. Of all the game he might have had when other women were near, Greyson seemed to always lose himself around Bree. "No," he finally blurted. "I won't take it personally. So does she know it's me yet?"

The dead air came into play once more. This time on Braden's end.

"You said you hadn't mentioned it last time we talked," Greyson reminded, "but that you would. I just don't want it to be a surprise, is all." That was an understatement. There was no telling what Bree might do if she discovered Greyson would be helping her run the orchard. What if she backed out of the thing entirely?

"Oh, of course, I told her."

He waited for him to elaborate, feeling oddly desperate for Bree's acceptance of his role. When he didn't, Greyson urged him on. "And..."

"She was good with it. Glad, really. Yeah, she thinks it's great."

Good? Glad? Great? Huh. Greyson could tell Braden

was holding back. Most likely Bree hated the idea. She was probably picturing scenarios akin to a creaky castle guarded by some hideous beast. That nervous feeling sunk beyond his skin now, seeped into his stomach where it twisted up into an achy bunch.

"Well I'm uh, really looking forward to catching up with her." He bit the words off there, wishing he hadn't said them at all.

"Bree's looking forward to that too," Braden said.

Yeah right. "I'll touch base once I arrive. We'll stay in touch on the guy's release. Get the surveillance going once he's out."

"Absolutely. Safe travels. Oh, and Greyson?"

"Yeah?"

"Thanks."

CHAPTER FIVE

Bree eyed the clock on the dash as she neared her destination. Barely three o'clock and the sun was already gone, lost behind a blanket of clouds and a sheet of rain that hadn't let up. She'd traded in her car the night before, surprised at how easy it had been. She'd prepared herself for another emotional breakdown – one more goodbye – the car she'd owned since the kids were born. Turned out it was nothing in comparison to the others.

At the mercy of her phone's GPS, Bree turned when she was told, following the directed route, a numb sort of haze keeping her emotions at bay.

In eight days Carl Ronsberg would take his first steps into freedom. Steps that had already forced Bree into a prison of her own. Of course there was a chance Carl had stopped obsessing over the years – that he'd rehabilitated and had no intentions where Bree was concerned. But they couldn't risk it. Not after the things he had done, or the things he had threatened to do if he ever got the chance.

A shudder rumbled through her at the thought. No, she was right where she needed to be. Far away from Montana. A very unwelcome voice told Bree she'd be with the *person* she needed to be with as well – something she was not prepared to admit.

Her mind drifted back to what Allie had shared with her the other night. It was right after her conversation with Braden on the back porch. Her well meaning sister-in-law had come bearing magazine articles featuring her soon-to-be warden, Greyson Law. Each highlighting the *Quarterback Turned Bodyguard* in all his stone faced, suited-up, muscular glory. Bree had tried to remain unimpressed, but it hadn't been easy. Not by a long shot. Even then – at the mere recollection – Bree could feel her cheeks flushing with warmth. The guy was handsome, she'd give him that. And probably quite capable too. She figured he'd do what Braden had hired him for just fine.

With that, she straightened her shoulders and eyed the misty scene ahead. She'd been hoping to appreciate everything Braden and Allie had told her about this quiet spot of land. Hoping to be charmed by the place as much as they had been. To have that warmth – the one she'd lost upon leaving her home – magically return once she arrived.

But as she approached Braden's orchard – rows of green-leafed trees on acres of green grass – she felt no such thing. The disappointment was heavy and cold. The bulk of it settling in the center of her chest. Perhaps once the rain cleared, she'd feel different. Perhaps once she could take in the view without squinting through a steady stream of thick, grey drops she would see the beauty of it. For now, Bree felt as if her insides had been hollowed out completely.

She flicked on her blinker as the rows came to an end, watching for the obscure driveway leading to the home. It was set far back, according to Braden. Hidden from passing traffic, and guarded by a tall wall of surrounding maples. The drive — also lined by towering trees — was even longer than she expected.

She proceeded down the driveway, the rows of trees like towering soldiers. The sound of the rain was different beneath their great branches. Gone was the spray of a million tiny drops. In came the scattered, larger thuds against the windshield and hood, drops that had gathered and joined among the leaves, multiplying in size.

"Where's the house?" she muttered, wondering if she had the right place. But then she saw it, a blurred spot of pale yellow. There would be a garage door opener waiting inside the home, but for now she'd need to pull up to the closed garage and make a run for it. She shut off the engine, clicked off the headlights, and pulled in a deep breath.

With keys and cell phone in hand, Bree pushed open the car door and bolted for the covered porch. Cool spats of water pelted her along the way, soaking her shirt in seconds flat. Her shoes were wet too, squishing as she made her way up the steps. *Stupid puddles.*

After unlocking the screen door, she fumbled with the two remaining keys on the chain – one for the knob, one for the deadbolt – and frowned when she got the two reversed. At last she unlocked the deadbolt. The knob next. And shoved open the oak door.

Exhausted, Bree trudged over to the window and searched the edge of the thick drapes until she found some tight, pulley cords along the wall. With arms that felt weak and shaky, she pulled the things until she exposed the entire window.

Pale, outdoor light penetrated the room, barely illuminating a mantel along the far wall. She shivered as she moved toward it, thrilled to see a switch beside it. *Thank heavens – it's a gas fireplace.*

She flicked the switch, smiled when the flames flickered to life, and sighed as she dropped into a nearby seat. The warmth hit her legs first, and then her sock-covered feet as she pried off her damp shoes. After warming her fingers by the glass, Bree sunk deep into the soft cushions and let her eyes close.

She hadn't had a decent night's sleep in a month's time – her focus set on checking off the dreaded list:

Pack up the house – check.

Say goodbye to the kids – check.

Get to the orchard house with her sanity intact – check.

At last, she was done. She recalled a time – years ago – when she'd pulled a thin green wire from one of the roses Dad gave Mom. As young as Bree had been, she hadn't known its purpose was to keep the head of the flower erect. She'd been horrified to see the heavy top droop sadly against the stem. Limp and lifeless. It felt as if that list had been her wire. It had served its purpose of keeping her strong and focused and awake through most hours of the night. But now it was gone, her limbs growing heavier with each breath. She gave into the bone-warming sensation, let it carry her into a deeper state of comfort, and at last, slipped into a very welcome sleep.

Greyson flicked on the windshield wipers one last time, clearing remnant drops from the passing storm. Throughout the long drive, his mind played a game of tug-of-war. At one side stood the great pull of Carl Ronsberg, the sick stalker behind Bree's secret escape.

The second side tugged from an entirely different place – a familiar yearning to know Bree Fox. To discover the mystery of the woman who'd quietly kept his interest throughout their school years.

Thoughts of his impending circumstance had taken Greyson back to that place of curiosity and intrigue, giving him a strange connection to Bree's stalker. Something he didn't want. But strangely – horribly really – he could see how one could become obsessed with such a girl. And now here she was, placed right before his path in what he might call fate, if he believed in it.

With a fresh spark of interest, he peered over the orchard in the fading light, admiring the beauty of it. Unlike the peach and cherry orchards he was familiar with, this layout was more like a vineyard. The full, reaching limbs creating long corridors, walls of leafy green and bright, colored apples.

Once the headlights were aimed at the trees, he surveyed the area with a watchful eye. He'd already downloaded a layout of the property from a birds-eye view, printed it out along with other online shots he'd found. In the headlights' glow, he recognized the outskirts of the orchard, the shed at the southeast corner of the lot, the guesthouse on the north end.

He approached the turn at a slow pace, and inched down the driveway with his eyes set on the car parked outside the garage. A knot of irritated heat shot up his throat. Why had she not parked in the garage? Sure, the guy hadn't been released just yet but that wasn't the point.

An inner voice told him to let it slip; it wouldn't be worth causing a rift over. But that voice was silenced when he realized that the front door of the home hadn't even been closed. Beyond that, the house looked completely dark.

He scanned the shadowed depths of the large porch. Surely if she'd gone to bed she would have locked up the front door. Or at least closed the dang thing. His heart punched a beat out of place, his irritation shifting to fear. Worry over Bree and just what might have taken place before he arrived.

It took less than five seconds for him to shut off the engine, grab his gun, and climb the front porch steps. He hadn't harnessed up today, had doubted he'd make a habit of doing so at this particular job, but now he was starting to think better of it.

The wide screen door made the softest of creaks as it opened. He was glad his headlights were still on; their white glow lit up the farthest wall, illuminating most of the rectangular room. A sofa. Love seat. A glowing fireplace. His brows arched up in surprise. The beam from his headlights had kept him from seeing the small flicker of fire lighting the room, but he could easily feel the effects of it now. The thick heat permeating the room.

The flickering flames lit a corner chair that hid in the shadows, but there was still no Bree. He was just about to call out her name when he spotted a curled back and a splash of pony-tailed hair in that very chair. He took one step closer, seeing that her legs were tucked onto the seat, her head propped along the large, rounded armrest.

His heart jumped into a panicked rhythm, his palm growing sweaty beneath the grip on his gun. He remained motionless as he watched her shoulder rise. And then fall. Rise, and fall.

A deep exhale pushed through his lips. *Thank heavens.* She was simply asleep. Hunched in a ball on a sofa chair by the fireplace – asleep. He hoped the wood floors wouldn't give him away as he took a step closer. The back of the chair blocked the headlights from reaching her, so Greyson relied on the sparse fray of firelight, coupled with the adjustment of his eyes as he looked over her further. Her cheeks – or at least the one he could see - looked flushed, covered in a sheen of sweat from the fireplace. Sparse strands of hair clung to the back of her neck as well. Too hot. She'd been sitting there too long.

On the cushion beside her leg he saw a set of keys and a phone. The image made him recall the appearance of Bree's car. A silhouette of a tall suitcase handle stuck out in his mind.

Without another thought Greyson leaned down for the keys, securing the tallest corner of metal between his finger and thumb.

Bree stirred a bit and rubbed her nose with a sigh. A soft, cute little noise.

Greyson's heart thumped louder in his chest as he waited for her breaths to come evenly once more. It'd be rude to wake her, but it'd also be inconsiderate not to help with her luggage.

After snagging the keys and making for the car, he secured a puffy pillow beneath his arm, a thin, pink blanket in one hand, and her suitcase in the grip of his other. He rolled the case until he got to the stairs, and lifted it from that point on, not wanting to startle his new client. In this case, he was grateful for the quiet creak of the old screen door. But he couldn't help but feel concerned by it as well. If someone cut into the mesh screen to unlock it, the least it could do is let out a creak to alarm the lady of the house.

With a quiet touch, Greyson set her things down, flicked off the fireplace, and locked up. The front door wasn't any louder than the screen door, he realized, another beat of concern gripping hold of him. Tomorrow morning he'd install an alarm in the place.

Once settled behind the wheel of his SUV, Greyson roared up the engine once more. He backed up just enough to round the home, and pulled into the far end of the property. On the opposite side of the bordering fence stood a woodsy lay of towering pines. The guesthouse looked small in comparison. It was a narrow home with two floors and a pointed roof.

With his bag secured over one shoulder, his work case in hand, Greyson approached the front door. The pale glow of moonlight glistened over the narrow strip of cement, lighting his way as he went. Pine needles from the wooded area behind the guesthouse littered the ground, dry and fresh ones alike, crunching beneath his shoes.

The main house had been large with light siding. This one was small with dark siding. It was possible this house was built first, years back, and that the main house had been a new addition. Perhaps after a few good years of profitable harvest.

A flash of uncomfortable heat shot through him as he pictured Bree in that house alone. Why had he been okay with this scenario? It didn't seem right for her to be alone. Not with this nut-job on the loose in just eight days.

Another concern came to him then as he recalled the way he'd turned off the fireplace. She was going to freeze. Who knew what the temperature was set at in that house? Clearly she hadn't settled in yet.

He shook his head in helpless frustration and twisted the knob. This door creaked. *Really* creaked – it seemed to be making up for the ones at the other house. He slid a hand along the wall until he found a switch. On went the light. A bright yellow glow, shining light on … what was this?

Greyson squinted his eyes, widened them, and cocked his head to one side. Puddles. The place was drenched.

He lifted his chin to view the ceiling. There was a loft of sorts, and a vaulted part that went right to the roof overhead. There, just off from the highest pitch, was a jagged hole. A bizarre view of the star-lit sky, framed by a silhouette of small square shingles. At one side of the hole lay the culprit: a giant pine. Flat, spiky needles jutted from a broken branch, the top half dangling by a shred of bark.

His gaze shot to the floor where remnants of the damaged roof lay scattered just beneath. *Great.* He was supposed to call Braden right when he arrived. He'd get his call all right. Greyson only wished he had better news for him.

CHAPTER SIX

Muffled music. Bree could hear it, practically feel it as she worked to open her eyes. *My phone,* she realized. She reached for her nightstand, but something felt off: she wasn't lying in bed. The thought made her gasp and straighten all at once.

Darkness surrounded her. Strange and unfamiliar. She looked down to see the muted glow of her phone, resting facedown next to her, the ringer still playing its country song. The screen nearly blinded her when she turned it over, but at least she hadn't missed the call.

"Hello?"

"We've got a problem."

"Braden?"

"Yes, it's Braden."

Bree was coming to her senses. She stood up, moved blindly toward the entry of the home, and felt along the wall for a light switch. When her fingers slid across two by the door, she flicked them both on. "What's wrong?" she asked, closing her eyes against the brightness.

"I guess Oregon has seen a fair share of rain the last

few days. And you know how there's a forest-type area behind the guesthouse?"

"Not really," she said through a yawn. She forced her eyes open after a few blinks. "I haven't taken a look at the property ye –" The sight before her cut the word short. "How did my luggage get in here?"

"What?" Braden's reply sounded muffled, nearly muted through the pulsing panic in her head.

Her heart sped up to a painful sputter, throbbing wildly in her chest. "My luggage." She took a step back, reaching behind to feel for the door. The one she'd left *open* – not closed. "Someone's been here," she breathed. The phone fell from her grip as she spun around and wrestled with the old brass knob.

Braden's voice spilled from the dropped receiver, words she could barely distinguish. That is, until it clicked... *Greyson*. In a rush she stooped to pick up the phone.

"Bree?"

"Yeah, did you say Greyson's been here?"

"Yes." He sounded out of breath. "It's only Greyson. He brought your luggage inside and locked up."

Bree put a hand to her heart, eyeing the display before her. Her suitcase, pillow, blanket and keys. "He came inside while I was sleeping?"

"Yes," Braden said again.

"Why?"

"Because he noticed you didn't even close up the house. He was concerned."

Bree was about to say something back but her

rebuttal took flight. Truth be told it wasn't like her to neglect such a thing. "I fell asleep," she mumbled.

A light chuckle came through the line. "Yeah, that's what I hear."

Bree gritted her teeth, hating the idea of Greyson seeing her hunched over in that chair while she slept and snored and drooled all over for all she knew.

"Listen," Braden said, "I need you to let Greyson in."

"In *here*? Why?"

"The ceiling in the guesthouse fell in. I've got an insurance agent coming first thing tomorrow to take a look at it. But until it's repaired, he's going to have to stay with you."

Bree's hand flew to her mouth as she gasped. "The roof caved in?" A gold-framed mirror hung above a mantle on the far wall, allowing her to see the stunned expression on her face. "You're kidding me. Please say you're joking." The fireplace was off, she noticed. Must have been Greyson as well.

"I'm not joking. Now would you hurry and open your front door? He's waiting right outside."

"Why didn't he just knock?"

"Because he wanted me to ask you if it was okay. I told him I knew it would be but he insisted I call and check."

"Huh."

"Seriously, Bree. Would you let him in already?"

"Of course." She swiped the few frayed strands of hair from her face, wishing she didn't look so hideous, while simultaneously wishing she didn't care. "Jeez," she grumbled, striding to the door. "I'm opening it right now." With that, she swung open the door and flicked on the porch light.

Bree had expected to see him there on the patio; what she *hadn't* expected was the seriously attractive appearance of him. Yes, Greyson had always been handsome in that I-play-football-and-date-whomever-I-want sort of way. And she *had* just seen magazine photos where the man's looks had put most stars by his side to shame, but surely photo enhancements had played a part. Hadn't they?

Her heart did odd, sputtery things while she looked over his sandy blond hair, just long enough to show hints of a natural wave.

And that face – even more stunning than it'd been in print. Strong, solid jaw. Perfectly sculpted chin. And eyes caught somewhere between blue and gray, like a stormy sky. Ah – *there* was an imperfection. A small scar along the bridge of his nose. Of course, she mused, some might argue the mark only added to his rugged quality.

"Hi," he said with a businesslike nod. Though he'd spoken merely a single word, the rich, raspy tone of his voice filled the room.

Her heart jerked from the sputtering rhythm into an outright race. She pushed open the screen door and propped it with her shoulder. "I'll call you back," she said into the phone before dropping it onto the sofa chair. "Hi."

Greyson extended an arm. "It's a pleasure to see you,

Bree. It's been a while."

Bree straightened her arm toward him. "Yes," she agreed, "it has." His hand was warm. Firm. Strong. And the touch of his skin on hers, exhilarating beyond reason.

It took her a moment to recall why he was standing before her, a duffel bag draped over his shoulder and a sleek silver case in one hand. "That was Braden on the phone. He, uh… said your roof caved in." When she sensed her phrasing hadn't come out just right, she gave in to a nervous laugh, feeling like she was back in high school. Quiet. Awkward. Inept.

She stepped out of his way and gulped. "Come on in."

"Thank you," he said, stepping in and walking past her. A spicy, masculine scent drifted through the air as he went, and Bree inhaled it with a shameless breath. *Yum.* It had been a while since she'd been in the company of a man. At least one she wasn't related to.

"I'm sure sorry to inconvenience you this way. I told Braden I could stay at a nearby hotel but he didn't like the idea."

No, Braden would definitely not go for a thing like that. "It's no inconvenience," she lied, straining to come up with a different option. Anything that put Greyson anywhere but in the same home as her.

He stepped around her luggage and glanced around the place. "I've seen a layout of the home and noticed that all the bedrooms are upstairs," he said, heading into an adjacent room. "Unless we could make this work…" He flicked a light on, illuminating a dining room of sorts. An oak table surrounded by sturdy matching chairs.

Make *what* work, she wondered, hope rising in her chest. Was there a room he could stay in down there? *Oh, please say there is.* She followed him through the dining room and into the next as Greyson flipped on yet another light – the kitchen, it turned out. A smaller, less formal dining set stood next to a large window.

She surveyed the layout as Greyson continued toward an old door. Though wood panels made up the bottom half of the door, the top half was glass, like a screen door of sorts, yet it didn't lead outside. Just to some dim-looking space with empty shelves.

"Hmm," he mumbled, stepping back into the kitchen. "I figured it was probably a storage room." His brows scrunched, his expression thoughtful as he set his eyes back on her.

Whoa. Her chest filled with warmth, a rushing sensation that snatched her next breath. Bree couldn't fathom why her body would react in such a way. It was obvious, by the look in his eyes, the man was a thousand miles away. But just what was he thinking about? Her face warmed as she made for the closest cupboard, hoping to get out from under his gaze. Cups. Perfect.

On went the faucet, in went the water, and up to her lips went the glass.

"I don't want to intrude on you," he said from behind. "I know this is a tough situation, and that you weren't expecting me to stay here. I'll just camp out on the couch for the night so you can have the upstairs to yourself."

She forced down a gulp of lukewarm water, fully expecting to tell him that that wasn't necessary. Only the words wouldn't come yet.

"I'll see you to your room." He walked out of the kitchen and strode back toward the front room.

Bree set down her glass and followed, knowing she should not let him sleep downstairs. Not if one of the extra rooms had a bed. But she hardly knew the guy. Sure, Braden trusted him. And for that reason alone – she was certain he could be trusted. But that didn't mean they had to be so close. Separated by only a wall between them.

He fisted her keys, tucked her blanket and pillow beneath one arm, and then gripped hold of her suitcase. It felt odd, watching her personal items being held by none other than Greyson Law. He set those stormy eyes back on her. "Once we find out how long the repair on the guesthouse will take, we can see about me moving into one of the other rooms."

Bree nodded, but there seemed to be a purpose behind those words. As if he were easing her into levels of discomfort. First he'd be in the house. Then he'd be in the room beside hers. What next?

The staircase was wide and bright, the light fixture overhead spilling its generous glow over each step. It was the only part of the home, from what she could tell, that had vaulted ceilings, offering a limited view of the bedroom doors as she rounded the first, small landing.

She followed Greyson, trying very hard not to look at him from behind. The situation couldn't have been more awkward. Stuck in the same house with a guy from high school. Her complete opposite at that. She hated having people in her space. And now he had no place else to go.

He led her around a wooden railing at the top of the stairs, through a spacious, rounded walkway, and into a nice-sized bedroom. A big bed took up a good portion, its white, lacy duvet adding a charming touch. A hope chest stood at the foot of the bed, a lavender cushion covering the top. On the nearby nightstand stood a brass lamp, but it wasn't on just yet. For now, the decorative glass fixture on the ceiling lit the room.

"This is the largest bedroom in the house," he assured, "but it doesn't have its own bath." He set down her suitcase, glanced around the room a bit more, and then strode directly toward her where she stood in the doorway. He gave her one short, distinct nod as his gaze fell to the floor. "Excuse me," he mumbled, shuffling out of the room. He was careful not to nudge her as he squeezed between her and the doorframe. Realization hit – she was in the way.

Ugh. Why didn't I move?

"There is one bathroom up here," he said, pointing to an open doorway. "The other is just off the garage next to the kitchen. That's a bedroom there. One there too." It was odd to have him explaining the place, knowing he hadn't even been there before either.

"All rooms have windows," he said after a brief pause. "None have balconies though, which I was glad about." His ramblings seemed to be more like inner thoughts he spoke aloud.

Her brows furrowed. She just wanted this conversation to end. The *night* to end. Heck, the sooner this whole thing was over and she was back in Montana with her kids the better. "Well," she said, pointing a thumb into her room. "I'm really exhausted. You don't mind if I just go onto bed, do you?"

Greyson shook his head. "Not at all. See you in the morning."

"Night." The word was no more than a whisper. An afterthought as she watched him round the wooden railing toward the stairs. Guilt was rising from all sorts of places. She wasn't being much of a host. If she had any semblance of manners she would see that he had a bed for the night. See that he didn't feel obligated to camp out on the couch.

Say something, an inner voice pled. "Thanks for bringing up my things," she blurted.

Greyson gave her a subtle nod and made for the stairs. He got to the landing, took two more steps, and then paused to look up at her where she stood in the doorway, paralyzed.

"Bree?" Tingling warmth gushed through her chest at the sound of her name in his deep, raspy voice.

"Mmm?"

His eyes locked on hers, and Bree was certain – by the look on his face, the very air about him – that if Greyson Law wanted to own the world and everyone in it, he could.

He lifted his chin, squaring his face with hers. "I'm going to see that you're safe."

———— ~⁓⁓⁓~ ————

Greyson bit into a large apple, appreciating the tangy-sweet flavor. If he was going to intrude upon Bree for a while, at least he didn't have to worry about where his breakfast would come from.

He rested an elbow onto the picnic table he'd discovered, and looked over his list. The wooden table – shaded by the neighboring pines – stood right along the fence bordering the property. Finding it had been a stroke of luck. This would be his office for the time being. His place to think and plot out his day. A task that was proving to be much harder than he'd anticipated. When out on a job, Greyson had a rundown of his client's activities from sun-up to nightfall. Most often, he would have spoken with the security staff at each vendor or location and discussed the best approach for escorting them on and off the premises. With Bree, it was different.

He took another bite of his apple, catching a drop of sweet juice with the side of his thumb, and pondered the list. It looked like more of a façade. All centered around the orchard he and Bree would manage for a time. A fine one, at that, he'd admit. One that required a great deal of work this time of year, being harvest as it was. But that was just it. Greyson was used to having a list of things to cover and check – assuring all was safe for his client. His mind was caught between finding efficient ways to harvest the fruit, and techniques he might use to alert himself of danger in this strange, new circumstance.

His phone let out a buzz, and Greyson checked the screen before pulling it to his ear. *Braden.* Seeing the name reminded him of the other issue prodding at his mind: the guesthouse.

He came to a stand, walking toward the shed as he answered. "Hi there, Braden."

"Morning," came his reply. "I finally heard back from my insurance company. The local agent is out of town until Thursday. If they can get someone else out there before then, they will. But that's the best they can do."

"Thursday, huh?" Greyson said with a nod. "No problem."

"Of course that's just to get someone to take a look at it. From there they've got to send out their guy to give a bid. Schedule a date for repair." Braden let out a sigh. "I'm afraid we could be looking at a large chunk of time."

"But will it be covered by your insurance?" Greyson asked, concerned for Braden and his finances.

"Oh, yeah. Between my insurance and the property insurance of... whoever owns that neighboring land, we shouldn't have to come up with much."

Greyson nodded. "That's a relief."

"Yeah, but I still feel terrible for the inconvenience," he said. "So, how is Bree taking it?"

The question made Greyson's insides twist. "Taking what?"

"You being in the house with her."

"I'm not really sure. I just grabbed a sheet and slept on the couch last night. Got out of there before she woke this morning. I'm trying to stay out of her way, I guess."

"The couch? Why? There are two other bedrooms upstairs. One's more of a game room, but the other is furnished with a dresser, bed, and an office desk, if you'd like to use that."

"Alright," Greyson said, "that's good to know. Thanks." Of course, he wouldn't take him up on it until Bree encouraged it herself. He didn't want to do anything to make her uncomfortable. Yet he had to admit, the change in circumstance gave life to something he'd been entertaining for the last few days. With him being in the same house as Bree, the two could actually pose as husband and wife, which would provide Bree with an added level of protection.

He didn't mention it just yet, only followed the conversation as it moved to things concerning the orchard.

"You can always hire a few locals to help pick if it becomes too much," Braden said. "We pay by the pound. You'll find the payment log in your email, along with a list of locals who've helped out in the past. Most of them students."

"Sounds great," Greyson said with a nod, heading back toward his makeshift office.

"About Bree," Braden added, his voice changing to a more casual tone. "She plans to help out quite a bit, so be sure you allow her to do so."

He nodded. "Will do."

"I know there's a lot of lifting and that involved," Braden continued, "but she's stubborn and doesn't like to be coddled. If something is too much for her, she'll back off on her own. But not if she thinks she has something to prove."

"Gotcha." A small smile tugged at the corner of Greyson's lips. Just why did this make him like the woman even more? An image of her lovely face rushed to the forefront of his mind. High cheekbones and a well-earned grin. Even the image of her fighting that grin caused his blood to blaze. His thoughts had taken him from what Braden was saying, but he focused back in soon enough.

"...if she goes hurting herself it will be her lesson to learn," he said in an almost a fatherly tone. "Take it from me – there's no stopping her anyhow. You'll have her hurt and mad at you all at once."

Greyson paused in replying. Not sure if he was finished just yet. This wasn't the first time he'd been given a warning where Bree was concerned; he was starting to wonder if she should have come with her own instruction manual.

"Think that's just about it..." Braden said, his voice fading off.

"Alright, then," Greyson said. "Oh, but Braden?"

"Yeah?"

A thought came to Greyson; one he felt was only fair to mention. "Maybe you can give Bree a bit of a head's up where I'm concerned."

"Sure." Braden said.

"I'll let her help with physical work around here, as long as I believe she's not asking for injury, but I'd like a little cooperation on her end too."

"Fair enough." Braden sounded amused.

"She needs to understand that protection is my life. When I have a concern – whether from intelligence I receive, a sign that something's out of place, or based strictly on gut-instinct – I'm going to need her to cooperate. You wanted me to let her lead a normal life here – as best she can under the circumstance – and I plan to do that. But there won't be a time that I'm not thinking about her safety. She should know that I can be just as stubborn as she is, if it means keeping her safe."

One small chuckle sounded from the line. "Precisely why you're the best man for the job."

CHAPTER SEVEN

A warm burst of sun welcomed Bree into a conscious state. Her eyes flicked open, revealing a sideways view of the unfamiliar room. The lamp on her nightstand she recognized. The dresser and closet, she didn't. Light, lavender paint covered the walls, matching the tiny flowers on the sheets. She turned onto her back and stretched, wondering where Greyson had ended up. The idea made her cringe. She'd behaved badly last night and she knew it. Still, she'd learned something about the man, in the moments he'd spoken to her from the stairwell.

If there had been any question as to why Braden picked Greyson Law to watch over her, it had vanished after that very encounter. To some it might not have been much of an encounter at all. Just an exchange of a few simple words. But none had ever carried so much weight. So much fervor. *I'm going to see that you're safe.*

That sentence had played out in her head countless times as she'd readied herself for bed, filling her with a much-needed assurance. It reminded her of the craft she'd made with the daycare kids just a few months back. Paper flowers in a plastic cup. She hadn't realized they'd run into a problem with the weight of the flower in that big, empty cup. Knowing that water would ruin the stem, Bree had set out to collect rocks. The kids helped, each digging into the soil in the backyard until their cup held enough weight to stand upright and sustain the unique, handmade flower inside.

Greyson's words had done that for her. They'd filled her insides with something she hadn't even known was missing. But now it was clear — Bree had been falling for days. Weeks even. It wasn't just the pending separation from her kids and family — it was the looming *what if* question, knocking her off balance at every turn. *What if Carl Ronsberg found her?*

As much as she dreaded the idea of having someone in her space, she felt relieved in an entirely different way. It was a trade off: her solitude in exchange for the protection he could offer.

Bree yawned as she sat up, stretching an arm high over her head. The gold, ornate clock on her nightstand said she'd slept in. Really slept in. It was past ten in the morning. That meant the kids had already left for school. She wondered how their first morning had gone with their dad and Wendy. Were they going to like school? Be scared of their new teachers? Make new friends? How wonderful it would be to get their call once they got home.

She sighed, willing time to move faster. Perhaps if she

allowed herself to fall back to sleep, she could kill a few more hours. And – bonus – she wouldn't have to run into Greyson.

The very idea filled her with an immense amount of dread. She had been awful to let him sleep on the couch last night. She vowed that if he had to spend another night there, she'd let him sleep in one of the bedrooms. The thought caused a ripple of nerves to bristle over her skin. She just couldn't imagine saying the words out loud. *Hey, Greyson, if you'd like to, you can sleep in the room next to mine.* It sounded way too much like a come-on. And Greyson would not get a come-on from her for as long as she lived. She did not want that pompous man thinking she was falling all over herself in love with him like every other female on the planet. The fact was, she would never love a man like him.

Still, there were two very distinct characteristics Greyson possessed. Admirable ones. He was trustworthy. That much she knew based on Braden's measure alone. But the second was something she'd discovered on her own. He would do almost anything to keep her from harm. That sense of duty was etched in his face as he'd spoken to her, and for that, she was grateful.

Bree climbed out of bed, turned full-circle to view the charming, sun-lit bedroom. Light seemed to love this room, and Bree suddenly loved it too, for that reason and more. She pulled in a deep breath and moved to open the sheer drapes. The large window – centered just above her bed – showed a view of the front yard. Her spirits lifted a little at the sight.

She barely recognized the trees lining the driveway, the branched giants looking friendlier in the light of day. The driveway – made up of cracked, moss-covered cement – was dotted with a sparse array of fallen leaves. The rooftop jutted out over the front door, and Bree recalled seeing a big porch out front. Oh, she hoped that her memory was correct.

After retrieving her cosmetic bag and freshening up for the day, Bree set out to discover the rest of the home. Another bedroom stood at the opposite side of the bathroom. The next room held only a couch and an entertainment center filled with board games and knickknacks. She imagined playing games with the kids on the large oval rug in the center of the floor.

She hadn't noticed the great window above the staircase landing. It was massive, and offered a clear view of the orchard. Her eyes widened. Walls of gorgeous green accented by rich, colorful fruit. *You're kidding me.* Her first view of the place hadn't done it justice. What with the rain and the clouds and the sadness hovering over her. But in the sunlight, sparkling hints of dew glistening like diamonds, the sight was stunning.

She spent the next twenty minutes admiring the rest of the home. The charming – though rather small – kitchen, the custom woodwork framing the lovely dining room, and the cozy front room she'd overlooked upon entering the home. But better than all of it, was the front porch.

After shrugging into a soft, warm hoodie, Bree sunk deep into the hammock and sighed. *This* was something she could get used to. The stray thought made Bree sit up straighter, shifting uncomfortably beneath the guilt she felt for thinking such a thing. How could she possibly *get used* to life without her kids? She couldn't, Bree assured herself, climbing out of the hammock while the guilt took root.

Something occurred to her then – she had a job to do. That gorgeous orchard was more than a pretty view. It was a paycheck. And now was the beginning of harvest. *Perfect.* Just the distraction she was looking for.

She pictured Greyson in that moment, musing he was a bit of a distraction himself. The romance-deprived side of her seemed to yearn for him and all of his handsome, manly splendor, despite her aversion to guys like him.

He's a business partner, she reminded herself. A fellow worker she'd be polite to. And – she assured herself as she spotted him steering an old tractor along the orchard – someone she would invite to sleep in the room upstairs until his place was fixed.

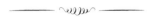

Greyson pulled the old tractor to a stop and killed the engine. He'd attached two rolling crates onto the back, figuring they could most likely fill them up by tomorrow's end.

The humming of a soft melody drifted through the air, alerting him to his company. Bree. Stubborn Bree who would fight to work like one of the boys and gripe if he treated her differently. *Humph.* Heaven forbid he treat her like a lady. He stiffened with irritation. Usually his clients respected him. In fact, he'd dare say a mutual admiration existed between them, each having appreciation for what the other had achieved in their respective fields. In this case, he felt as if she was forced to tolerate his presence, and he couldn't avoid the annoyance that caused.

The humming stopped. But as a soft breeze picked up, it carried one uttered word on its wings. "Hi."

Soft. Unassuming. Almost sweet. He tightened the straps on his pack. "Hey."

"Sorry it took me so long to get out here. Mind if I help pick?"

Again. Kind. Non-threatening. Perhaps Braden had warned him for no reason. "Not at all. I brought you a picking basket. It's just inside that last bin there." He looked over his shoulder. "You see it?" If she'd said yes he hadn't heard, because he'd only then caught sight of her. Looking even more lovely than she had the night before. Rich olive skin, gorgeous brown eyes, and a shade of pink accenting those high cheekbones.

Bree stepped closer to the crate, rested her hands along the edge. "Oh, yeah. I see it." The bin was nearly to her waist; he didn't want her tumbling in or getting a sliver as she reached for it, but if she wanted help she'd ask.

He gulped, wishing he could force his eyes away from her – not knowing quite how. He couldn't figure out what made her so lovely. She had two eyes, a nose, and mouth like everyone else. It was just that hers – combined with whatever she had going on inside – made up something truly unique. He knew she was standoffish, even a bit cold. But all he could feel from her then was warmth, and it was magnetic.

Once she snagged the strap between her fingers, Greyson approached the first tree of that particular row. He'd gotten only three apples into his pack before Bree spoke up once again.

"Okay, I'm trying to figure out how this thing goes on, but I swear it doesn't even have an opening."

She was asking for help? That was a surprise. "Here," he said, backing away from the tree. He moved toward her, assessing her reaction as he neared. He'd studied body language in his line of work, learned just what it revealed about people, whether they knew it or not. And the arm that Bree had pinned across her chest, the way she held the carrier between them – said she didn't want him anywhere near.

He stopped walking, looked into her deep brown eyes, inwardly wishing she wasn't so guarded with him. Wondering what it would take to get close to such a woman. To have her want him near.

Her brows lifted, and then furrowed. "Are you going to help, or..." Her cheeks flushed red, contradicting every other thing her body said.

"I will if you'd like me to."

"Pff. If I could figure it out on my own, I would. But we're wasting time, so..."

Hmm. "Are you okay if I put it on for you? Like, showing you by placing it on?"

She took a step back, twirling the strap she held so the carrier spun. "Unless you can just, turn around and let me figure it out by looking at yours." A splotch of sweat dotted her upper lip. She was uncomfortable. Why was she so uncomfortable? Had the mere idea of him touching her made her upset? It bothered him. Forget the fact that she'd had some crazy stalker after her. Greyson was not that stalker and she needed to trust him.

"I guess you can look at mine but you said yourself we were wasting time, so suit yourself." He spun slowly in place until he faced away from her. A smile crept over his face as he realized the awkwardness of the situation. Jeez, this woman was something else. A light sweeping sound of fabric told him she was giving it a try. A quick glance over his shoulder said she was failing. Her arm was caught through one loop, while she was trying to force her head through another.

A chuckle snuck up his throat. He pinned his lips to keep it in, but knew the bouncing of his shoulders would give him away. At last he spun around in time to see her drop the carrier right onto the ground.

"Something's wrong with that one. It's designed for a small child or something."

He could not get the grin off his face as he eyed the

picking basket at her feet. "You just need to undo the straps."

"That one doesn't have any clips," she assured.

In one swift move, Greyson snatched it off the ground. "They're hidden," he explained, sliding the fabric toward the seam. "The sleeve is to make it more comfortable against your skin. You have to move it in order to see the clasp." Once he had the thing unlatched, he motioned for her to come closer. Her to him this time; not the other way around.

She kept the one arm crossed against her chest, and folded the other over her stomach as she neared. She stopped once she was at arm's length, dropping her gaze to the ground. "Okay," she mumbled.

He hadn't smiled this much in years. "You'll have to put your arms down," he said.

"Alright." Bree let out an annoyed huff.

What was with this woman? "You'll make sure the X goes across your back." He brought it over her head. "Go ahead and lift up your arms."

She did, the floral scent of her competing with the apples as he inhaled. Greyson tried very hard not to touch her as he slipped the openings around her arms. Parts of his knuckle grazed her shirt, the slightest touch, but it still made his pulse pound. Once the oblong carrier hung loosely across her chest, he stepped around her to secure the clasps. One, and then two.

"How does that feel?" he asked, stepping back to look at her. She shifted it awkwardly over her chest, and

Greyson realized she had a bit of an obstacle there.

"Is there any way we can drop this a little lower? Or just…" she pulled it away from her chest, "maybe get a little more slack on top?"

"I'm sure there is." He walked behind her once more, reminding himself – when his eyes wandered over the prominent curve of her waist – that she was a client. His heart stood no chance of settling down now. The physical and visual stimulation keeping the rapid pace. After forcing his attention to the upper part of the straps, Greyson found an adjustable piece and worked to move the clip on one side.

"How about there?" he asked.

"Yeah," Bree said, her voice soft like a whisper. She cleared her throat. "That's perfect."

Something about the unsteady sound of her voice made Greyson more aware of how close he was to her. "Good," he replied. "I'll uh, do the same on the other side." His knuckles grazed the back of her neck the slightest bit as he moved to the other side. Soft. Silky. Warm. The wispy tips of her ponytail brushed against his wrist as he adjusted the second strap. And then he was done. But that didn't mean he could get himself to move. Not yet. Something was happening between them. Something more than two people standing side by side. It felt as if a current in the air – alive and pulsing – held the two in place. Pulling. Drawing.

His heart sputtered and lapsed in time with the magnetic pulse. He wondered what it might feel like if they touched. *Really* touched. Him holding her hand in his. Or running a palm along her lower back. Around that curve of her waist.

"Thanks," Bree blurted, stepping away from him. She shifted the carrier and cleared her throat once more. "This will be fine."

Greyson snapped out of his daze. *She's a client,* the voice in his head hollered again. *A client!*

"Which apples are we looking for?" she asked, approaching the tree next to his.

He stepped toward the one he'd been working on, reached for an apple that looked ready. "You want to make sure there's a full face of red," he explained, twisting the fruit for her to see. "We won't just pick all the apples off one tree and move on. We'll have to come back through daily and pick what's ready.

He reached for another apple that was ready to go. "To pick, you take hold of the bottom and lift up until it snaps free." The stem plucked off the branch with ease.

"You'll set them gently into your tote, and once you have that filled, I'll show you how to put them in the bin without bruising the fruit."

She nodded, her brown eyes shifting away from him back to the apples. He watched her pick the first few, relieved to see she'd seemed to learn the technique with ease.

They worked in comfortable silence, each filling then emptying their tote in turn. Greyson couldn't help but look over to watch Bree unload her case. He liked the way her delicate-looking hands moved over the apples, keeping the movement down to a minimum. Gentle. Almost loving.

"So," Bree said, securing the base of her tote into place once more. "How's the situation with the roof? Any word?"

Greyson shook his head. "Sounds like it'll be a few days before the insurance agent can get out here." He looked up at the sky, glad to see an endless stretch of blue, dotted with only puffy, harmless looking clouds. "I went back and shut off the electricity, so no one would get shocked. If the rain comes back before they take care of it, I'll have to climb onto the roof and secure a tarp over the hole."

"That sounds dangerous," she said.

"I'll try to do it before the rain starts," he promised with a laugh.

She let out a small chuckle as well. "And the lightning too?"

"Yes, the lightning too. So I guess the bad news is, I'll have to intrude on you until they get the place suitable for living."

"Is it really bad," she asked, "the damage?"

Greyson tilted his head, glancing over to catch her eye. His heart clunked out of rhythm. "I guess that depends on how you look at it. Some pines are massive. I'm sure they take out roofs all the time. I think we're looking at minimal damage compared to what it could have been." He shrugged. "Even still, I'm just glad your brother has the place insured."

"Me too," she agreed.

A look passed between them. One that had nothing to do with broken roofs, pine trees, or insurance.

A splash of warmth spread over her cheeks.

His heart skipped a beat, a tug pulling at one corner of his mouth.

Just as evidence of a similar grin showed at her full lips, Bree turned away from him, shifting her focus back to the tree she was picking from.

The exchange, though short-lived, caused heat to stir low in his belly. A sensation that simmered as he finished up with the tree before him and moved to the one beyond Bree. They continued to work side by side as Greyson thought over the strange situation he was in. As frustrating as it was, not knowing just how things would go with him and Bree, he had to admit —inwardly anyway — that he was anxious to find out.

CHAPTER EIGHT

Bree slid the fabric carrier along a heap of red, gorgeous apples, guiding them into place as she moved. The fragrant fruit had tempted her for hours, but she'd promised herself she wouldn't sample until lunchtime.

"You about ready for a break?" Greyson asked over his shoulder.

"Yes," she said. "I think so. Why don't we head into the kitchen and I'll…" She stopped there, remembering that she hadn't brought any groceries. "You know what? I don't have any food." She chuckled. "I planned to make a trip to the store this morning, but forgot all about it."

She worked to secure the clasp Greyson clamped for her, hands fumbling blindly as he spoke up.

"I packed a few cans of soup," he said. "Why don't you let me warm that up and we can go pick up some groceries this evening."

We? She didn't like the sound of that. But the soup part was tempting. "That would be nice," she said, still patting around the straps.

"Here..." Greyson's voice came from behind. He wrapped his large hand around hers, solid and strong, and guided her to the end of the sleeve. "See this right here?"

Bree froze, her body letting out several involuntary reactions at once. Her heart – though Greyson had no claim over it – fluttered and skipped out of beat. Warmth spread over her cheeks. And when she felt his touch along the inside of her wrist, goosebumps spread up her arms. She looked down, was barely able to see the strap along the back of her waist. Inwardly she was more concerned with his touch. Wondering if she could squirm her way out of it.

"You'll push this cloth back. And then..." He moved her hand gently, allowing her fingertips to feel along the way. "You grab onto this clasp and pinch, right here." He tapped his finger and thumb over hers.

Bree nodded while stepping away from him. He was too close. And she didn't need all the physical reactions playing with her mind. Once in her own space again, she pinched the clasp, glad when it released the strap around her waist.

"And now you can just shrug out of it," he said.

She pulled it over her head, sliding her other arm out completely, and then rested it on top of the apples. "Hey, do you know what time it is?" she asked, glancing at the bright sky above.

"Just after one."

Hearing the time put fire into her legs. She took off in

a sprint toward the home, calling over her shoulder. "The kids have early-out for their first day. You don't mind if I jog ahead, do you?"

"Not at all," Greyson mumbled behind her.

Bree moved faster, the frantic pace of her heart urging her forward. Once in the house, she grabbed her phone, noting she'd missed a call from Dallin's cell. With a few taps of her screen, the phone dialed back. She scurried onto the front porch and waited for someone to answer. Her heart thumped out in protest over the sudden stop in motion; she countered it by pacing along the large porch.

"Mom?" The sweet little voice belonged to Carter.

Bree smiled. "Yes! Hi, Carter boo! How was your first day of school?"

"It was awesome!" With great enthusiasm, Carter spilled details through labored breaths, unable to get the words out fast enough.

Bree ate up every bit of it, the words seeming to heal the splintered parts of her soul. Parts that had fractured and split at their separation. Next came her conversation with Sophie. Stories ranging from what she ate for lunch, to the *kinda cute* boy who sat next to her in class. All of it supplied Bree with an extra level of comfort and peace. By the end of the call, she was strolling along the far-reaching drive beneath the massive trees, chuckling aloud at one of Sophie's wild tales about their baby sister.

"You should see, Mom. Chloe is saying a ton of words now! I can't wait until baby Jacob talks like that."

The comment made Bree realize how much Braden's

baby would change while she was away. Not to mention Dallin's baby, Chloe. "Yeah," she said. "I'm looking forward to that too." In the quiet moment that followed, Bree sighed in content. "Oh, Sophie bear, I've been looking forward to this call all day."

"We have too," Sophie assured, her soft, high-pitched voice a comfort all its own. "How do you like the house you're in?"

Bree spun to face the two-story home. "It's beautiful." She took in the country appeal of its pale yellow siding, large covered porch, and pointed pitches along the rooftops. A new, warm burst of peace burrowed into the center of her chest.

"I want to see it. Can you send me a picture?"

"Sure," Bree said, "just a sec." She navigated her way through the phone settings until the camera came up. Framing the home within the small screen made it appear fake – like something out of a storybook. "There. You should get it any minute."

Dallin's voice bellowed in the background. "I gotta go," Sophie said.

"Okay." She fiddled with the necklace Allie made for her, remembering how she'd had each of them kiss the heart-shaped trinkets with their respective birthstones. She brought them to her lips, pressing a soft kiss to each. "Love you, Sophie bear."

Her shoulders dropped once the line went dead. Not with despair or disappointment, but with relief; saying goodbye wasn't nearly as painful as she thought it might be. The kids sounded happy — and that caused her spirits to soar.

Bree made her way back up the creaky porch steps and sunk into the hammock with a sigh, feeling — for the first time since she arrived — a sense of absolute peace.

In that very moment, a small voice reminded her that Carl Ronsberg would be out of prison in just six days. Would her peace be lost then, lost in a sea of worry and fear? A light sound of whistling carried through the front screen door, causing an image of Greyson to seep into her mind. *No*, she decided. She was miles away, in a place he would never find, thanks to Braden. Beyond that, she had an extra wall of protection. If Carl managed to hunt her down — if he appeared in this town to gawk through her windows or stand on her porch or leave cryptic notes that threatened her safety — Greyson Law would make him regret it.

The screen door made the slightest creak as Greyson stepped onto the porch. The quiet sound of it reminded him that he needed to install the home security devices on all the windows and doors before the day was through.

He scanned the porch before realizing Bree was just yards away, her slender body cradled within a knit hammock. Quiet. Serene.

While warming soup on the stove, Greyson had overheard parts of her phone call. He had to admit – he'd been surprised by the way she'd come to life. While talking to her kids Bree had been laughing heartily one moment, and joking around the next. He'd heard bits and pieces of advice she'd given to one of them, something about showing manners to their teacher no matter what. That it would get them far in life.

A deep feeling of admiration took root in him; he liked discovering the kind of mother she was. Loving. Concerned. And playful, too, he mused, remembering the way she'd teased them. Bree was a mystery to him. And it seemed the more he got to know of her, the more intrigued he became.

A plank in the patio squeaked as he stepped onto the porch, but Bree didn't budge.

"How did your phone call go?" he asked, veering toward a patio swing across the way.

"It was wonderful. They both loved their first day." Her smooth, rather low voice sounded dreamlike. "Carter got a little mouthy with the teacher, but I could hardly get after him for it."

"Oh yeah?" Greyson lowered himself onto the swinging chair, leaned his elbows onto his knees. "What happened?"

Bree was lounged back, her gaze set on the beams overhead, but she straightened up once he sat. She turned to look at him, tucking the hammock's edge beneath her knees so her feet dangled. "Well he's in first grade, okay?

And his kindergarten teacher last year was like a dream. Never raised her voice or anything. So when he gets in *this* class and sees the teacher go off on some poor girl for not bringing her supplies, Carter speaks right up." She shook her head, laughing as the most splendid smile spread over her face. A smile that put heat in his belly in a blink.

"He tells the teacher to leave... her... *alone!*"

"The gal she was getting after?" Greyson asked with a laugh.

"Yep." Bree sighed. "Oh, I tell you. Just when you think you've taught your kids all they need to know about manners and being polite."

"Well it's kind of hard to be mad at the kid when he's just sticking up for a fellow classmate," Greyson pointed out. "A girl, no less."

Bree waved an arm toward him. "Exactly." She held his gaze, a thoughtful look in her eye. "This might be good for them," she said.

He hadn't expected that. "Oh yeah?"

She nodded. "Yeah. I think until now they sort of resented their little half-sister."

Greyson gave her a questioning glance.

"My ex-husband remarried. He and his wife have a baby girl. Big blue eyes. Thick, blonde hair. A real cutie. Her name's Chloe. Anyway, I think they went into their weekends with him thinking it was either them or her. That – during those days – their father had to choose them. But now that they know they'll have all this time with their dad, they're more willing to accept her. Let her be their baby sister, not their competition."

Greyson nodded, impressed with the insight she'd gained from a fifteen-minute phone call. "How old did you say your kids are?" he asked.

"Seven and nine. Sophie, the oldest, just had her birthday over the summer. She's in third grade now and said she already has homework. And she said it like she was all proud of it. Something about living in the real world now." Bree shook her head. "Hilarious."

There were several things swimming in Greyson's head. A curiosity about kids already having homework in the third grade, the first day of school, no less. A desire to know more about the kids. To meet them one day, even. But louder than all of that was an acknowledgement of how changed Bree was after speaking to her kids. Physically, even. The guarded tension he'd seen in her posture was gone. The looming look of reservation in her eyes had vanished. And what was left – after all that had melted away – was something Greyson could only call beauty. True and undeniable.

"So did you find that soup?" Bree asked, yanking Greyson from his thoughts.

"Oh, yeah. Got it all warmed up and ready. I've got a box of crackers too, if you'd like to have them along with it."

"Sounds good. I'm starving."

Greyson stood up, offering his hand to assist her. Bree glanced down at it, that shield of reservation rising between them once more. He'd extended it with an absent mind, and wished then – in the lengthy pause – that he hadn't.

"I've got it," she assured, holding the sides of the hammock as she climbed out.

Greyson let his hand drop and resisted the urge to sprint for the door and open it for her. Instead he followed leisurely behind, nodding when she propped the door for him. *Baby steps,* he reminded himself as they headed into the house. He would need to be patient with her. She wasn't the type of person who would just let anyone into her life. After what she'd been through who could blame her?

**

"So how is your family doing?" Bree's question took Greyson off-guard.

He pushed his empty soup bowl away and stretched his arms with a yawn. "They're doing alright," he said. "It's just Todd and my old man, you know."

Bree nodded. "That's right."

Greyson wished he hadn't pointed that out. After all, what remained of his family might have been small, but she had even less. "Todd's helping my dad run the place for now. My dad's hoping it can heal their relationship, having this time together." He wasn't sure how much she knew about Todd's drinking problem. Anyone up on his or her gossip would be well aware. Those who stayed out of the loop wouldn't have a clue.

A question formed in her eyes, but she didn't ask it. Probably because she didn't want to offer anything personal in return. She took a few spoonfuls of soup before speaking up once more.

"And what do you do now? I mean, I know you've been in the security business, but..." she drifted off there, lifted another spoonful of soup to her lips and blew on it.

"I own a training center in Washington."

"You train people to become bodyguards?" she asked.

He nodded. "Train, certify. We also give courses about safety and potential pitfalls to those already in the industry. I work with a large network of people in the business. Several agencies have expressed an interest in heightening the skill level of their staff," he said. "In fact, I'll be building a new center back home soon. Bought a nice chunk of property about fifteen miles from my old man's. There, we'll focus on the latest technology available. There are some very sophisticated teams out there, nations even, willing to do just about anything to get what they want. We have to use every advantage we can to keep our clients safe."

"Hmm. You umm... used to work with a lot of folks in Hollywood, right? But not so much anymore."

"Right," he said. "I'm not one for the spotlight." Boy was that ever true.

Bree nodded quietly, an unreadable expression on her pretty face. It seemed as if the sunlight from the window had seeped into her skin, the radiant glow reflecting off her cheeks even brighter than the window itself.

"What made you want to become a bodyguard in the first place?" she asked. "It's a pretty unique occupation."

Greyson leaned back into the chair, cradled the back of his head in his hands. "A number of things," he said. "Well, three, to be exact. First, my father's love for Kennedy. His study of the assassination is one of my earliest memories. So that encouraged one aspect of it."

Suddenly Greyson's phone started to vibrate and buzz. He glanced down to see a number he didn't recognize, and then brought the thing to his ear.

"Greyson Law," he answered. The caller identified himself as Amelio, the local produce buyer for the grocery stores in town – someone Greyson had been waiting to hear from. "Excuse me," he whispered to Bree.

She gave him a nod while coming to her feet, collecting the glasses and bowls from the table.

Greyson stepped around the corner and into the storage room, where he kept the conversation short and sweet. He confirmed they were right on schedule to deliver two bins by tomorrow afternoon, another two on Thursday, and three by Saturday evening. It would take consistent efforts on his and Bree's part, but by the looks of what they'd accomplished in just a few short hours, they'd meet their targets just fine.

"Sorry about that," he said, stepping back into the kitchen.

Bree had cleared up the dishes and was now wiping down the small dining room table.

"No problem." She eyed the yard out back, a glint of curiosity on her face. "I'm curious about the guesthouse. What does it look like inside? And how bad is the damage?"

Greyson tucked the phone back into his pocket. "I can show you, if you'd like."

"Yes," Bree said. "I'd like that."

CHAPTER NINE

"So you didn't finish telling me about why you decided to become a bodyguard," Bree said. "And is that an outdated term or do people still use it?"

"People still use it. But we often refer to it as the personal protection business as well." Greyson held the backdoor open for her.

"Personal protection," she mumbled while stepping into the backyard. The outdoor air was cool, but as she stepped from the shaded patio onto a sunny patch of sparse grass, a layer of sun-drenched heat seeped into her skin. "The first was your father's interest in the Kennedy assassination," she said. "What are the other two?"

He squared his large shoulders toward the guesthouse and looked down at the ground. "Your brother had something to do with it, believe it or not."

"Braden?"

He flashed her a grin, and parts of her body

responded again. An electric zing sinking deep into her chest like a dart. *Stop,* she scolded her betraying body.

"Yeah. I made the junior varsity team during my freshman year – earlier than most. Coach even let me step in on one of the varsity games in a pinch. A few of the guys didn't appreciate that. They started giving me crap about it."

She and Greyson had been walking at a slow pace, small steps while he talked. The ground cover had changed as they neared, the grass growing more sparse as the sight of pine needles and pinecones increased. Bree liked how the main home offered cover with its enormous oaks, but she appreciated the wall of pine trees out back as well. Along with their fresh, woodsy smell they offered a level of comfort. She liked knowing that they were shielded from nearly all angles.

Once they stepped into a shaded area in front of the guesthouse, the crunch of fallen debris beneath their shoes, Bree stopped walking altogether, wanting to hear him out before entering the home.

"Anyway," Greyson said, "I wasn't looking for a fight, so I just tried to play it off, you know?"

She nodded. "Mm, hmm." Inwardly she was wondering what kind of idiot would start a fight with such a specimen. All muscle and mass, Greyson Law had always looked like one of those mess-with-me-and-die types.

"So one day they handed out practice updates, and mine had an extra practice scribbled onto it. I remember thinking it looked suspicious. Wondering if coach had written on there, or if it was that particular group of guys, setting me up." He cleared his throat, looked up at the blue sky for a blink before setting his matching eyes back on her. "That's the weird part. I had a hunch it might end badly, but I still went. Mostly because – as much as I didn't like confrontation – I was sick of being afraid."

Sick of being afraid. The words pulsed and swayed in her mind, resonated in every fiber. A swell of emotion flooded her chest, causing a certain kinship to rise between them. One she hadn't anticipated. Bree had lived in fear half her life, but the idea of Greyson Law fearing anyone... it was hard to fathom.

She must have had some noticeable reaction to his wording, because Greyson elaborated on that point. "There were five of them. One of me. So yeah, I was scared. Anyway, I headed onto the field. No cars in the lot. No other players around. And no group of guys ready to jump me. Lame, right? Their joke was to just get me to waste my time?" He leaned a shoulder against the guesthouse, just off from the front door.

"Yeah," she whispered, knowing there was more to come. "That *is* lame."

"Once my guard was down, I headed out of the stadium." He paused there, a darkness falling over his face. "Suddenly, I got jumped. Felt like I got hit with a wall. They'd been hiding behind the concessions stand – wearing masks over their faces – and they just started whaling on me. I mean, here I am, several years younger than them, outnumbered five to one."

An icy ache rippled up her back, making her shiver as a breeze blew in.

"It was your brother that put an end to things. He'd caught wind of their plan through one of the teammates. He'd tried to call and warn me first. When that failed he raced right down to the field."

A memory stirred at her mind as he continued. Had she heard about this back when it happened?

"All I remember is bracing myself for the long haul, and then being surprised when it came to an abrupt end. Braden had alerted Coach Brown. He got there within minutes of Braden. Two of the guys tried to run." He chuckled. "You should've seen Braden take them down. They should've known better than to mess with our best lineman."

"Wow." Bree had barely moved, as captured as she'd been by Greyson's story. "I think he told me something about it. He didn't say it was you," she clarified, "just that it was a younger player. Braden came home with a bruised up face, I think." The memory brought a horrible question to her mind. "How bad was it? The damage they'd done to you?"

He pointed to the bridge of his nose. The small scar she noticed almost each time they talked. "They broke my nose," he said. "Had a black eye. Split lip. Few cracked ribs. Word went around that I was in an accident, but everyone on the team knew better."

Bree grimaced, giving thought to what he'd shared. Something was clicking together in her mind, giving clarity to how she'd viewed Greyson in the past. She'd always believed that her brother defied the stereotype where jocks were concerned. That most were not only mindless but also capable of things like the attack Greyson explained. She'd been wrong. On both counts. It was obvious Greyson was intelligent. But it was evident to her now as well that he never would've taken part in something like that.

She thought of her drive to Oregon. Of how filthy the windshield kept getting between bouts of rain. Dust and dirt clinging to the glass in a grimy film. She'd had to clear it off several times just to see straight. It seemed that now – though Bree hadn't asked for it – someone was wiping off a smeared layer of mud, allowing her to see Greyson Law clearly for the first time.

"Anyway," he said, reaching into his pocket. He pulled out a key ring with just two keys on it and proceeded to unlock the door. "I was impacted by that event in so many ways. But the main thing that kept sticking in my mind is the cowardly way these guys went about it. Some sneak attack when I'm alone. Practically helpless against them. I wanted to stop people like them from hurting others. To save someone, the way Braden saved me that day."

He looked over his shoulder, making her realize how close she'd gotten to him. Warmth permeated the cologne-scented air between them. Bree pulled in an intoxicating breath of it, realizing she was now subject to all of his charms. Thanks to the distorted filter she'd been viewing him through over the years, Bree had built up a shield of sorts, a mental block to prevent even the slightest hint of desire for a man who would – in her mind – bring her nothing but misery. Yet as Greyson's eyes locked on hers, the filter no longer in place, his gaze burned holes through that block, melting her resistance in one, smoldering shot.

Her heart skipped a beat, then picked up in an odd sort of flutter, like the flapping of a hummingbird's wings.

She *wanted* to know him better. *Wanted* to be closer. *Wanted.*

The door swooshed open. Her eyes went to the sight within, not really seeing it at all.

"When I came out to shut off the power," Greyson said, "I sopped up most of the water to minimize the damage."

She remained silent, willing herself to pull out of her mental slumber.

"I know. It's pretty bad," he mumbled.

Bad? Yes. The damage. Bree cleared her throat. Shifted her gaze toward the roof. A giant hole with a tree branch coming through it. "Oh. Jeez, I didn't realize the tree was still there."

"It won't be for long. Someone's coming to remove it this afternoon, before it does any further damage. Hopefully they can get the place fixed up soon." He was looking away from her when he'd said it, and Bree couldn't tell if he hoped it was soon for her sake or his.

"Huh." She stepped away from the house, suddenly not wanting to walk inside anymore. The towering trees behind the property swayed along with the breeze. Bree felt like she was swaying too. Tipping toward something she'd been determined to avoid. She was starting to like Greyson Law. She could feel it. Here she'd made it all through her school years without being sucked into his charms, only to spend less than one day with him and get reeled in by his deep voice and alluring eyes.

It was more than that, she assured herself. So much more.

She shook her head, pulling in a deep breath. If she didn't watch out she'd become just like that fallen pine. Crashing down. Destroying itself while damaging everything in its path.

Suddenly the heart flutters stopped — shifting into mean, anxious thuds. Each seeming to speak to her as the pace increased: *Run. Run. Run.*

"You okay?" Greyson asked, catching up to walk alongside her.

"Yeah. I just thought maybe we shouldn't go in there until the agent takes a look at it. In case it's not safe." It probably sounded dumb but she didn't care. She had lost something very valuable to her and she needed to get it back. She'd lost her ability to see Greyson through her old eyes. Calloused, non-Greyson-liking eyes.

"Actually," she said, switching gears. "I'm not feeling so well. Do you mind if I go lie down for a bit?"

A sharp look of concern rushed over his face. "Not at all. Would you like me to escort you back?"

Bree got snagged on the word *escort*. It sounded so...

business-like. It made her feel like one of his clients. She stopped mid-stride and turned to look at him. "What was that?"

Greyson furrowed a brow, looking like she'd asked him a trick question. "If you're not feeling well, it might be best for me to see you to your room."

Oh no. The warm feelings were coming back. "No thanks," she blurted, her concern rising to a new level. What did the months ahead have in store for her? Being in that orchard with Greyson day-to-day, hearing him open up about his past, reveal things about his present – it all made her wonder what it might be like to be a part of his future. Stupidly. Ridiculously.

Suddenly Bree felt ill, just like she'd said she was. She walked quicker toward the home. Perhaps Greyson *was* a terrific guy, that didn't mean she needed to like him. It didn't mean she needed to hear about the third thing that influenced his decision to do what he does.

No, it would be better for everyone if she steered clear. Avoided personal conversations, casual smiles, and gently guiding hands helping her find hidden clasps on her picking tote. There would be no more of that.

Bree nodded, grateful she'd gotten hold of herself before things got out of hand. From this point on, Bree vowed to be less open, more aware, and far less susceptible to the alluring qualities of Mr. Greyson Law.

CHAPTER TEN

Bree smiled to herself as she wedged her earphones into place. She'd ordered one of the longest audio books she could find and was determined to listen to all sixteen hours over the next few days. Surely there were enough audio books out there to keep her busy for the entire nine-month duration.

The idea had come to her while talking to Carter last night. Dallin had been reading to the kids, which reminded Bree of how much she missed reading. That thought tapped into the steady loop cycling through her brain – the whole having-to-be-around-Greyson dilemma, and *voilà* – the perfect answer to her problem.

She pushed open the back door, feeling in control of herself once again. Sure, she'd been forced away from her life for a time, but she'd get it back soon enough. And she'd do it as a single, independent mother who was not pining after the guy who'd agreed to watch over her.

The sun seemed to assure her in that moment. Beaming its approving light on her back as she strode toward the not-even-as-magnificent-as-she'd-thought-yesterday Greyson and the beautiful orchard of fruit.

Bree grabbed her picking basket as she neared, put it on by herself (thank you very much) and strode over to the tree *two* down from Greyson. When she saw him turn to look at her she gave him a polite smile. "Good morning."

"Morning," he said. "Sure is beautiful out today. Seems like there's a bit more autumn in the air this morning, doesn't it?"

Now that he mentioned it, it was a bit chilly. "Yeah," she agreed, plucking a fragrant apple from the nearest branch. "It does." There. Polite conversation. Easy. She reached for another apple, trying to dodge the cord that went from her earbuds to the phone in her front pocket. It felt awkward, having to work around it. In fact, by the time Greyson stepped over to the bin to deposit his apples, Bree's carrier was less than halfway full.

"So what are you listening to over there?" she heard him ask from behind. The question was muffled, but she'd heard it well enough.

"Oh, it's…" she broke off there, realizing she couldn't remember the name of the book she ordered. But then another, more important realization struck her: she hadn't even pressed start on it yet. Was simply working with the buds in her ears, no sound coming out. "I can't remember the name of it." A warm wave of embarrassment swept over her cheeks. She'd been relying so heavily on the look of being preoccupied, that she hadn't given any thought to why she'd put the earbuds in to begin with. Of course, dodging conversation with Greyson *had* been the real reason.

Immediately she pulled her phone from her pocket, navigated through the screens until she clicked *play* on her audiobook. She tapped the volume up, hoping it would be loud enough to drown out anything he might say. A voice in her head — one that sounded just like her mother's — said she was seriously rude for behaving in such a way. *Self-preservation,* Bree told herself, *must come above all else. Especially when you're a parent.* And with the narrator's smooth voice drowning out all the others, Bree proceeded to load up her basket.

Twenty minutes down.

Two-hundred-sixty-seven days to go.

There was one last countdown looming in her head, but Bree did her best to stifle it. Still, as thoughts of Carl Ronsberg's release simmered like sulfur in the back of her mind, an entirely different number came into play — one that made her pulse race with familiar dread — *six*. Just six more days and he'd be out.

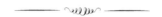

Greyson shook hands with Amelio, impressed with the guy's business savvy. The kind man had secured them a prime vendor spot at the farmer's market, an event held every Saturday morning throughout the harvest. The side job would generate extra income and give Bree — if they opted to run the booth themselves — a much-needed outing, allowing her to meet a few people in town.

Of course they'd need to take precautions, which was something he'd been meaning to discuss with her. Trouble was, Bree had been making that nearly impossible with her evasive behavior the last two days. The mere thought caused a sharp point of frustration to rear up his throat.

Greyson pushed his anger aside, said goodbye to Amelio, and fired up the small tractor. In the warmth of the morning sun, he steered it down the dusty trail toward the orchard. He'd traded two full apple bins for an empty pair, the two bumping behind him as he went. The path in his mind was even bumpier.

Thoughts of Bree owned his mind more than he wanted to admit. Just what in the world had gotten into her? Day one might have been a little rough, with him having to intrude on her right when he arrived. But day two had gone very well. At least he thought it had. Picking apples with her while they talked, sharing bits and pieces of themselves. They'd had lunch together, talked a whole lot more and then... it all changed.

Bree had said she didn't feel well and had hidden in her room the rest of the night. Well, that wasn't entirely true. She'd snuck out while he was in the shower and pasted a sticky note on the bathroom door. He could still see the pale yellow page, her rather simple print penned across the square.

Feel free to stay in the spare bedroom.
I warmed up some soup.
It's on the stovetop.

He'd found that promising, until the last two days happened. She'd done all she could to avoid anything beyond formal conversation. Blasting her audiobook through those ever-present earbuds. Busying herself through lunch. Calling her kids just before he and Bree sat down to dinner. It was maddening.

He shook his head as a new frustration came into play: Carl Ronsberg. Bree's deadly stalker would be out of prison in just four short days. True, he'd be miles away with no knowledge of where she lived, but that didn't mean his release wouldn't affect Bree. The very idea could knock her into a tailspin, making Greyson's already complicated job all the more difficult. The dilemma – on top of everything else – made his head hurt. Boy, had this job proposal come from anyone but Braden – asking him to watch over anyone but Bree – he would've gladly turned it down.

While pulling in front of the house, the picture perfect orchard just beyond, Greyson mulled over the idea that had been stirring in his mind for a while now. The one where he and Bree would pose as husband and wife. Had they been able to stay in separate homes as intended, convincing Bree would have been a much greater feat. But now, with the two sharing the very same home, they may as well gain the advantage the appearance of marriage could offer.

Sure, they already had a list of advantages. Being out of the state among the greatest, but Greyson knew how widely a man's connections could stretch. Even a man like Carl Ronsberg. In a situation like this, one couldn't be too cautious. A groan of frustration rumbled in his throat. Just how was he supposed to go about it anyway? They were all moot points if Bree continued to ignore him. Up until now, Greyson hadn't been able to find the opportunity (or the courage) to discuss it with Bree.

No matter; today was a new day. Bree couldn't possibly listen to that audio book all week long. And even if she did, he'd find a way to discuss the things they needed to address.

His shoulders lifted, his heart and mind feeling lighter already as he pulled the tractor through the leafy lanes. The sweet-tart scent of apples hung strong in the air, and Greyson swore to himself that it would be a good day. A day when he and Bree would get past whatever barrier she'd put up. A day when he would bring up the things he needed to address.

The mental checklist ran through his mind: he would tell her about the farmer's market, talk to her about meeting people in town, and see if she was open to going by her middle name. Lastly, he'd present the option of appearing as a married couple.

A jagged knot of anxiety formed in his gut at the very idea. She'd never go for it. Either way, Greyson planned to open the lines of communication, and possibly, if the stars aligned in the heavens, become a friend to her too. Whether she fought it or not, Bree needed that much. They both did.

CHAPTER ELEVEN

Bree kept her gaze on her feet as she trudged over the long, damp grass. The sight of the orchard wasn't one she liked to miss, but she had no desire to meet Greyson's eye. She'd done a fine job of staying the course the last two days, and inwardly smiled at her success.

The deep sound of the narrator's voice played loudly through her earphones as she secured the picking tote around her waist.

Greyson – having just pulled the apple bins into place –climbed off the tractor. She flashed him an obligatory grin before nearing the tree she'd marked the day before. The turquoise ribbon she'd tied around the branch on day one had now become her trusty marker, always showing her just where they'd left off. Of course, not all of the apples had ripened before they'd passed by, so she and Greyson made a habit of going back through to check at the end of each shift.

She reached into the fragrant limbs, an unsettling

image poking through her shield of comfort. It was just that – the look on Greyson's face was different today. Usually he wore a mask of professionalism and courtesy. Giving her a cordial nod and a slight grin. Today it was not so slight. One side of his lips curved up much higher than it normally did, causing a hint of that dimple to show in his roughly shaven cheek. And his eyes... Bree risked a glance over her shoulder, bothered when his gaze met hers. This time she could not force a polite smile or nod in return. She only turned her head back to the apples and dissected the new look on his face. It almost reminded her of when they were back in school. Confident. Pompous even, which had made it very easy to steer clear of him during those years.

Well, good. If he wanted to strut around as cocky as the biggest bull in the pen, that was fine by her. It would only keep her unpredictable feelings from surfacing once again.

The fruit was firm and smooth beneath her fingers, the perfect crisp texture to bite into on an early morning. She told herself she'd do just that once she picked her first three totes.

As she tuned in to the words of her audiobook, wishing she could stay focused for more than two seconds, a high-pitched voice took her by surprise. She spun around, yanking one of the buds from her ears and saw an older woman approaching. Thin, tall, and dressed like she was headed to a tennis match, their visitor called out once more.

"Hello, there." A strong Dutch accent hung on the words.

Bree smiled, charmed by the sound of it already, and freed her other ear as well. "Hi."

The woman extended her hand. "My name is Mila. I understand one of the trees on my property caused you two some trouble."

You two? Bree couldn't muster a simple response. Was too caught up on the idea that she and Greyson appeared to be a couple. Should she correct the woman?

"Oh, it's no trouble at all," Greyson piped up, striding toward her. He reached out and shook her hand. "My wife and I weren't going to rent it out for another month or so anyway."

Wife? The word was an unexpected bomb exploding in her brain, leaving it fuzzy and achy and... and... Bree shot a look at Greyson, shifted her blurry eyes back to the woman, and then set her gaze back at Greyson once more. Shocked. Stunned. Speechless.

"I'm Greyson Law," he continued, "and this is my wife, Elizabeth."

What the... he knew her middle name?

Certainly he could feel the heat of her dumbfounded glare, but he didn't even flinch.

"I'm glad to meet you Greyson and Elizabeth." Their visitor gave Bree a nod, eyeing her and Greyson like they were a new set of grandkids. "I'm happy to see a nice young couple move in here. Do you have any children?"

"Not yet," Greyson blurted, striding toward Bree, "but

we're working on it." He wrapped a solid arm around her lower back, leaned his head toward hers, and pressed a kiss to her cheek. *An actual kiss!*

Bree felt her eyes widen as sparks flittered over her skin. Sparks of shock and pleasure, anger and want, colliding into one, foreign intruder. His touch. His wholly avoided, all-too-affecting touch! It was everywhere. His breath reached a ticklish spot by her ear, and goosebumps raced up her arms like someone had just shouted *go*. Yet within seconds, two new words exploded in her head as she identified the last bomb he'd dropped:

No. Kids.

The words sounded terrible together. Ominous and bleak. If Bree had no kids, she had no identity. None.

"As they say," Mila said, "trying is half the fun." She tucked her neck into her shoulders and laughed, nearly snorting in the process. "Sorry. I should not say such things."

"Naw, we don't mind," Greyson assured, pulling Bree close once again. "Right, Elizabeth?" There was a smile in the tone of his voice. She could hear it. A slimy, just-closed-a-shady-deal grin.

Mila was watching for her reaction. It could be found in the hammering of her heart. The fury pushing through her veins like fire climbing a short fuse. "Mind?" Bree managed. "The comment?" Some manic sounding giggle burst from her own lips. "No. We...hmm," she died off there, unable to remember what she could possibly have taken offense to besides Greyson's bold, assumptive manner. Who gave him the right to tell this woman a pack of lies about the both of them?

"Will you two be selling at the carnival next week? Caramel apples from Townhome Orchard. Amelio had me reserve a booth, just in case."

"That's something the two of us are still discussing." Greyson stepped away from Bree and walked briskly toward a nearby tree. He reached out, plucked a perfect looking apple off the branch and handed it to Mila, avoiding Bree's gaze all the while. "How about I take your number and let you know by tomorrow evening?"

Mila grinned, her skin pale next to Greyson's. "That would be just fine, son. Thank you." She held on to the apple with both hands while Greyson logged her number into his phone. And soon he was walking her back to her property. All manners and ease.

Bree was on the opposite end of the scale. Her fuse growing shorter and shorter still. She felt like an idiot. Had that been Greyson's plan all along? To act like they were husband and wife? *Jeez.* He was probably glad the stupid tree fell on the guesthouse. Just went right along with his plan, didn't it?

Her eyes narrowed in on Greyson as he threw his head back in laughter in response to something Mila said. Bree's shoulders tensed tighter. She wanted to punch or kick something. She wanted to snatch a rotten apple off the ground and send it flying toward Greyson's stupid head. In fact...

"See you soon," Greyson called out, waving over the

high-set fence beyond the maples. His voice was distant. Mila's even more so. But she could see him as he neared, a good twenty yards away.

Fifteen yards.

Ten.

She half-expected him to look like a frightened animal, tail between the legs and all, but not Greyson. No, he strode toward her with his posture high and even. His chin centered in just the same carefree manner.

Bree's eyes shot to the ground. How quickly could she round up a few squishy apples? And how many would she have to throw before one of them actually struck him? *One,* Bree assured herself. She may not have tossed a softball since her days on the junior high league, but the angry heat within her frame assured her she could hit him square on the head if she wanted.

She zeroed in on one in the grass. A real winner. One that was oozing brownish juice from a wormhole by the stem. She bent at the knees, ready to grab the thing off the ground when a new thought came to mind. *No. He won't take me seriously if I'm throwing things at him like some little girl.*

Five yards.

One.

"Boy, we were thrown into that one, weren't we?" he said.

"*Were* we?" Her voice sounded more like whistling steam from a boiling kettle. "I know *I* was thrown into that, but it looked like *you* were the one doing the throwing."

Greyson tilted his head as a beat of contemplation ticked by. "You're upset."

Bree propped herself on her toes to peek toward Mila's property, making sure she hadn't made another appearance. "Gee, I don't know, Greyson. Why would I be upset about having to pretend I'm married to a man I hardly know?" A bit of hurt flared in his eyes, but the momentum had already built up. "Why would I possibly be upset over denying the *one* thing that has identified me for the last nine-plus years of my life?"

She held his gaze, watched as his dark brows furrowed.

"I'm a mother, Greyson. First and foremost and above all else. And now..." She fought the tremble of her lower lip. Feeling as if she'd just been robbed. Stripped of everything dear to her. "Now I'm forced to not only live without my kids, but to deny their very existence to everyone in town." She tore off her carrying tote, sunk it – along with the apples it held – into the bin, and took off down the aisle, the long grass brushing over her shoes as she went.

"Bree, wait."

The sound of her name only reminded her of another fine detail Greyson had messed up. "Oh," she snapped, spinning around to face him. "What did you call me? That's not my name, remember? Why don't you try again?" She folded her arms, tapped the toe of her shoe. She had him now. There was no backing out of what he'd done. None. And the very least he could do is fess up and apologize for…

"You gave me no choice."

"What?"

"What did you expect me to do, Bree? We've been here only a few days. I'm racking my brain, trying to take every measure and precaution I can to keep you safe, but I can't make all the decisions myself."

Bree squinted her eyes. Tilted her head. "Exactly. So why are you doing it?"

"Because *you* forced me to by ignoring me the last few days." His pitch was building now, gaining in volume with every word. "What did you expect me to do? Introduce you to her and the entire neighborhood as Bree Fox, proud mother to Sophie and Carter; loving sister to Braden, the carpenter? May as well just add soon-to-be-repeat victim of Carl Ronsberg while I'm at it."

That did it. Bree wasn't about to squelch the urge a second time. Without another thought, she hunched down and grabbed the first apple she saw. When her thumb sunk into one side of it, she smiled inwardly with satisfaction. Channeling her inner shortstop, Bree let Greyson's face serve as the open mitt, hearing the coach's voice in her head. *Short. Fast. Hits.* Heat rushed through her veins as she reared her arm back and let it fly.

The apple – caught somewhere between its normal reddish pink hew and a brown, rotting cast – whirled through the air toward Greyson so fast she had no time to regret throwing it.

Greyson's arm shot up to guard him as it neared. Elbow bent. Palm toward her. A stone-cold glare visible between his tensed, waiting fingers. The overly ripe fruit exploded when it hit, as if his hand were a brick wall.

Wet, juicy chunks flew in every direction. Up, over his long fingers, settling along his sandy blond hair and finely chiseled face.

A bubble of laughter snuck its way up Bree's throat as she took it in. She tried to resist it, her unrepentant gaze locked on him.

The look of disgust marred Greyson's face as he gave the blocking hand a good, hard shake, sending more chunks flying. Juice dripping.

Laughs threatening to surface.

"You deserved that," Bree said through a laugh.

Greyson's eyes widened. He took a step closer.

She backed up with two, even steps. "Admit it. You deserved that."

"If I deserved that — for simply telling Mila that we're married..." He stepped closer, his blue eyes holding hers in a way that made it hard to back away or even blink. She saw a challenge in them, and she would rise to it. Legs firm. Fists tight. She waited for him to finish the thought. A thought that looked to be balancing on his parted lips.

"Then you deserve *this* for ignoring me." He reached out, slid the tips of his dripping fingers beneath her chin, and gave her the grin she pictured him pulling earlier. Smug. Satisfied.

A mixture of embarrassment and guilt poured through

her; a bitter blend. She gulped it down, hating the heat that rushed up her neck and into her face. All she could think to do was run. It was familiar. It was reliable. It was... already in action.

She bumped his shoulder as she passed, feeling the heat in her shins now through the fast-paced stride toward the house. She wanted to break into an outright sprint, but didn't want to give him the satisfaction.

"Nice choice, Bree," Greyson called. "Go back to ignoring me. Good solution."

He hadn't yelled, simply spoken loud enough for her to hear. But the words themselves were piercing. Sharp enough to cut through the defense she stood on. Sharp enough to tear a hole clean through it, leaving her with no ground at all. She *had* been ignoring him. She *had* made it impossible to discuss the situation they faced. Her feet stopped moving, but she couldn't force them to spin back around, let alone carry her back to him.

But then she heard something – the steady hush of strides through the grass building behind her. She waited there, dropping her gaze to the ground at her side. Listening. Waiting. Wondering what he would say. Or did he expect her to speak up? He'd be waiting all day. She had nothing...

"I'm sorry." If his earlier statement had been sharp and piercing, this one was soft and encouraging. It carried warmth with it, something that settled over her shoulders and spread straight to her heart. She felt sorry too. But she couldn't form the words just yet.

"You have to understand my position," Greyson continued. "I've thought of little else since I accepted this job. I've spent literal hours learning about who this guy is, what he did, and what he might be capable of next. I've considered just how many people he must have met while behind bars. How many people he's spoken to about you."

She lifted a brow while spinning to face him. "What do you mean?"

Sensitivity. That's what she saw on his face. Plain and simple and pure. "The chances of him ever finding you here are slim, okay? They are. But there are *still* ways he could find you." Greyson licked his lips before continuing, looking as if he were staging the order of his words carefully. "You meet people in prison. People who come and go. Ronsberg could have said that you were his ex-wife. Ex-girlfriend. Someone who took off with the kids and didn't tell him. It all depends on how fixated he is. How determined to finish what he started."

Greyson shook his head, his face scrunching as his gaze shifted to the distant sky. "It's possible he has people on the hunt for you already. Looking for a woman matching your name and description. Ready to tell him the moment he gets out." He shrugged. "Between visits, phone calls, and post cards... he could already have all sorts of information about you."

It took everything in Bree to keep his words from sinking too deep. She'd never considered that Carl could actually get others on his side. That he could have good, decent people out there looking for her. She pinned her lips between her teeth, testing her level of panic. What Greyson shared could easily throw her into a world of anxiety, but it hadn't struck; there was a protective barrier – like wax to water –keeping it at bay. But she knew all too well that the barrier could dissolve at any moment.

"I don't want to live in fear of him." Her sentence dangled in the air like a confession, because it was one; she didn't want Greyson to see her afraid.

Greyson held his hands out before him like he was approaching a dangerous animal. "I don't want you to either," he said, taking one step forward.

Her gaze dropped to his shoes. "Sometimes I think I'm more afraid of living in fear my whole life... than I am of Carl himself."

Another step closer. "That makes sense. You know, Bree," he let out a sigh, and she let her eyes drift up to his face. "If I could go back, I'd do this differently. I'd sit down with you in the very beginning and discuss our options. I apologize for not doing that." He took another step closer, his defensive stance reducing to something more natural. "But since it's too late for that, we've got to take it from where we are. I'm confident I can keep you safe. But we've got to get on the same page. Okay?"

She wasn't sure how he'd done it. How he'd saved her from the humiliation she was certain would be hers upon facing him. Upon facing how she'd treated him over the last two days. Whether it was the reassurance in his words, the admission of error on his end, or the understanding in his eyes, Bree wasn't sure. She only knew that she did not feel like running or hiding or backing away. In fact, she had the unmistakable urge to close the remaining gap between them.

She stepped back instead, just a little. "Okay."

The grin that spread over his face this time was far from cocky. More like relieved. Unassuming. Reaching.

She wasn't sure what her own expression showed. If it matched the struggle she felt, it would look confused above all else.

"Let's start with this whole marriage charade." He lowered his chin until she met his gaze. "Are you going to be able to –"

"It's fine," Bree blurted. "I mean, yes. I can do it." Her face flushed with heat.

He nodded. "Okay. The carnival. Would you like to sell caramel apples there? We've got to let Mila know as soon as possible."

At the mere mention, a wave of inspiration rushed in. Candies and nuts. White and dark swirls of chocolate, making each caramel apple a unique creation. "Yes. I'd like to do that," she said.

Another nod. "Alright. And would you like to participate in the farmer's market? We can man the booth ourselves, or send the apples with Amelio. He's been running it for a small percent all summer."

"It's every weekend?" Bree clarified.

He nodded. "For the next ten weeks."

"Maybe we can let him keep running it for now," she said, watching for his reaction. She didn't want to disappoint him, but she was still affected by Greyson's assessment of things. Committing to a weekend was one thing, but an ongoing obligation was a different story.

If Greyson was disappointed he didn't show it. "Sounds good to me."

Bree gave him a single nod before setting her eyes back on the orchard. "Well, I guess we should get picking, right?"

Greyson nodded. "Right. But uh... why don't you get started? I'm going to take care of a few other things around here. I'll be close by."

"Okay." Bree gathered – by the way he'd said it – that he was trying to give her space. The strange thing was, Bree suddenly didn't want space. After ignoring him the last couple of days, and finally getting past a few obstacles she hadn't realized were there, she found herself wanting his company. Still, she quietly watched as he headed toward the shed at the east end of the orchard.

After a silent moment, she made her way back to the bins, retrieved her picking tote, and clipped it back on. While picking one ripe apple after the next, she thought back on the things she'd learned about Greyson. It seemed as if the more she got to know him, the more mysterious he became. Which wasn't necessarily a good thing; it was that very element most women found themselves drawn to – the dark, mysterious man with a past. Bree had always been different that way. She'd simply filled in the blanks herself. Trouble was, she'd done so by painting the ugliest picture she could create for them. It was easy to assume her imaginations were close enough to the truth, which allowed her to dismiss the guy with ease. All to keep herself safe from unpredictable guys like Carl Ronsberg. A man whose true colors hadn't shown in his striped polo shirts and un-tattered jeans. Nor had they been evident in his polite manner and quiet ways.

She reached for the next apple that caught her eye, nestled among a cluster of lush green leaves, and plucked it from the branch. Upon inspecting the reddish pink skin for holes or bruises, Bree rubbed it over her sleeve, impressed by how beautifully it shined. Years back, Bree had thought she was doing that same thing for the terribly awkward, painfully shy Carl. Back in junior high she was different. Open. Outgoing and unafraid. She'd seen some of the guys pick on him. Cocky, obnoxious creeps who were bigger, louder, and anything but cool. She'd hated them for picking on weaker targets in school. And one day, she'd decided to do something about it. Who knew it would backfire on her the way it had?

Carl Ronsberg wasn't harboring a warm and gentle soul, worthy of the kindness she'd shown him. His outside appearance wouldn't show it, but he was a very bad piece of fruit. Poison. A dose he'd inflicted on her for years.

A prickly chill slid over the surface of her skin, but Bree refused to let it sink any further. She shook it off instead, and took a bite of her freshly picked apple. The fruit was bright white, tangy and sweet, and the perfect crisp texture. At least apples were more predictable than men. Turns out she'd been wrong about Greyson too. Of course she didn't know everything there was to know about the bodyguard from Montana. But what she did know – after hearing of his passion for protecting those in need – was that he was good. He was more than that. It seemed as if he was sensitive too. Courageous. Humility might not be among his greatest qualities, but perhaps he wasn't as arrogant as she believed. Just sure of himself. Which wouldn't be such a bad thing had she not mistaken it for the same attitude carried by those who bullied and pushed and created quiet monsters who would dream about killing the one girl in school who dared defend him.

She couldn't help but be saddened by it even still. By the way it changed who she was. How she would trust. How she would live her day-to-day life. *Trials make you a more compassionate person,* her father would say. And after he passed, her mother – enduring a tumultuous battle of her own – would repeat the phrase. Without question, adversity had done that for Bree. But it had also made her a more fearful person. Slow to confide. Cautious to trust. Terrified to love.

And now, after she'd fought for years to move past her fears, the object of that ongoing fear would be on the loose in just four days, free to – if the urge still festered within him – terrorize her once again. And the magnitude of it was nearly crippling.

It was that very conclusion that brought her back to a place of compliance. To a spot where she was willing to play along. Here in Oregon, she wasn't Bree, a divorced mother of two. She was Elizabeth, a married woman who was helping her husband run an orchard. She brought a hand up to the charms at her necklace, two hearts – one for each of her kids – and remembered her desire to put all of this behind her. If it meant playing along for the remaining two hundred and sixty-five days, she would. Bree tried very hard not to get hung up on that number. She could do this. If it meant she and her kids could live safely, happily, she could do it. Besides, with as kind as Greyson seemed to be, perhaps it wouldn't be so bad.

CHAPTER TWELVE

"Well," Braden's voice came through the line in a flat, grim tone. "He's out. It's official."

Greyson nodded as he eyed his watch. Just before noon. He climbed off the tractor, having just moved the apple bins further down the aisle when the call came. "Have you talked to Bree yet?" He only asked because Bree had gone inside moments ago to prepare lunch. He'd be joining her in the next few minutes.

"No," Braden said. "I spoke with her the other day though. Guess she was coming to grips with the idea of posing as husband and wife?"

Greyson's face went hot. "Yeah, well, I just kind of threw it on her. She didn't have time to think it over or even agree to it. Poor thing. I think she's forgiven me by now."

"Oh, yeah?" Braden sounded amused.

"Yeah. She's starting to realize that she'll only have to play my beloved in public. And the truth is, we're not mingling with folks too often." Greyson had meant what he'd said, but still, something felt… unresolved about the issue. "You know, I really went about it the wrong way," he admitted. "Though I hadn't meant to."

"That's something I wanted to talk to you about," Braden said.

Greyson wondered if a lecture was coming his way. Something about being more sensitive to his baby sister.

"Allie and I agree that you probably did it in just the *right* way," Braden said.

Greyson tilted his head. "How so?"

"Whether you meant to or not, the last minute approach forced Bree into it, and you might not have gotten her to agree any other way. You know, the whole ask-for-forgiveness-rather-than-permission approach."

Braden's statement made Greyson feel better for about two seconds. After that, the guilt returned. "Perhaps," he said.

"It's got me thinking though," Braden added, "the two of you will most likely need to stay under one roof to pull it off."

Greyson gulped. "Yes."

"Who knows when the guesthouse will be fixed anyway, right? Maybe this whole marriage charade was written in the stars." He chuckled. "At least now you can settle into the main house and get comfortable."

More guilt. "Sounds good." Only he wasn't so sure it did. Bree was intimidating at best and seriously moody beyond that. He'd actually been looking forward to getting some space. And giving her the distance she needed too. Of course, an equally compelling side of him longed to eliminate every shred of distance between them, little by little, until she trusted him. Liked him. Wanted to be near. Just thinking of her ignited a strange sort of fire low in his belly. That familiar desire for her.

He cleared his throat and got his mind back on track. "How are the surveillance cameras coming along?"

"Right on track. All up and running," Braden answered. "Got the one at her old place, Dallin's house, one outside my place, and the one watching his parents' property as well. We don't have anything on that just yet but I expect some activity pretty soon here."

Greyson nodded, grateful for the discovery Braden had made; Allie's family owned the property that butted right up against the street where Carl's parents lived. It was just ranch land, of course, but it gave them a set of eyes on the place, a camera secured in an old dead tree by the road. Greyson couldn't wait to get a pulse on the guy's activity. What vehicle he'd be driving. When and if that vehicle ever slithered through the streets where Bree used to live.

"The next few days will be telling," Greyson said. "We're about to learn whether or not Carl Ronsberg plans to go back to his wicked ways." The very idea sent a slow shiver to ripple over his skin. "Either way, we'll be ready."

"Damn right," Braden agreed.

There was a sober pause. The moment thick with a deadly promise: If Carl chose to come after Bree, they'd be waiting. Ready to make him regret it.

"You'll call Bree now, won't you? Let her know?" Greyson asked.

Braden cleared his throat. "Yes. Is she nearby or..."

"Just in the kitchen getting some lunch ready. I'm out picking."

"If you don't mind," Braden said, "I'd like to do it when you're a little closer. When do you plan to head in?"

"I can head in now if you'd like." Greyson unclipped his picking tote. "I'll be there in two or three minutes."

"That'd be great. And hey... thanks, Greyson."

"Sure thing." He strode toward the house, the grass much too long beneath his boots. He'd need to trim it up soon. Maybe after lunch while Bree picked. It'd give her another chance to be alone with her thoughts. He'd been working to do that over the last few days. Heck, first he moves out there with her, next he moves *in* with her, and *then* forces her into playing his wife. Heaven knew the woman was probably sick of him by now.

Once at the back door, he listened for Bree's voice, wondering how long her conversation with Braden might last.

When he failed to hear anything, he stepped inside. "Bree?"

"In here." Her voice barely made it through the space; what little did carry, sounded tired and frayed.

He made his way into the kitchen with hurried steps. She stood next to the large window. Her slender arms were folded over her chest; she rubbed them with her hands, looking cold, though to him it was anything but. He spotted her jacket on the back of a chair. Quickly, he snagged it and walked toward her.

"Did you um... talk to Braden?"

She remained locked in place, her lovely lashes fluttering as she nodded.

"You doing alright?"

Bree nodded again, but her chin quivered. "I think so." She trembled, reminding Greyson of the jacket he held. He took another step closer, cleared his throat to let her know he was near, and then draped the thin, knit jacket along her shoulders.

"It's going to be okay," he said. "No one's going to lay a hand on you, Bree, I'll make sure of it."

She took a backward step, bringing her back closer to him. He paused there, considering. It seemed as if she wanted to be comforted by him, but he couldn't be sure. He let his eyes trace over the slender curve of the back of her neck as she hugged herself once more, bowing her head slightly.

He reached out with tentative hands, wrapped his palms around her delicate shoulders, and released a shallow breath. She backed into him further, closing the gap completely. Her back barely grazing his chest.

Greyson put a little more into his touch. "It's going to be okay," he assured, his fingers cradling the bend at her elbows. So small. So warm.

At once Bree spun around, surprising him with the action. She didn't look up at his face, only kept her chin down. But her hand had found his arm. Her fingers loosely curled around his bicep.

Greyson froze in place as his pulse spiked. He let his gaze sweep over the beauty before him. The pale pink of her cheeks and eyelids, the soft flutter of her dark lashes. The sweet floral scent floating up to him as he pulled in a careful breath.

"It feels awful to know he's out," she said in a whisper. "Terrifying." Her fingers flittered over the sleeve of his flannel shirt. Toying with the fabric. Grabbing at it, as if keeping him near. "I've known this day was coming since ... since he was sentenced. We've been preparing for it for *years*." She glanced up at him, her brown eyes harboring an intensity she hadn't shown before.

Raw.

Real.

Revealing.

His heart seemed to slow along with his breathing, for fear he might scare her away; this was a side Bree did not let him see. Would she suddenly realize she'd forgotten herself and panic? Run away and hide? His forearms hovered in mid-air, inches from her touch. He wasn't sure whether to wrap them around her again or let them drop.

"I mean, look how prepared we are. Right?"

He gave her one short nod. "Absolutely."

"We're in a place where nobody knows us. They don't know *my* name, anyway. And nobody from home knows that you and I are together." She stated each fact slowly. Evenly paced. Nodding her head the slightest bit with each truth. "You mentioned he could have people on the outside looking for me, but even still, they can't know where I am right now, right?" She looked up at him.

Greyson swallowed another helping of guilt as he nodded; perhaps he shouldn't have been so open with her. "Right."

"How sure are you that nobody — besides Allie and Braden — know where we are?"

He discounted Todd and his father as well, knowing they were included among the exceptions. "One hundred percent." It was close enough to ninety-nine; and would keep Bree from focusing on that measly 1 percent.

"Me too," Bree said. She licked her lips, shifted her gaze to her hand. She pressed her thumb into a tight muscle along his upper arm, and though it was obviously an absent act, the feel of it was like a massage. "I'm positive that there's no possible way Carl could find us right now. But it's like...that only speaks to my brain. The thinking, rational part that knows I'm safe. For now," she added. "But there's this whole other side of me that I can't even reach or talk to. It's this crazy panicky part that has me wanting to just..." she licked her lips, "run. Fast and forever. Take the kids with me and forget they even have a dad. Go someplace out of the country, you know?"

His body responded to her words before his mind could even make sense of them. A sharp clump of fear working its way through his chest. "And not see your family again?"

Her gaze had drifted to a low corner of the room, but

at his question, she looked back to him. "If that's what it takes."

The clump became more jagged. It seemed to be working its way down his ribcage, ricocheting off each bone along the way. Did he have to worry about her running? About her disappearing in the night? Just how could he protect her if she did a thing like that?

Bree shook her head dismissively. "Like I say, it's not a rational side of me. Just a very real, very loud, growing-larger-with-every-second side." She followed it up with a tiny laugh, as if she were only joking. He only hoped she was.

He needed to get her mind on a different path. A more realistic course. A thought came to him suddenly. "Have you taken any self-defense classes?"

Bree's lip twisted. "I've taken a few, but it's been a while."

"Well, I don't think you're going to come face-to-face with him, but that's beside the point. Sometimes, being prepared for the worst-case scenario helps eliminate the fear of it. You know?"

She nodded, taking a step back from him.

The space where she'd been felt cold suddenly. Greyson ignored the thought and continued. "Having confidence can do a lot for a person's nerves. Often, what women fear the most about being attacked by a man is not having the strength to fight him off. The truth is, you can't battle strength for strength. So you need to know a few key techniques that can help you fight off an attack no matter your difference in size."

"Okay."

"I can show you some if you'd like. We could even start with a few before we eat."

She took another step back, her shoulders lifting as she pulled in a deep breath. "Okay. I think that would be good."

He scanned the room a bit. "You know what? Let's go out to the porch. We'll have more room there."

Bree spun to look at the counter. Sandwich condiments stood next to a loaf of bread. Deli meats and cheese lay nearby. "How long will we be?"

Greyson shrugged. "About ten minutes is all. I could show you a couple things each day if you'd like."

"Okay," she said again. Bree walked determinedly past him and through the front room where she pulled open the big oak door. Greyson reached in, pressed open the screen door, and motioned for her to precede him. He couldn't help but feel as if he'd just escaped something disastrous. Evaded the strange path her mind had been treading.

Bree wiped her palms over her jeans while stepping along the creaky porch. The T-shirt she wore matched the blushed color of her cheeks. The soft sheen of her lips. So lovely. Always.

"So what are some of the techniques you learned? Can you recall any off the top of your head?"

She scratched the back of her neck. "Hmm... Oh, yeah. There's this one they showed me for like, stopping a guy who grabs me from behind."

"Perfect. Let's start there." He clapped his hands together and rubbed them a few times. "You go ahead and walk along the porch. I'll come up, grab you from behind, and you make your move."

"Got it," she said with a nod.

Greyson took a few backward steps and motioned for her to start.

She did. One step. Two step.

He moved up behind her and wrapped his arms around her body from behind, pinning her arms in place. "Okay," he said. "Show me what you've got."

Instantly Bree lifted a foot and – with a loud *hi-yah* – rammed the heel of her shoe against the toe of his boot.

Greyson barely felt a thing. "Is that it?"

Bree grunted and squirmed, and then tried to stomp on his foot again. This time she missed.

Her body went limp. "Yes," she said with a sigh. "What are those, steel-toed boots?"

"Uh, probably. But that's not the problem." He loosened his grip and stepped back. "The loud sound you made – the hi-yah kind of noise – was perfect. It empowers you while drawing attention to the scene. But the move itself isn't going to work. See, the attacker's goal is to get you someplace else. Let's say, a woman on her way to a parking lot passes an alleyway. He'll want to drag her into that alleyway and out of eyesight. Possibly into a vehicle he has waiting there."

A flicker of fear sparked in his chest. He shot her a

stern look. "Always avoid that, okay? Never get in a vehicle, no matter what. Most say you should die trying. That you're dead once you're in there anyway."

Bree's face went pale. She nodded. "Okay."

"So say it. I'll never get in a vehicle."

"I'll never get in a vehicle."

He shook the tension out of his arms, hoping to calm the anxious thoughts in his head. "Okay. Now if I'm stepping back, my feet won't be planted in one spot. You'll be stomping all over the place before you make contact, and the chances of hurting me enough to loosen my grip are slim."

A small furrow pulled at her brow. Her plump bottom lip turned down the slightest bit. "Okay. What if I kick your shins?"

"You'd probably have better luck with that, but I'm going to show you a way to get him where-it-counts."

He recreated the scene by wrapping his arms around her. Instantly he could smell that sweet floral scent again. "Now, your arms are pinned below your waist, right? So your mobility is limited. Yet your hips, if you notice, can move from one side to the next."

She shifted them to the side, and then back again. "Okay."

"So what you'll do is shift to one side and reach into the groin area with your keys or fist to cause as much pain as you can. Of course, we don't actually want to rehearse that part, but can you see how easily you gained access to that area?"

She shifted her hips to the side once more and glanced down for the briefest second. "Yes."

He released her and straightened up. "Good. Now if you get him to release you, you don't want to start running yet because you won't get far. You'll need to further injure him so you can gain distance. Let's say you've got him doubled over in pain," he said. "You have a momentary advantage to take one more shot. You could jab him in the eyes or neck with your keys. Take an elbow to his head. Take a knee to his face. We'll work on those later."

"What about pepper spray?"

Greyson tilted his head from one side to the next as he considered his reply. "It's better than nothing, but to be honest, the guy's adrenaline will be pumping so hard it might not phase him. I've got a tool for you to put on your keychain," he said. "It's a metal tube that has pepper spray inside, but the device that holds it could do a lot more damage than the spray. I'll give that to you when we get inside. It'd be perfect for the last situation I showed you."

She nodded, her wide eyes seeming to take in his words piece by piece. They were kind eyes, and he hated having to be so plain with her.

"Let's do one more. Do you recall any other defense moves?"

"I think they taught one about choking, but I can't remember it."

"A front chokehold?"

She nodded.

He glanced over his shoulder. "Okay. Let's walk over to the side of the house. That way if someone drives by they won't think we're trying to kill one another." Of course the yard was private; the chance of someone seeing them was slim, but it was better to be safe.

She followed him along the side of the house facing the orchard.

"Put your hands around my neck," he instructed, "and I'll show you what to do."

Bree did as he said, her thumbs meeting in the middle as she wrapped both hands solidly around his neck. Her fingers were slender, but strong. Greyson ducked his chin against his chest, moving her thumbs slightly away from his skin.

"Did you see that? With that quick, short move, you can take some of the pressure from those thumbs off your throat. It's much better if you can move your chin down before he can get a grip, but you don't always see it coming."

Greyson wrapped his hands around both of her wrists, and then pulled her arms so they bent against his chest. The move made her bend forward at his mercy. Gently then, he lifted a knee, making light contact, just enough to demonstrate the reason he'd pulled her against him.

"I'll do that again," he said, straightening back up. He secured her hands on his throat. "Tuck the chin. Pull the arms in. Thrust your knee to the groin."

"Okay," Bree said, dropping her arms, "let me try it."

She spread her feet apart and leaned her shoulders

slightly toward him in a challenging stance. The words *strong, beautiful, courageous* floated through his mind.

Bringing his hands to her throat was a sobering act. He tried to block out the new words that came to mind with her delicate neck in his gentle grasp. *Small. Fragile. Defenseless.* He stifled a curse, hating the man she feared. Hating him enough to choke the life out of him right then and there if he could. He'd make sure Bree was anything but defenseless.

"What do you do first?" he prompted.

She tucked her chin as she said it aloud. "Chin. And then I grab your wrists and yank your arms down..." She did just that, with a good amount of force, too.

"Nice."

"And then I just *wham!*" She brought her knee up, dangerously close to Greyson's groin, making him jump back.

Bree laughed out loud. "Sorry. That was close."

He cleared his throat. "No problem. Just uh, hoping to have children one day if you know what I mean."

She blushed, her smile triggering that dimple of hers. Greyson mused it was one of the most magnificent sights he'd seen.

Bree gave him a wink, and his pulse bolted like a racehorse. "I'll be careful," she promised.

They rehearsed the technique again and again. And with each round, she seemed more confident. She was also growing more comfortable with him. Holding his gaze as they spoke. Shoving him in the chest when she teased him, the teasing itself something new.

"Well that's probably good enough for today," he said after another close call. The last thing he wanted was to get dropped to his knees by a blow to the crotch.

Bree nodded.

"The thing about vehicles?" he quizzed.

"Never get in them."

"Right. And will you ever try to stomp on a guy's toes again?"

"Nope. I'll go for the crotch instead."

He laughed. "Good girl. Now let's get some lunch." As Greyson followed Bree back to the kitchen, he was reminded of the confirmation they'd received earlier. Carl Ronsberg was officially out of prison. The thought of that man laying his hands on her sent a mean streak of fire through his veins. So help him, if he ever messed with Bree again, Greyson would take him down without a second thought. Who knew if the guy would still be on the hunt after serving his sentence? Only the weeks ahead would tell.

CHAPTER THIRTEEN

Bree took a sip of her iced drink, her gaze set on Greyson across the table as she considered him. A little over an hour ago, she'd received news that Carl was a free man. Years of preparation hadn't stopped the panic that gripped hold of her at the receipt of Braden's call.

But Greyson had been just what she needed. A solid rock of surety. A deep form of comfort. She could hardly believe how natural it had felt to accept his soothing words and gentle touch. Somehow he'd been able to distract her from the anxiety that threatened to take hold of her, and she was grateful for it.

"Thanks for the lunch," he said, sliding his small plate away from him. "That was delicious."

"You're welcome. You know," she said, "I actually miss cooking for a houseful of kids, if you can believe it."

"You do?"

"Yeah. I mean, for breakfast and lunch most days I was feeding close to a dozen kids, including the ones who came before school for an hour or two. Anyway, it came to me when I was at the store yesterday, buying things like feta cheese and rye bread and roasted pecans. Grown up food," she said with a laugh. "I felt kind of sad that I wasn't buying things like chicken nuggets and bologna."

"I can see that." A smile spread over his face, but his sea-colored eyes were thoughtful. "That leads me to a question. I've told you what inspired me to go into the security field. But you haven't told me why you chose to do daycare of all things. House filled with other people's kids – not sure I could do it."

"You're not alone in that opinion," she said, her gaze veering toward the sight out the window. "But the decision was really a no-brainer." She was very aware of his eyes on her in that moment. Could nearly feel the caress of it warming her skin. Warming her insides too. She glanced over in time to see him raise a brow. She added it to the list of things Greyson did that her body reacted to. "You do realize that you only told me two of the three reasons you went into your line of work."

He gave her the slightest nod. "Okay. I'll tell you the third once you dish yours." If the head nod had been subtle, his smile was beyond. A small quirk in just one corner of his lips. She couldn't imagine why, but it made her wonder just what it would feel like to have those lips on hers. The thought made her face hot, and suddenly she wanted to hide.

Without another thought, she brought both hands up, cupped her face in her palms and sighed. "Just a second," she said, the words echoing against her hands.

"What's the matter?"

"Nothing. Just a nervous habit." She moved the tips of her fingers down until her eyes showed, unable to stop the small grin forming on her lips at the sight of him.

"So you're nervous right now?"

Bree shrugged, forced her hands from her face, but kept her head down, willing the blush to leave her cheeks. What was wrong with her that she admitted that to him?

Greyson remained quiet and still as she lifted her chin, degrees at a time. The linoleum floor. The table. Crumbs, napkins and plates. His broad chest. And then him. His warm and inviting face. Comfort. Kindness.

Her heart skipped a beat or two.

She gulped as her embarrassment drained away. Her limbs loosening all at once. "My kids. They're why I chose to do daycare. I wanted to stay home with them, but because I'd just gotten a divorce, I had to get a job." She shrugged. "It was perfect."

"So now that your kids are in school, you could get an office job though, right? Are you tempted to do that, or will you keep doing daycare?"

Bree sighed. The question felt like a hypothetical one. If they determined Carl was no longer a threat, and she moved back once the school year was through, Bree worried that she'd never feel safe. She couldn't imagine having kids come to her home, being put in a possibly dangerous situation. "No," she finally said. "As much as I love daycare, I don't think I'll be doing it again. No matter how this turns out."

He took a moment to respond, seeming to read into her answer. "So, what's your favorite part of the day — while you're doing daycare, that is?"

"Story time," Bree said. "Definitely. You wouldn't believe how many wonderful books there are for kids. Stories that make them think, make them laugh, make them want to be someone who can, I don't know, take on the world. One simple book, no matter the size, can shape a life for good. Imagine what hundreds can do."

Greyson held her gaze, a thoughtful crease owning his brow. "I bet you're a terrific mother."

His comment sunk into a deep, needing nook in her heart. A place that felt barren and dry until then. She smiled. "I try."

———

"How in the world did we manage to pick three apple bins today when we took more breaks than ever?" Bree could hardly believe they'd actually filled a third bin, on that day of all days. When they'd taken time out to talk longer and eat longer and even goof off while picking.

"Surprises me too." He laughed, the surrounding crickets seeming to mimic the sound.

She didn't want to say it aloud, but Bree realized that the two had been in sync, acting as a team. That was bound to make a difference. Of course, it didn't hurt that they'd picked clear until nightfall. It seemed neither one wanted the day to end. Picking, instead, beneath the massive glow of the old floodlight by the shed.

"Maybe we need to make each day like this one. We'll clean house at that carnival."

The *carnival*. That was this weekend. Bree had almost forgotten all about it. She followed Greyson back to the shed to hang up their carrying packs, watching as he shut off the outdoor light. A lively energy settled over them as the light went out, the darkness somehow heightening the draw between them, wrapping them up in a whirl of sparks and allure.

He nudged her shoulder as they walked. A gentle, playful nudge.

"You know something else I love about doing daycare?" she asked, staying right by his side.

"What?"

"Crafts. I loved thinking of fun crafts to do. I like using as many real materials as I can. I've been thinking about drying a whole bunch of apple peels. Trying a few different soaking methods to see which best preserves their color. And then I think I'll go at them with a hole-punch and make a bunch of teeny tiny apples. I'll dry some leaves, gather a few twigs, and let Sophie and Carter create their own orchard so I can frame it. And then I'll have a piece of this orchard on the wall, and in my heart. Forever." Oh, we'd make one for Braden and Allie too, since they had their honeymoon here."

"When did you come up with that idea?"

She grinned. "Just while I was picking."

"Ah," he said. "I knew I was boring you with my fishing tales."

She laughed. "Oh, no. My mind can be in two places at once. Trust me – I'm a woman. We're made that way." She could hardly believe the day had turned out to be so great. And it was all due to Greyson.

"You keep dodging that final reason, you know? About why you picked your job. I'm never going to forget, so you may as well just tell me and get it over with."

A splash of moonlight spilled over his face as they walked toward the house, illuminating the most adorable grin easing onto Greyson's face. Her heart melted into a gooey, tingly heap.

"I haven't been very anxious to talk about that one, you're right. But uh, that's just because it's hard to talk about. My mother was everything to me because… she made me feel like I was everything to her." He shook his head, a small chuckle at his lips. "Once I got my license, was old enough to stay out late and go on dates, she'd wait up for me. She'd be in the recliner, doing crossword puzzles in the lamplight. Chewing on the eraser as she struggled over a particular word." He laughed, tucked one hand into his pocket, the other flat at her back as he guided her toward the house. A small light glowed from the porch, lighting their way.

"Some nights I was glad to know she'd be there waiting for me. Asking for details about my date. Who I went out with, on the off chance she didn't already know. How it went. Some nights it made it hard though. I'd want to get fresh with a particular gal, go further than I knew my mom would like. If I'd have known I was coming home to an empty house – or at very least a sleeping one – it would have been a whole lot easier to do what I wanted to do. Answer to no one."

Upon climbing the porch steps, Greyson led her to one of the patio chairs. Not where they normally sat, rather a bench along the side of the home. It was a bit darker in the quiet nook, the area catching only a fray of the porch light's glow. Bree sunk onto the seat beside him, a warm, inviting energy dancing over her skin.

"Anyway," he continued, "knowing that I was coming home to her each night – that she'd be fighting off sleep to hear about my evening – made it a whole lot harder to do wrong, I'll tell you that much. And she had big opinions about who I dated, too. In fact..." He put his head down, and a splash of red colored his cheeks.

Whoa. That was a first. Bree was positive she hadn't seen him get embarrassed before. "What?" she prompted.

"The dance. You remember when I asked you?"

Oh, no. She'd always prided herself on saying no to Greyson when he'd asked. Was she about to regret it now? Bree managed an encouraging nod, but nothing more.

"Well, she was excited about that. Said she thought we'd make a perfect match." He threw her a bashful looking grin. "She didn't know you'd go and turn me down."

A rash of heat broke out over Bree's chest. She pinned her lips between her teeth. Let out a deep breath, and mustered one, simple word. "Sorry."

He shrugged. "Don't be. Anyway, partway through senior year she died of a brain aneurysm. Was a cruel, sudden death. No warning."

Bree felt her heart crack, a sharp and sudden sting. "I'm so sorry."

"Left us stunned," he said. "And lonely too, house full of men. Two of us still living like boys for the most part. Anyway, my mother is that third motivation, or reason I should say, that I do what I do. Two nights before the aneurysm, she and I were up talking after I'd come in for the night. We were talking about the car trouble I'd been having with this uh... Toyota my old man had bought. And all of the sudden she set her hand on top of my arm and said, 'you need to protect people for a living.'" Greyson shook his head. "I was shocked. She had no idea that I had been considering that very thing. And it's odd because I'd been meaning to talk to her about it, but it just hadn't come up."

A deep chill rippled over Bree's body. Not a creepy cold chill that surfaces just beneath the skin. This was a lifting, inspiring burst in her chest. A good feeling that swelled as she breathed. "That's incredible."

He nodded. "I'm just glad she brought it up. I think — had I not had that conversation with her — I might feel like something was missing. You know?"

"Mm, hm." There was gratitude in that statement, and Bree admired him all the more because of it. He looked back on the tragedy of losing his mom and found a way to focus on something positive.

"When your father died, it was sudden too, right? Shortly after graduation?"

She nodded. "Yes. Was terrible."

Greyson nodded back. "I hope you don't mind my asking, but when did your mother lose her battle to cancer?"

"Just after I had Sophie. It's odd," she said, replaying the sequence of events in her mind. "She beat it the first time, when my father was still alive. But after he died and it came back a second time, I don't think she had the strength anymore. I lost them way too early, there's no doubt about it, but I'm grateful my dad was there for my graduation. He would've hated to miss that. And I'm so glad that my mom was here to see me get married and welcome her first grandchild into the world." Bree's eyes welled up, something that would normally cause her to hide her face. But this time she didn't feel the need. "Anyway, the loss, it's a pain that never quite goes away. I miss them all the time."

Greyson nodded in agreement. "I know what you mean."

She turned to him, admiring his face in the pale glow. Crickets chirped in the distance, playing a song for their guests in the night. Two wounded souls finding comfort in one another. Soon Bree felt herself leaning into him, a hunger prodding at her from the inside. She recalled her first encounter with the ocean – the constant, reckless tides – and mused she was getting a taste of that gnawing, needing, yearning.

She glanced down, saw his hand resting on his lap, and reached for it before she could stop herself. Solid, rough, and warm, his palm slid beneath hers until their fingers linked in a solid grasp. *Crash*, like a mighty wave against the ocean shore.

That energy – the current that seemed to hang in the air – pulsed through her body at his touch. He might have only had a grip on her hand, but Bree felt it most in her heart. The rapid, swelling thumps. Feelings she hadn't experienced since… since junior high, if she were being honest with herself. She cared for her ex-husband of course, dearly – but Bree hadn't been capable of truly letting go back then. She was surprised to discover that now – she was doing it with a barely conscious effort.

She hadn't thought the connection could get any stronger, yet as soon as their eyes met, every sensation intensified. It felt as if someone held onto a rope, one that was wrapped snuggly around the two of them – and was slowly pulling it an inch at a time. Drawing them nearer. Bringing them closer.

"Thank you for sharing that with me," Bree whispered.

Greyson nodded, leaned slightly toward her, and dropped his gaze to her lips. The sparks between them sizzled and cracked, building into something bigger and bolder.

She didn't know what to do with it – these new, addicting feelings. All she knew is that she wanted to kiss him. To lean into those full and inviting lips and –

A muted song burst into the night. Only this time it wasn't the crickets. It was her phone. Greyson backed away – just an inch – and looked at her. Gauging her response. If she was willing to ignore the phone and go back to business, he was too.

Oh, how badly she wanted to do just that.

In that instant, an image of the kids' faces came to mind, and Bree reached deep into her pocket. "Sorry." She shot to a stand, strode across the creaky porch as her kids greeted her with revved up voices. Two engines at the start line and the flag had just dropped. It hadn't been a distraction she'd wanted, but none better existed in all the world.

Bree guessed eighty percent of her mind was set on the conversation – eating every word with an appetite for more. But twenty percent – the remaining portion of her mind – noticed the way Greyson busied himself nearby as she spoke with them. Watering plants beneath the porch light one minute. Sweeping the walk with a push broom the next. And though he managed to give her privacy in the conversation, Bree was fully aware that he did not leave her alone, and she was glad.

After saying goodnight to the kids at last, she tucked the phone back into her pocket and folded her arms as she walked across the porch. Greyson – hunched over a garden hose he was winding into a coil – was just feet away from the back door. A nearby hanging plant dripped a fresh stream of steady drops. Bree set her eyes on the plant, wondering if their intimate moment was too far gone.

Greyson straightened up, wiped his hands on his jeans, and rocked back on his heels. Their eyes met. Held. Then faltered.

"How were the kids?" His voice sounded like he hadn't used it in hours. Cracked. Quiet, and unsteady.

"Great." She wanted to elaborate, could almost feel the words balancing on the tip of her tongue like scared little kids on a diving board. Should they jump or not? Would the conversation lead them back to where they'd been moments before the call? Suddenly, a few uninvited words pushed their way to the front.

"Well... goodnight." It was far from gracious – the awkward way she spit out the words. Even worse was the way she shifted around him to get to the door.

Greyson took a backward step. And then another, each more graceful than her own, and opened the door for her. The smile he gave was impossible to read. "Goodnight, Bree."

CHAPTER FOURTEEN

Greyson shuffled down the stairs with a yawn, wondering just how in the world he had slept in. Sure, he hadn't gotten too much sleep, with as tempting as thoughts of his housemate had been, but he wasn't one to make up for lost time in the morning hours. It seemed as if the effects that woman had on him were stretching into new areas of his life.

Moments earlier, he'd heard all sorts of rattling and banging in the kitchen, yet as he moved closer, an entirely new sound picked up – humming. High, soft, and lovely.

A sweet, butter aroma coated the sun-drenched kitchen as he stepped in. Dust particles hovered in the glowing beams, obscuring his view.

"Good morning," Bree called, drawing his gaze to the stove. She flashed him a smile before turning her attention back to a pot on the burner. He blinked, rubbed his eyes, and focused on the item in her hand. An apple. A large one, coated in caramel.

"What do we have here?"

"I'm just experimenting." She spun the speared fruit as she lifted it, thin streams of caramel dripping off the base. "You're here just in time for the fun part."

He raised a brow. "How's that?"

Bree motioned to the dining room table. Diverse bowls and plates rested in the center, each filled with a different food item. Though his eyes still worked to adjust to the brightness, he recognized crushed peanuts in the nearest bowl. "Are these toppings?"

"Yep. What we need to do now is set this over here..." She walked the caramel-filled pot to the table and rested it on a plate-warmer. "You'll start with this one while it's nice and sticky and I'll dunk the next one."

Greyson washed up quickly, drying off with a hand towel while she readied the next speared apple.

Bree moved to the bowl with black and white crumbs in it. She proceeded to dab the base of her apple into it until it was coated with a thick layer.

"What's in that one?" he asked, reaching for the one she'd prepared for him.

"Oreos."

"Mmm. That sounds good."

She turned the apple on its side and drizzled melted chocolate onto the mid-section. She finished it off by sprinkling some white, crumpled treat on top.

"And that?" he asked.

"White chocolate covered pretzels. Oh, that's a pretty one, huh?"

He ran a slow gaze over her. A colorful apron wrapped snuggly around her waist. Hair pulled loosely back, exposing the lovely curve of her shoulders. "Yes," he finally said. A memory of their almost kiss rushed to his mind – the very moment that replayed in his head throughout the entire night. Of course, in the thick of his dream-ridden night and the fog of his lovesick mind, he'd moved in for the kiss. And oh, how good it had felt.

"You better get working on that one," she said, "don't want it to cool too much."

He was surprised that she wanted him to help at all, with as perfect as her apple looked. "I just, do whatever I want?"

"Uh, huh. Do what you think will taste the best." She was coating the next apple in caramel.

"Mine isn't going to look that fancy," he warned.

Bree laughed. "It doesn't need to."

Greyson went for the crushed peanuts first.

"You know, I'm so glad these apples are tart. I thought that only green apples were good with caramel but these taste perfect."

He glanced up at her. "You've already been sampling?"

"I had to make sure it would taste good before I made a batch this big. Here."

At once her hands were next to his. "You'll need to

kind of press them into the coating a bit. Like this."

Her touch sent him back to their time on the porch once more – to the way she'd actually reached out to hold his hand. How many guys had he razzed for bragging about holding a girl's hand? Too many to count. Of course he'd held his share of hands, he just never thought it counted for much. But after last night, Greyson knew just what all the fuss was about. In addition to being a comfort during the tough conversation, the feel of her silky smooth skin on his had kindled flames of desire for her, the burn of it evident even still, a lingering heat in his belly.

She went back to her own apple, drizzling what had to be melted white chocolate on top. There was a look of satisfaction on her face. The same look that came over her when she'd told him about the craft she wanted to do with her kids. Helping them make miniature orchards she could frame. She liked creating things with her hands. Came to life whenever she did.

Greyson tried to keep up, pressing colorful candies onto one, and salted crushed pretzels onto another. With the last one, he decided to have a little fun. M&M's for eyes. A dot of white chocolate for a nose. And a row of chocolate chips for a smiley mouth.

"Okay," Bree said, setting her final apple down. "Looks like we're ready."

Greyson wouldn't deny that Bree's looked a lot better, but he was sure his would taste just as good. At least, they couldn't taste bad. "So when did you get all these ingredients?" he asked.

"While you were sleeping."

A nervous streak zipped up his back. He didn't like hearing that she'd gone out while he was sound asleep. He'd figured– after the difficulty Bree faced yesterday – that she would be more careful. Of course going to the store wasn't reckless by any means, but alone? Without even telling him she had gone? Greyson sensed a headache coming on. He didn't want her to live in fear her entire life. But her lack of fear was almost frightening on its own.

"We should probably do a few more self-defense moves this afternoon," he said.

Bree reached for his crushed peanut-covered apple. "All right," she said. "Now let's dig in."

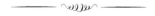

"Well, it looks like we've got a few winners here." Bree jotted their favorites on a notepad, glanced up at Greyson, and tapped at the smiley faced apple he made. "This one has inspired me. I think we should definitely do a few of these. Kids love anything that smiles at them."

Greyson laughed. "Ah, that's the trick, huh?"

"Yep." Bree sighed, loving his playful manner. His willingness to participate in such an activity with her. And he hadn't gone halfway, either; Greyson had really dug in and contributed. "I think I'll get a few more candies to mix it up though. Some candy corns, if they're selling those yet. Maybe some thin licorice ropes too."

He nodded, looking at her with thoughtful eyes.

Her face grew warm beneath this gaze. She wondered if he was thinking about how close they'd gotten the night before. The way she'd reached out to hold his hand. The magnetic feeling of his skin on hers.

"I was thinking," he said in that raspy, deep voice of his.

She felt herself lean toward him from across the table, though she hadn't meant to. "Hmm?"

"We're really going to need to get our story straight. About when we were married and all that."

"Oh." She hadn't been expecting that. "You're right." A small knot of nerves twisted in her gut at the thought. "Okay, let's see. We could say we got married like, four years ago."

He lifted a brow. "Four?"

Bree shrugged. "Yeah. That's a good number."

"What month?"

"December." She'd said it without a moment's delay. "In reality I'd want a spring wedding, but Braden got married in the winter and it was the most beautiful thing ever."

Greyson gave her a nod. "Yeah. I remember."

"You do? I mean, you went?"

He nodded again, looking embarrassed. "I must have really made an impression," he joked.

Bree watched as his face reddened. She'd noticed that happen once before too. For a reason she couldn't explain,

Bree loved it. Maybe because it made her feel like… like someone capable of making a guy like Greyson Law turn red.

"I don't do a lot of mingling in crowds, Greyson. You shouldn't take it personally."

The slow smile that pulled at his lips revealed lingering hints of embarrassment. But as it curved up on one side more than the other, Bree saw that playful side of him.

Her heart stirred into a new rhythm She flashed him a smile in return, suddenly wanting to hide her face or leave the room or start rambling about whatever she could think of.

"The family Braden married into is incredible," she said. "Do you know them? The Emersons?"

He nodded. "Not personally, but I used to watch them bull-ride in the rodeo when I was younger. Seemed like a real close-knit family."

"They are." Bree felt her heart calm at the new topic. A level of comfort falling over her as she spoke of them. "They just have this way of making you feel welcome."

"That's nice."

"Mm, hmm. Especially for someone like me. I'm kind of an introvert. I don't really like being among big groups of people. And when I'm forced to, I usually walk away feeling socially inept." She shrugged, surprised at herself for sharing so much. "Anyway, the Emersons never make me feel that way. It's just a big ol' group of people that own up to their flaws faster than you can think about your own. Makes me feel more normal, I guess."

Her comment seemed to spark something in Greyson, an ember of new interest burning in his blue eyes. He leaned in, like she'd done earlier – a furrow at his brow. "I'm glad you have them," he said, "but why would you ever feel abnormal?"

Hide. She wanted to hide again. She bit her lip while fighting the extraordinary urge to put her face in her hands. At last she blew out a pent-up breath and shrugged. "I'm just a lot more comfortable when I go unnoticed."

"I doubt a woman like you goes unnoticed very often."

She didn't like that. "What do you mean?"

"Do you really not know?" He tilted his head the slightest degree, his gaze unyielding.

Her face was getting warmer. She felt like she might break out into a sweat. Was he saying that she acted too strange to go unnoticed? Her palms were getting hot now too. A tightness building in her chest.

Greyson rested an arm onto the table, a slight smile at his lips. "You're beautiful, Bree. You're going to turn heads wherever you go."

Bree fought an eye roll as she shot to her feet. With hurried hands, she began collecting the toppings, stacking bowls as best she could. "I don't think that's true at all."

She heard his chair slide along the floor, and soon Greyson was walking up from behind. He reached around her, rested a few items he'd gathered on the counter, then cupped her upper arm with one, large hand.

Her blood tingled beneath.

"Whether you choose to believe it or not, it's true."

Bree knew exactly what head-turning women looked like. Tall, confident, and curvy. Bree was short, quiet, and lacking the curves she used to wish for. Now she was only glad for her lack of them. Didn't mind being plain if it kept her where she was comfortable – fading into the crowd when she had to be in them.

At once she spun to face him, wanting Greyson to know just how unnecessary his comment was. "I don't want you to say stuff like that to me, okay?"

He tilted his head. "Why not?"

"Because I'm not saying things to fish for compliments. I'm not like that. I'm just trying to speak real with you and I'd appreciate it if you'd do the same."

"You think I'm lying?"

She pushed past him, irritated with the conversation. Furious was more like it. She plunked the bowls onto a tray, one after the next, spilling sprinkles in her rush to get through the task.

"I'll prove it to you," he said.

"You can't."

He laughed. "Oh yes, I can."

When she only heard quiet behind her, Bree spun around to see Greyson had pulled out his phone and put it up to his ear. "Todd?" He waited. "I need to ask you something. Just a second." He pulled it away from his ear, tapped the screen, and then walked toward Bree.

Three long strides.

They were standing face to seriously-stunning face,

the small device between them. Bree sucked in a shallow breath. He was too handsome. Unnervingly so.

"Who did I always say was the hottest girl in school and she didn't even know it?"

"Bree Fox."

Whoa. It felt as if Bree's heart had been given a jumpstart. The beat rushing so hard and fast it nearly took her breath.

"And how upset was I when she said no about the dance?"

"You bawled like a baby," Todd said with a chuckle.

Greyson's eyes got wide. "Be honest, man." He shook his head. "I did not cry."

Laughter came from the line. "Oh, yes he did," Todd assured, his voice pouring from the small speaker. "Oh, I can't believe someone would actually say no to *me* – Greyson Law. How could this happen?"

"Yeah, right," Greyson said, a reluctant smile giving way.

Bree felt a smile work its way onto her face as well. The situation was comical for sure, but something else was happening inside her. She was beginning to believe him. And the mere idea that Greyson Law truly thought she was the prettiest girl in the school – that he really had been upset when she'd said no – all of it filled her with a sense of empowerment. Confidence. Something she hadn't felt for a very long time.

"Alright, alright," Greyson said. "That's enough, punk. I'll talk to you later."

Todd chuckled. "Did you tell her about the –"

Greyson disconnected the line and ran a hand through his sandy blond hair.

Bree watched him tuck the phone back into his pocket. He looked ruffled, and she couldn't help but enjoy it.

"Tell me about the what?" she asked.

"Nothing."

"No, really. What was he going to say?" She was enjoying the unexpected moment. Enjoying the fact that Greyson looked like he wanted to hide *his* face now. She stepped closer, tipped her head to one side until their eyes met. Cool blue wonders that looked almost boyish now.

She let the grin slip through. "C'mon."

He scratched his roughly shaven jaw. "Fine. Back in the fourth grade, I wrote a poem about you."

She gasped. "You did not."

He nodded, taking a step back while raking fingers through his hair once more. She was making him nervous. Bree could hardly believe she made this guy nervous.

"It was some lame assignment in Mrs. Wilkon's class. We had to pick a topic. Write a poem. Draw a picture." He shrugged. "I wrote about you."

Satisfaction, mingled with undeniable delight, flooded her chest.

"You don't have to enjoy this so much," he grumbled, making Bree aware of just how wide her smile was.

"That's so cute," she said.

He groaned. "Cute?"

"Yes. It's the cutest. I wonder when Sophie's going to have her first crush. And Carter. I would love it if they wrote a poem like that."

The tension seemed to drain from his shoulders. "Oh, my mom went crazy over it. It's probably part of the reason she was so happy about me asking you out. She always liked the idea of us getting together."

"Hmm."

"And while we're making confessions..." he said. "I've got something else to tell you."

The tidbit should have made her nervous, Bree knew that much. But the events leading up to that moment had her feeling at ease. "Let's hear it."

"You and Jane Fillmen showed up to Mike Tower's party freshman year. Do you remember?"

A rush of heat flared up in her chest. She gulped. "Yes. I was braver back then." She didn't elaborate, but as things with Carl escalated, Bree became more reclusive. Less likely to do things like hang out at crowded parties and... and kiss unknown boys.

A look in Greyson's eyes caught her attention then, planting a thought in her head. A mind-blowing thought. The heat in her chest roared hotter, deeper.

There was no way.

There was no way Greyson was about to say what she thought he might.

"They divided you girls into rooms. Blindfolded. And then they had a guy come into the room, where we'd get three minutes of heaven together."

Oh, yes. She remembered. It was something she'd secretly kept with her throughout the years. Something she'd even compared her own husband to.

"No one knew who they were getting paired up with. Mike was sure of that. Except …" Greyson looked down, slid one of the chairs with the side of his foot. "Except me. Mike owed me a favor. So he paired me with you."

The heat in her chest pooled over, spilled into her limbs, making them weak and wobbly. "How do you know?" It came out in a whisper. "He might have said he was bringing you to me, and then taken you to someone else. There were six rooms with six other girls." She knew this without a second thought. Like it had happened only yesterday.

"Seven, including Mike's girl in the pantry. And… I *know* it was you." The fierce look of desire smoldered in his eyes as he held her gaze. He had to see it in hers as well, because in that moment, it was all she could feel. Warm doses of desire.

"You wore a silky top that night. You had a little ring on your pinky finger, and some, lacy hairband around your wrist. All details I noticed about you before you were led away. All things I made sure were there before I kissed you."

Before I kissed you… The words echoed in her head again and again. Greyson Law had kissed her. Strong hands, certain lips, and a tenderness she hadn't thought a mere freshman could conjure.

"That was you?"

He nodded silently, his gaze falling to her lips.

Bree's heart thumped in some wild, erratic beat. The rhythm like strong, encouraging hands, urging her toward him. She wanted to kiss him again right then and there. To wrap her arms around him and repeat one of the most exciting moments she'd had in her life. She'd used that night to remind herself that she *was* normal. She *had* lived a typical teenage life. She'd been desired – truly desired. By someone she'd never really know, granted, but she'd been okay with that. Had liked it, really. In fact, secretly Bree had always feared that – had the mystery man known it was only her, and not one of the other girls at the party – he may not have kissed her in the same way.

But Greyson had known all along.

Had been the one to arrange it, even.

Because he wanted her.

And as he stood in the sunlit kitchen before her, all sincerity and longing, she could swear he wanted her even still.

The look in his eyes changed then, to some unreadable expression. "I'm sorry if you're upset about that."

Upset? "No, I'm not."

"Or if you were hoping it was some other guy this whole time."

"I wasn't." Her voice was small. Almost lost in the sandwich of his words.

"I probably shouldn't have told you that." He began tucking the chairs around the table. "Well, I'm going to head on out and check on the orchard." He threw a thumb over his shoulder before turning away from her and toward the pantry, where the back door was.

The door creaked open.

And then closed.

She watched the window as he walked by.

As soon as he was out of sight, Bree backed up to the fridge, felt the solid support at her back, and then slid to the base as her knees gave out in a dreamy, hazy, spell. *It was Greyson.*

CHAPTER FIFTEEN

Greyson watched as Bree stepped onto the patio, wondering – for just a moment – if she might join him on the porch swing. Instead, she opted for the hanging seat across from him. A crocheted hammock hooked to a large loop in the awning overhead.

"You favor that spot," he said as she sunk into it.

"I know," she said. "My grandmother used to have one of these." She wrapped her fingers through the loops along the edges. "I love that you can lay back in it, or just sit upright like this and spin." She demonstrated by using the toe of her sneaker to push off. She spun full circle in the suspended seat – once, twice.

He grimaced, feeling sick just watching. "I don't know why you'd *want* to do that."

"Fifty caramel apples!" she blurted before stopping and spinning the opposite direction. "That. Is. Awesome!"

He grinned, enjoying her celebration of sorts. "Sure is.

We'll more than double it by this time tomorrow."

"I can't believe the carnival is actually tomorrow," she said, stilling herself in place with her feet. "It's not like me to look forward to something like this. But for some reason I'm excited about it."

He liked hearing that. He liked hearing anything Bree said. The last week had been a series of good conversation on the orchard by day, and even better conversation on the porch once the stars were out. He could hardly believe he'd revealed as much as he had the other day. Calling Todd on the phone, letting her hear just how smitten he'd been over the years. And the kiss – he'd had to throw that in there too, hadn't he?

A breeze blew over the porch, rattling the leaves on the nearby trees. Wisps of dark, silky hair drifted across Bree's lovely face as she glanced up at him, and a deep yearning burned low in his belly at the sight of her. Of that playful grin that showed the dimple in her cheek. He'd been relieved that his admission hadn't sent her running in the opposite direction. In fact, ever since that very morning, she'd been more open with him, revealing new parts of herself.

Who could have guessed that – after Carl Ronsberg's release – Bree and Greyson would make a connection that put her more at ease than she'd been in the days leading up to it. Yet while her paranoia of what could come seemed to be waning, Greyson's was just starting to brew. Sure, he kept it at bay by tracking the surveillance tapes. They had enough on Carl to know exactly which car he drove – a rusty white Oldsmobile with a loose grille and an easily spotted license plate. So far, that car had not shown up in any of the areas they were monitoring. Braden had caught wind of the guy getting a job at a towing company, though it hadn't been confirmed just yet.

Still, Greyson worried that his determination to protect Bree – his desperation to keep her from harm – might rob him of rational thought altogether. Turn him into some paranoid lunatic.

Bree climbed out of the hammock. "What are you thinking about?"

Greyson was surprised to see her stepping toward him. At once he stopped the porch swing from rocking, waiting until she sunk into it. Her sweet floral scent, as subtle as it might be, flooded his senses every time. Add to that the warmth of her body, the silky touch of her skin as her arm grazed his, and he could barely think to answer her question.

"Not much." He mused on the unique development between them. On some levels they felt like nothing more than friends. Two people who got along well and enjoyed one another's company. It was moments like these – the way her hand found his, her slender fingers gliding up the length of his, up and back (dear heavens did that feel good) – that kicked things into that more-than-friends zone.

Several times a day, Greyson imagined sliding a hand along the back of her neck, drawing her close to him, and kissing those pouty lips until he'd had his fill. He was pretty sure she wouldn't stop him, either. It was what Bree might do *after* the fact that cooled his jets every time. Would she regret it terribly if they kissed? Go back to ignoring him like she'd done back on their second day there?

If Greyson were being honest with himself he'd say his concerns went deeper than that. He wondered if getting involved now – under these unique circumstances – was a terrible idea. After all, Bree was vulnerable here without her loved ones. Hell, she didn't even have her own kids. If she let herself become involved with him now, would she come to her senses once it was all said and done, leaving him all but forgotten?

A smaller part of him wondered if he was holding back for even more reasons than that. Was he afraid of losing her in an entirely different way?

He didn't know how to answer all the questions in his head. What Greyson did know was this: he could not move as quickly as he'd like to.

No, he assured himself while planting a kiss to the back of Bree's hand. If things stood a chance to work out between them, he needed to take it slowly.

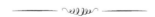

"So are the two of you all ready for tonight's carnival?"

"Yep," Bree said, thinking she could listen to Mila and

her accent all day. "Greyson and I have quite the showing of caramel apples setting at just the right temperature – ready to go."

Mila climbed off the patio chair, gripping the box Bree had given her. Two caramel apples lay tucked beneath a layer of clear wrap. "Oh, my mouth waters just thinking of it. I bet they're as tasty as they are lovely."

"Well *I* think they are," Bree said. "We really gave it our best."

"*We?*" Mila had been adjusting her thin sweater, but she'd abandoned that and looked up at her, a surprised look in her eye. "Elizabeth, does Greyson help you with all that? The dipping and the decorating and making them look nice?"

"Oh, yes," Bree assured. "He's the sole creator of our smiley-faced apples. You should see them. Some look like zombies. Some like jack-o-lanterns. We got online for a few ideas and he didn't do half bad."

"Well good for him. Lots of men think they're too good for such things."

Bree nodded. "Not Greyson. We spent the whole day on it and he didn't utter so much as one complaint."

"Sounds like you picked a real winner with him. And a handsome one too." Mila fanned at her face with the wave of her hand. "Goodness he is big and hunky and good looking too."

"You're right."

"Course he never gives me a second glance but, *ieder kaasje heeft zijn gaatje.*"

Bree gave the woman a sideways glance. "What was that?"

"Just an old saying. It means every cheese has its hole. You know, nobody is perfect."

"Oh." She grinned. "Isn't that the truth?"

"Well, I'll be off now. We will set booths in one hour. Carnival starts in two." She stood, straightened her skirt, and headed down the porch steps.

Bree creaked open the screen door after saying goodbye, considering what Mila said about every cheese having its hole. That nobody was perfect. It was true enough, though she was starting to think Greyson was pretty close to it.

She walked over to the sofa and plunked onto it before dropping to her side. Her mind drifted back to their conversation from the week before; it had really done a number on her. With a deep sigh, she stretched across the cushions. Once her eyes were closed, she was back in that room, on that night, clear back in her freshman year. The room was dark, but the blindfold she wore made it all the more so – a silky sleeping mask with an elastic band. She had stood there, rubbing hands over her arms to warm them, wondering just who they would send into her room. She'd been much braver in those days; the effects of Carl Ronsberg hadn't taken their toll just yet.

She'd heard him come in, the guy she'd been paired with, when he entered the room. The quiet creak of the door. A soft shuffle of footsteps along the rug.

Bree had been standing near the closet in the corner,

shifting her weight nervously while she waited. The smallest hint of a whisper came once he joined her, deep and raspy. "Hey."

He smelled good. Really good. A manly, spicy scent of cologne. She pictured the samples she'd come across in magazines at the checkout line, recalling the accompanying ads of topless men riding horses or stepping out of glistening pools.

His hands found her hips first, but they didn't stay there. Instead, they moved up the length of her arms, slipping sensually, slowly until they followed the slope of her shoulders, and then back down to her wrists. A tingling rush of anticipation swept over her.

His fingers glided through hers. "Are you okay to do this?" he asked in that same, throaty whisper. She caught hints of mint on his breath.

He'd cradled her neck with one, large hand, so she nodded in reply, hoping that was assurance enough. She'd gone into the room nervous and uncertain, but the guy in that room with her – whoever he was – put her at ease. More than that, he set her skin ablaze. A sensation that was nearly foreign to her. She drank in the delicious tension as he lifted her chin the slightest bit, ran a thumb over her lips. At last he leaned in, pressed his own against them. Testing. Soft. Gentle. *Mmm.*

"Is this okay?" he asked in a whisper. After she nodded once more, he kissed her again, more certain this time. And then again, showing her the dance of a kiss. The warm push. The tender pull. Each press of his lips urging the kiss deeper. Coaxing her to do the same. Not in an urgent manner, but in a patient, alluring sort of way. Kissing her as if he loved her.

Loved her. The mere idea sent a thrill through her chest even then. Bree squelched a smile as she turned to lay on her other side, propping her head on a puffy, decorative pillow. She loved knowing it had been Greyson Law. Loved it more than she could fathom.

While facing the back of the couch, she traced the pattern with her finger, that final thought still ringing in her head. She recalled the contrast in the other kiss she'd had with someone else at a similar party. After having such a positive experience the first time, Bree had agreed to participate in a game of spin the remote, where she and Danny Web got lined up. The two had snuck into a dusky fruit cellar in the basement.

If there'd been any question as to whether or not she'd kissed Danny the first time, the possibility had been ripped from her mind at first touch. The guy was all hands and tongue. Groping and groaning. She had not stayed in there until the timer dinged. Instead, Bree pushed him away from her, stomped up the basement steps and right out of the house. She shivered at the mere memory, the words *scarred for life* running through her mind.

The incident had only made her admire whomever she'd encountered first. Bree had sought after that type of tender patience in a man. She'd found it in her husband, Dallin. Sadly, there had been one very important thing missing – for her, anyway: Passion. Of course that hadn't played a part in their divorce. And it was nothing she faulted Dallin for. Mostly, she'd assumed the stalking incident had robbed her of the ability to feel such things altogether. Whatever the reason, Dallin had never been able to evoke the feelings Greyson *(wow, it was so crazy to know it was him)* had risen in her that very night. And to think that he'd already had feelings for her at that point, having written the poem for her back in grade school and all.

The next thought that rose to her mind made her face warm: What would Greyson's kiss be like now? A grown man. Stronger in body and passion. And experience too.

"You going to take a nap?" The sound of his voice startled her. The finger she'd been using to trace the floral print darted off course.

"Jeez," she griped. "Scared me." She worked her way onto her back, grabbed hold of the pillow she'd been resting on, and chucked it at him.

Greyson ducked impossibly fast, dodging the pillow with ease. He straightened up and grinned at her triumphantly.

"Wow. It's like you've got *spidey senses*," she said with a laugh, but she wasn't done trying. She reached for the other pillow, did a fake-out toss aimed at his mid-section, and then let it fly toward his face.

This time he caught it with one hand. "I do." He lifted a brow questioningly. "You want to have a pillow fight?"

"No," she said.

"Looks to me like you do." He held the pillow he'd

caught in one hand, secured the one that missed him with the other.

"I don't. I just… want to hit you with a pillow and not have you throw one back." Laughter coated her words.

His grin grew as he neared, each fist armed with a fluffy pillow. "That's not how it works."

She giggled. "It's not?"

Greyson laughed too. "No." He was getting closer.

Bree's eyes shot to the opposite end of the couch. She bolted toward a large, lacy pillow she spotted there and chucked it at him. She was certain he'd let that one hit him just to encourage her. It worked.

Greyson tossed the decorative pillows like he was pitching a game of little league.

More laughter filled the room as she caught the pillows, only to throw them at him once more. Back and forth they went, a chaotic bout of dodging and catching, aiming and throwing; Greyson drawing ever nearer in the process. At last he was hovered over where she sat, dangling the large, lacy pillow over her head.

"Admit that it was a bad idea to pick a fight with me," he urged.

Bree kept her lips tight while shaking her head. She ducked, barely missing the playful swoosh. "You admit that it was a bad idea to come in and startle me like that."

Greyson dropped the pillow, slipped his hands through hers, and propped a knee onto the edge of the couch. He hovered over her then, pinning her hands over her head. "From this viewpoint, I'd say it was damn-near genius."

Her heart seemed to swell as his gaze held hers. She worked to slow her breaths while her heart picked up its pace, a hammering, thunderous beat. She wanted him to lower himself over her, press his lips to hers, and take her to that place once again. To that world of longing. Of being longed for in return.

But suddenly his grip loosened. His arms dropped. And he straightened up, stepping away from her altogether. Still, he held her gaze, a pained look in his eyes. "The carnival's going to start soon," he said. "I better hit the shower."

He turned away from her then, the tingling effects of his touch still flittering over her hands and wrists. She wasn't sure why Greyson had shifted so quickly – gone from that predatory play, to running away like the hunted.

Bree mused over it in her mind, trying to make sense of his sudden shift. Perhaps she'd been misreading him all along. A strange ache settled into her gut as the unwanted thought took root. It could be that Greyson didn't feel anything for her after all.

CHAPTER SIXTEEN

"That was our last one," Greyson said, handing a few crisp bills to Bree.

Bree grinned, tucking the bill into the cashbox. "Man, we've made ten times what we spent on caramel and toppings. Not bad."

Greyson nodded in agreement, enjoying the way the carnival lights reflected in her gorgeous brown eyes. "I'm just surprised we actually sold some plain apples too. Who knew – with all the goodies this place has to offer – that folks would seek out food that wasn't battered, fried, or dipped in something sweet."

She shrugged. "Not me."

"So..." Greyson said, "what do you say we lock up this cashbox and go have a little fun before they close this place down for the night?" The question hadn't just come to him. It was one he'd been inwardly phrasing for the last hour. Wondering how he should pose it and what Bree might say in return. He held his breath while waiting for a response.

Bree looked over the crowd tentatively. "I don't know. It's late. And we've got to get up early to coat more apples tomorrow."

He nodded while considering his reply. Bree had taken a few steps back. Metaphorically, that is. Perhaps he'd made the right decision on the couch after all. While in the shower, Greyson had done a whole lot of inner grumbling. He'd been frustrated with himself for not making a move. There couldn't have been a better moment. The chemistry between them building into a thriving, pulsing, dominant force. He'd been certain she felt it too. So just why hadn't he acted on it? The answer was too complicated for him to pinpoint.

"How about this," he said, turning to face her completely. "If I had it *my* way, we'd snatch up some kettle corn and stay here until the place closes down."

"That's over an hour away." Bree looked horrified at the mere thought, her eyes wide and worried.

"Well, that's just if I had it my way. And I'm guessing that if we did things *your* way, we'd pack up and leave now, skip out on the festivities altogether."

"Definitely."

He smiled. "So let's compromise."

Bree's shoulders dropped. She let out a groan. "I'm tired..." she dragged out the word like a pouty teen.

Greyson's face scrunched in disapproval. "You're as

bad as a small child, you know that?"

His comment earned a grin from her. "Well in that case, I'll stay if you buy me some cotton candy."

"Deal," he said with a laugh. After securing the cash box in Greyson's SUV, the two headed into the crowd. Greyson put his arm around Bree as they walked, pleased when she rested her head against his arm. "We'll just play a couple of games. Go on a few rides. Call it quits in a half-hour or so. Sound good?"

"It sounds… doable," she said.

"Good. Because that Ferris wheel is calling my name." He stopped by the treat booth first, where Bree opted for cotton candy in a bag versus a cone.

"This way I can eat it later too," she said before popping a pink puff into her mouth. She offered some to Greyson next with a lifted brow.

Greyson took the offering, enjoying the sweet sugar crystals as they melted on his tongue. As the last few granules dissolved, Bree slipped her warm, silky hand into his. She didn't turn to look at him when she did it, simply kept her gaze locked before them as they walked. He could barely hide the grin that crept over his face; the action surprised him nearly as much as it pleased him.

"Not a bad wait," Greyson said as they stepped up to the back of the line.

With her hand still in his, Bree shuffled closer. One foot after the next. The toes of their shoes, separated by mere blades of grass. Greyson had never been so confused. It seemed one minute Bree was hot, the next she was cold. Warm and cool described it better, seeing that she wasn't extreme by any measure. Just a little standoffish here, a little more friendly there. And since when did Greyson go around dissecting every move a woman made? It was ridiculous. Worse than high school. At least then he'd had more confidence. Except where Bree was concerned.

"Oh, looky here," a familiar voice hollered from the front of the line. Mila. A handful of people separated them, so she leaned her head around the small group. "It is good to see you two getting out and enjoying some of the fun."

"Yeah." Greyson said, glancing down at Bree. "She had to drag me over here but I'm sure once we get on this thing I'll be thanking her for it." When Bree's eyes widened in surprise, he shot her a wink.

She turned her attention to Mila. "You should have seen him. He wouldn't even agree to come along unless we got some cotton candy first." She tightened her grip on his hand and giggled.

Mila tipped her head back. "Oh, the big baby. Had to bribe him, did you?"

Bree laughed some more. "Yep."

Greyson gave her a grin, bringing his mouth close to her ear. "Nice one."

"Thanks." She looked pleased with herself. But more than that, she looked comfortable. Not bothered by the large crowd as he thought she might be. He wanted to think that perhaps *he* was the reason she was so at ease.

His nearness. His ability to keep her safe. Perhaps that was the cue he needed to stop analyzing things and enjoy himself as well.

The line began to move, and Greyson looked up to see a couple climbing down from the cart nearest to the ground. A new couple took their place, and the giant wheel moved just enough to let out the next group. A mother and her two little kids. Their faces glowed with bright smiles and rosy cheeks. Without glancing over, Greyson knew Bree had spotted them too. Somehow knew of the pain she might feel over the sight. The reminder of what she was missing. A quick glance at her said he'd guessed right. Her gaze was fixed on the happy bunch, her pretty eyes growing glossy and red.

"I'm sorry," he murmured into her ear. "This must be hard for you. Being at a place like this without your kids."

Her chin quivered. "It's just kind of hitting me all at once. I loved talking to all the kids who bought apples and played the game in the booth next to us, but now it just... feels like I'm ready to go home to my own. I don't know if I can be away from them for so long." She wiped at the moisture gathering in her eyes.

Without another word Greyson switched the hand he held and wrapped his arm around her. He pulled her in close, kissed the top of her head, and sighed. "I wish I could change things for you, Bree. I really do."

Bree sniffed. "Thanks." She felt so soft and warm next to him. He wanted to keep her there forever.

"Hey, I would like you guys to meet my husband,

Travis," Mila said, gaining their attention once more. She must've allowed the small group between them to move ahead, because she was now right next to them in line. "Travis, these are our nice new neighbors, Greyson and Elizabeth." The gray-haired man reached out to shake their hands.

"Are you the ones Mila shoved one of our tree's onto?" he asked with a grin.

Mila gave him a playful slap.

"You've got to watch out for this one," Travis continued. "She wanders in her sleep, weaving through her grove of trees out back, and then knocks one over to prove her strength."

Mila laughed some more. "Oh, you tease."

Travis threw Greyson a knowing grin. "Are you two here with any kids or is it just the two of you?"

"Just us," Greyson piped up, rubbing Bree's arm once more.

"They don't have little ones yet," Mila said. "Remember?"

Travis nodded, a thoughtful look in his pale gray eyes. Eyes that reminded Greyson of his father's. "Oh, that's right. You told me that, didn't you?" He pointed to a group next to the face-painting booth. "That right there's our daughter and her kids over there. Her husband's manning the cotton candy booth. Then of course we've got our two other children here with their spouses and all eleven of our grandchildren."

"How wonderful," Bree said. "They all live in the area

then?"

"Yep." Mila beamed. "We bribe them with Sunday dinners and Friday night pizza at our place. The benefits are just too good for them to stray from."

"Oh, there are the rest of them right over there." Travis pointed to a rowdy cluster, kids and parents alike, some waving over at them. "They're hoping we get stalled up at the tippity-top."

"They are?" Bree asked.

"Oh, yes. If a couple gets stalled while on top, they have to smooch." Travis gave them a wink.

Greyson glanced down to see Bree's face redden. "Well in that case I hope *we* get stalled at the top."

Bree did not look up when he said it, only swiped a dark lock of hair behind one ear, her face burning an even deeper shade of red. When Greyson said he hoped they'd get stopped, he'd meant every word. But now – after seeing the look on Bree's face – he wasn't so sure. Talk about mixed signals.

"Whoops," the man said, "looks like we're up. And lucky you, looks like you'll be on this round as well." He guided Mila toward the ride as she spun to call over one shoulder. "Have fun!"

"You too," Greyson mumbled.

Not a word was spoken between them as they stepped forward, waiting for the ride to move and the next cart to empty.

"On you go, you two," the ride operator said. A plump man with a red beard and wide grin.

Greyson didn't break their silence, only nodded before helping Bree into the old-fashioned looking seat. Forget about old-fashioned – it looked more like an antique. A copper-looking cage with red vinyl seats. White lights with vintage bulbs cased the entire caging, making each seat glow.

"You guys are the last of this bunch," the operator said. "Enjoy the ride."

Once they were off, Greyson leaned over to whisper in Bree's ear. "This thing looks a little rickety, if you ask me."

She pulled away to look at him, a glint of amusement in her eyes. "Are you nervous?" And there was that dimple sinking into her cheek. Greyson's belly stirred.

"A little."

"Here," she said, taking hold of his hand. "I'll protect you."

He chuckled under his breath. "Thanks." They were nearing the top now. His pulse rising along they way.

Closer.

Closer.

And over.

Whew. As much as he wanted to kiss Bree, Greyson didn't want her to feel rushed or forced into it. He leaned forward to see the ground below, and his stomach did a new sort of twisting. How long would this thing go? He worried about getting stopped on top for the kiss. But he also worried the entire contraption would collapse at any moment.

Get a grip, man. What was with him? In his occupation, Greyson consistently faced very real dangers. Bullets, bombs, attempted kidnappings. Heck, he'd scaled walls, for crying out loud. This small amusement ride was nothing to worry over. But still he felt unsettled. Almost sick.

The ride circled around once more. Greyson closed his eyes as they neared the top, sucking in a deep breath. He began letting it out in a slow, paced breath through pursed lips.

"You are not really afraid of this ride, are you?" Her tone was that of humor mingled with concern. He glanced over to see her expression matched the tone. A hint of that dimple was there, but a slight crease furrowed her brow as well.

"Here," she said, untying the twist tie on her bag. She tore off a tuft of cotton candy and handed it to him before popping a piece in her own mouth. "That should help."

He couldn't imagine how eating cotton candy on an ancient death wheel would make anything better, but he ate it anyway.

"Just focus on the taste," she said. "Mmm." She closed her eyes and leaned into him. Just like she'd done in line. He liked it. Focused on that along with the taste, wondering if the sweet candy tasted the same in her mouth as well. Heat burned low in his belly at the thought, curing any sick feeling that'd been there. Leaving nothing but a simmering desire for the woman by his side. He didn't know how she'd done it. Caused such a fast and fevered switch, but as they neared the very top of the wheel once more, Greyson wanted it to stop so he could kiss her there and then – consequences be damned.

A group of spectators chanted below. "Stall. The. Ride! Stall. The. Ride!"

"Must be rooting for Travis and Mila," Greyson said, recognizing the group – young parents with their small children.

"That's sweet," Bree mumbled. "Do you think he'll really stop it? Just so two people can kiss at the top?"

"Don't know. I didn't notice if he'd done it earlier or not."

"Hmm. I didn't notice either."

Suddenly something rattled and clanked. The motion of the ride began to slow. They were nearing the top now. Closer. Closer. Inwardly he wished that it would. Wished because he was suddenly certain – by the chemistry smoldering between them – that she wanted it too.

The growing crowd cheered some more. A new cluster of folks joining in.

Slower. Closer. Nearing the top.

Right at the very height of the ride, the world disappearing beneath their feet, the massive wheel screeched to a halt. Greyson's heart did a similar thing as he realized the ride had actually stopped. With them on top.

The hum of electric lights buzzed in the breeze.

A lone voice cried out from the crowd. "Kiss her!"

Others joined in. "Kiss. Kiss. Kiss." Greyson's pulse

rushed at the thought, speeding until it double the pace of the chanted word.

"You must kiss her, Greyson," came Mila's voice. "It's tradition." Through slats in the bars supporting their feet, he caught sight of Mila and her husband looking over their shoulders.

"Go get 'em, tiger," Travis hollered.

Bree pulled away slightly, straightening as his gaze turned to her.

Mila and Travis joined in. "Kiss. Kiss. Kiss."

The carnival lights did wonders for Bree's already brilliant face. Glowing skin. Flushed cheeks. And an encouraging look in her eye that caused his belly to burn hotter with desire.

Greyson brought a hand to her neck, delicate and warm, keeping his gaze on her as he leaned in. With the warmth of her breath filling the space between them, Greyson paused to lift a brow. A silent question. Was she okay with this?

Bree gulped. The desire he thought he'd seen in her eyes looking more uncertain with each hammering beat of his heart. She looked down at his lips, adding to the confusion.

He needed to act. To at least get Bree out of the spotlight if nothing else.

At last he swooped in, bringing his lips between her rosy cheek and the corner of her mouth, and kissed her there. He held it there to please the crowd, raising a triumphant arm in the air. The onlookers cheered as he straightened up, but Greyson could only think about Bree. She looked away from him, avoiding his gaze as he glanced over her face. His heart sunk like a cold, heavy stone.

"Sorry," he mumbled. "I didn't know what to do."

She didn't reply. Only swept another lock of hair behind one ear.

Regret sunk through him, sharp and sudden. He'd wanted to taste her kiss more than anything in that moment. Yet – again – he hadn't dared make the move. It was obvious Bree was troubled, that the moment had bothered her to the point she couldn't hide it from him. But still, one very important question remained: Just what exactly had made Bree so upset? Did she believe he had gone too far by faking the kiss, by coming so very close to that lovely mouth of hers? Or was it possible the offense was in not really kissing her?

As the wheel came full circle, bringing them back to the height of it once more, his frustration swelled enough to fill the dark, open sky above. He was certain that final question would haunt him until his lips touched hers at last: Had he been the only one wanting the kiss, or had Bree – like Greyson – wanted it as well?

CHAPTER SEVENTEEN

Bree fiddled with the trinkets on her necklace as Greyson steered the SUV down the long, quiet driveway. The headlight's beam illuminated each massive trunk as they crept slowly beneath the trees' branches. Deep shadows accented the rough, bark-covered surface. Her mind was shining a light of its own – a glowing beam aimed right on a replay of that moment on the Ferris wheel. *So close.* He'd been so close to kissing her, and then stopped.

Suddenly.

Horribly.

Only to offer the taunting touch of his lips to the corner of her mouth.

The lonely, needing part of her thrilled at even that. She could hardly keep from rehashing the short coarse feel of his late-night shadow, that trace of facial hair against her skin. She wondered – for the millionth time – just what had caused him to change course. And there was no mistaking – he *had* changed course. Bree knew that – at least for a moment – he planned to really kiss her.

She couldn't be sure, but Bree was almost positive that he'd simply been too scared to act on it, unsure of what she might think or do in return. The crazy thing was, Greyson's rare moments of vulnerability seemed to give Bree equally rare bursts of courage. Times where she felt capable of doing things she might never dream of. Like the time he'd told her about his mother. Open, raw, and exposed. It had caused her to want to reach out to him. Touch him. Take his hand in hers, even. Something she never did. Something most people didn't dare do with her, as if she sent out signals warning people to keep their distance.

It made Bree wonder if *she* was the problem; the very reason he hadn't put his lips to hers. The thought only gave merit to an idea running through her mind. A dare, really. If Greyson didn't know whether or not it was okay to kiss her, Bree would show him that it was. After all, she'd been dreaming of his kiss since discovering it was *Greyson* she'd met in darkness at the party so long ago. *Greyson* who had swept her off her feet and made her feel wanted. Special. Desired.

She squeezed each trinket on her necklace one last time before bringing her hand to the door handle.

"I'll get that for you," Greyson said as he shut off the car. His voice was oddly quiet and unsure. And for a reason Bree could not begin to explain, it fed her confidence, made her look forward to what she was about to do all the more. She only hoped his reaction would be what she expected.

Nope, she told herself. *Don't worry about that.* She was right about this one. Could feel it in the fibers of her being. She let out a calming breath as Greyson opened the door for her. He took her hand as she stepped onto the running board of his SUV. "Thanks," she said with a confident grin.

He gave her a slight nod, his gaze shifting around the yard behind her. A warm breeze picked up, causing the leaves in the trees to rustle and stir.

"Heard anything from Braden?" she asked, though she already knew there was no news, having talked to him after speaking to the kids earlier that day.

"Nothing new," he said, resting a hand along the small of her back. He pressed at the key to lock his SUV and led her up the front porch. Her nerves kicked into gear as he unlocked the front door.

Calm, Bree, calm. By the energy surrounding him, Greyson seemed ready to rush off mad. Or at least wounded. She wouldn't let him. They had unfinished business, and she would not sleep until she addressed it.

While propping the screen, he pushed open the front door and motioned for her to go ahead. She stepped into the warm light of the lamp they'd left glowing in front of the window. The security alarm Greyson installed let out a series of beeps. Bree quieted the thing with the press of four simple keys, and then moved aside, just enough to let him enter.

Her eyes ran over the plaid pattern on his shirt while he stepped in, her heart clapping like a crowd at an encore. She squared her feet and shoulders while he locked up the door and reset the alarm. At last he spun to face her, almost bumped into her, but then stepped back. The smell of his cologne drifted through the air. Of all the tantalizing scents at the carnival, that one had been her favorite. She inhaled a deep breath of it before taking one step forward.

Greyson's eyes met hers, a tentative look on his face. He folded his arms across his chest and took another step back, leaning against the door. "Is this about the kiss?"

Bree felt her face flush with instant heat. Before she could even guess at where he was going with that question, he continued.

"I'm sorry. I just... didn't know what else to do, you know?"

She held his gaze, registering what he'd said. His cheeks held more color than she'd ever seen on him. His eyes darted to the rug before meeting her gaze once more. He thought she was mad? *So cute. So endearing.*

It urged her forward as she nodded in understanding. "I know," she said, reaching her hands out to his waist. A voice in her head cried out in disbelief, *I'm actually doing this! My hands are on his waist!*

The feel of them there was electric. The solid build of his frame, strong and warm. The leather strap of his belt beneath her palm. Smooth. Cool. Masculine.

Greyson pulled in a rather shaky breath, his eyes

locked on her as his chest bulged, accentuating the muscles in his crossed arms.

She smiled as he unfolded them.

Held her breath as he proceeded to reach toward her in return.

Gulped as his hands slipped along the curve of her hips, gently, softly. Her heart skipped two solid beats. She cleared her throat.

"I don't mind that you kissed me on the cheek, Greyson," she said, taking one step closer.

Greyson leaned his head back; flush against the door now, a near pleading look in his eyes.

She lifted her chin, admiring the sculpted shape of his slightly parted lips, and leaned in until they nearly touched her own. *Mmm.* The heat from his breath teased her lips. Her hands wandered up his arms, over his shoulders, where they rested. A small hint of doubt crept into her mind. What if he didn't want this after all? What if she was forcing herself on him?

In the moment of hesitation, Greyson moved in, centimeters at a time, until their lips barely touched. *Oh, yes.*

Bree tilted her head and applied the slightest bit of pressure, the thrill of it drumming against her chest. Greyson ran his smooth bottom lip over the curved top of hers, and then pressed a gentle kiss to the pouted part below. He came in again with a series of soft kisses, each working up to something more. Encouraging her to meld into him. Become one with him.

Her hands knotted fistfuls of his shirt, as if she could somehow grasp onto the moment and keep it from slipping away. It was real. It was happening. And it was more glorious than anything she'd encountered.

His grip on her waist intensified as he deepened the kiss, a low groan sounding in his throat. Bree echoed the sentiment with a sigh of her own. It came out more like a moan. A pleading for him to never stop. He made her feel powerful and alive. Wanted and complete.

Breaking away from the kiss for a breath, he moved away from the door and took hold of her hand. Just when she thought he might lead her right up the stairs, he changed course, turned to face her once more, and pressed her against the door where he'd stood. And suddenly his lips were on hers again. A stronger, more certain kiss.

The switch in position seemed to say the tables had turned, and now he was the pursuer. That suited her just fine.

Bree sunk into the bliss of it, savoring the sweet taste of his mouth. The velvet-like glide of his tongue. And the tender way he trailed kisses toward her ear, whispering her name in a reverent tone. No one else had ever made her feel this way. Only Greyson Law sparked this amount of passion in her, and she couldn't help but think that he was her home away from home. That warm cloak of comfort she'd lost while leaving her life behind. *Him.* All him.

His lip teased her ear before he spoke up once more.

"It's late," he crooned, his warm breath tickling her skin. "And I am far too tempted to take you to my bed." He kissed her neck, longingly, tempting her as well. "So I'm going to say goodnight and lock myself in my room for the evening."

She giggled, and then let out a deep sigh. Her hands were in his hair – she hadn't even remembered putting them there. Carefully, Bree slipped them free, rested them at the back of his neck. "Okay," she whispered, her palms sliding lazily down his chest. She bit at her lip as he backed away from her, thrilling in the truth of what had just taken place between them. The raw, undeniable connection.

As Bree worked to calm her breath, her heart pulsed and throbbed. A testament to what he evoked in her. A deep and utter longing for more. But he was right. They didn't want to move too quickly. So she stepped past him toward the stairs, turning to look over her shoulder from the bottom step. Lamplight glowed in the depths of his stormy eyes. She searched his face, looking for the slightest hint of a smile but found none. All longing and devotion. Fervor and need. A look that made her want to throw caution to the wind.

Instead Bree forced a slight grin and set her resolve. "Good night, Greyson."

CHAPTER EIGHTEEN

Greyson woke feeling restless. Like he had a list of things to take care of as tall and wide as the largest maple in Oregon. And every one of those items revolved around keeping Bree safe.

He trudged out of his room, guided by the early morning light, and made for the bathroom. After running the shower until it warmed, Greyson stepped into the heated spray and let it beat against his back. Hopefully it could ease some of the tension that had every muscle in him flexing, as if there were an invisible fist ready and aimed right at him. Or, at Bree.

He clenched his jaw, forcing his tired brain to work — hoping the conscious part of him could make better sense of this new force warring within him. Greyson had been in this business for years. He'd learned to be a fierce, physical protector, doing anything to assure his client's safety no matter the circumstance.

But that wasn't the only side to him; there was his personal life too. There, Greyson had always been a different sort of protector. Never had he let Todd speak a mean word to – or about – their mom. He'd taken a swing at a kid who cracked an ugly joke about his dad. And even though his younger brother might have deserved some of the crap people said about him, Greyson defended Todd's name to anyone who dared speak ill of him.

Greyson reached for a bar of soap and lathered up, realizing just what his problem was: With Bree, those worlds had come crashing together, creating a deeper sense of caring and concern than he'd ever known. His feelings for the woman were like seeds that had taken root before he'd even written that poem about her in the fourth grade. They may have dried out over time, having not been a part of her life for so many years, but being there with her had brought them back to life.

Last night though... he shook his head, the mere thought hurling him into that place of need and desire. Last night had taken those roots and given them some sort of Miracle-Gro. Strengthening, lengthening, transforming them into a supreme, unstoppable life source. The fact that Bree had initiated the whole thing made her all the more intriguing. And beautiful. There was something about watching a woman own a moment. And last night, Bree had owned him, the moment, and the moon and stars too.

He groaned as he shut off the water, swimming in boyish adoration for her. But there was an equal level of frustration there too. Sure, he was in a difficult position, having to worry about this psycho coming back into Bree's life. But they weren't fighting a nameless, invisible enemy, like he so often did in his field. He was up against a man who lived in a different state. He had no known resources to find Bree, and they weren't even sure he wanted to. Still, a crazed desire to shelter her was taking sprout. He wanted to cancel their engagement at the carnival and spend the entire day training her like he would one of the agents in his training course.

Similar thoughts plagued him as he headed out to the orchard, Bree still quiet in her bed. As he filled his pack with ripe, fresh apples, the air cool against his skin, Greyson's thoughts turned back to their time together at the door. Her kiss had sparked a roaring fire deep in his belly. He could still taste the sweetness of her mouth, feel the slick heat of her lips, and hear the small sounds of pleasure forming deep in her throat. He blew out a short, quiet whistle, grateful they'd stopped things before going too far. Thank heavens for that.

If nothing else, Greyson would keep that line drawn in the sand: During their stay at the orchard, he would not take her to his bed. There was no telling where her head would be once she got back to her kids and family. Or if she'd feel safe moving back at all. Perhaps her ex could decide that it'd be safest for them all to relocate and then where would he be?

Madly in love with a woman he couldn't have in his life. No thank you. For that reason – and a whole lot more – Greyson would need to take it slowly.

For now, they had a big day ahead of them. More apples to coat, a full day at the carnival, and if he was lucky – a second shot at that Ferris wheel.

Bree's first day at the carnival had been a perfect beginning. She'd enjoyed everything from the tempting aromas, to the kind people who visited their booth. Today had been even better. The food more fragrant and rich. The amusement rides more vibrant in color. And after the sun set on their second evening, the lights on the Ferris wheel looked more sparkly and bright against the darkening sky.

On more than one occasion, Bree had told herself it was not due to her flirtatious encounters with Greyson each time they touched. She tried telling herself that the carnival itself just held an exceptional energy that particular day, but she wasn't fooling herself. His alluring smiles, playful winks, and teasing touches would be enough to keep her grinning clear into the following week. Add to that the memory of his kiss – the incredible way his lips had owned hers the very night before – and you had a grown woman acting like a giddy girl after her first kiss.

"Here's your change," she said, leaning to set the bills and coins into the palm of their current customer. The boy, probably seventeen or so, gave her a bold smile. "Thanks."

"Sure. Have fun." She'd never pictured herself in a job where she'd deal directly with customers and crowds. Bree had always preferred the peace of her own home, even if it was a little disrupted by the small children she watched. Yet today she'd not only gotten used to the change of pace, she'd enjoyed it as well. Bree could really get used to a job like this. Especially with Greyson by her side.

As if reading her thoughts, Greyson stepped up behind her, slipping his hands over her hips from behind. He lowered his chin onto one shoulder, causing goosebumps to rush up her arms. "I think that boy was flirting with you," he mumbled against her ear.

She giggled. "I doubt it. I'm way older than he is. Kid's still in high school by the looks of it." She nodded to his letterman jacket as he and his group of friends sauntered away.

"That's not gonna stop him," Greyson said. "Not if the guy's anything like I was back then. In fact..." Greyson straightened up, peering into the crowd while narrowing his eyes. "I bet you anything he and his friends will be back before the night's through."

"They will not."

"Oh, I bet they will. If I made myself sparse right now, those boys would probably swing back around real soon."

Her eyes shifted back to the group of teenagers. They

hadn't gone far, but they were wrapped up in conversation, laughing and talking.

"No way."

"How about we test it out?" Greyson pointed to one of the vendors a few booths down. "I'm going to go get us an order of nachos, leave you to run the place on your own for a minute, and see if they come back."

She lifted a brow. "Nachos?"

"Heck, yeah. Only this time you need to stop eating all the jalapenos before I can get any."

Bree rolled her eyes. "I don't touch those things."

He grinned. "Be right back." He gave her one flawless wink that made her heart jump, and then snuck out of the booth and toward the nacho stand.

A chuckle slipped through her lips. He was incorrigible. And devilishly charming. And capable of fanning desire in her with the sound of that deep, masculine voice alone. She was so preoccupied with the sight of him that she almost forgot the reason he'd left – the group of guys.

Her gaze shot to the cluster. Two in the group had their eyes on her, one being the boy who'd just purchased the apple. He'd already made a pretty nice dent in it, she noticed. One gave another member of their group an elbow bump, gaining his pal's attention before motioning toward her booth with the tilt of his head.

Bree hid a gasp. *No way.* There was no way Greyson was correct in his guess that they'd return when he left. Yet there it was. The group of ...five, six, seven guys headed her way, the one who'd purchased the apple leading the pack.

She dropped her gaze to the cashbox, straightening the metal case along the table as her face grew warm. When she lifted her chin once more, Bree moved her sights to the far corner of the grounds. A line of portable toilets lined the parking lot. She squinted, worked for a better view of a man in a wide-striped polo shirt, just like the ones Carl Ronsberg used to wear. The sight of them now — whether on mannequins or passersby in town — never failed to get her attention. Without a conscious thought, her physical response began following the old familiar pattern. Heat climbing up the back of her neck, creeping over her chest in a suffocating crawl.

She played the part of a casual browser as she searched the nacho stand. A large group of rowdy girls stood where she'd last spotted Greyson. She tilted her head, wishing she could see beyond the crowd. Bree was certain the man she'd seen was not Carl Ronsberg. He couldn't have been. But she couldn't fathom glancing back for confirmation until Greyson was safe by her side.

"Well, hello again," came a smooth voice. She turned her attention to the group standing before her, their presence like a sudden wall. Blocking her from other eyes.

Bree flashed the returning customer a nervous grin. "Hi. How can I help you?" Through a gap in the shoulders and heads, she peered back to the portable potties. Flashing bulbs from a nearby game spilled fluorescent green light onto the man, casting an inhuman tone to his bulky face. Were those dark-rimmed glasses? She could swear the guy wore dark-rimmed glasses.

"Yeah. My friends and I are trying to settle a little wager, and I'm wondering if you can help me out."

She forced her eyes back to the kid in time to see him hand his caramel apple over to one of his friends. He stepped closer and cleared his throat.

"Oh," she said through quickened breaths. "Okay. What is it?" Her gaze darted back to the nacho stand. Still no Greyson. A wave of sweat broke out over her palms and cheeks. Her skin suddenly felt flu-ish.

"I'd like you to accompany me on that Ferris wheel over there, and these guys say I don't stand a chance."

"'Cause she's older than you," one razzed.

"And probably with that guy," another said.

The persistent spark of confidence in the kid's eye was distracting. He placed both of his hands on the table and leaned in slightly, an assumptive grin on his lips. "You wouldn't mind coming on that harmless little ride with me, would you?"

"Mmm..." Bree smoothed the back of her hand over her forehead while risking a glance toward the striped shirt once more. Gone. *Gone!* She tilted her head, moving to see in the small spaces between the large crowds. *There.* He hadn't moved far. Was simply faced away from her, lined up at the game with the flashing lights. *It's not Carl, Bree. It can't be.*

"Don't do it," one kid blurted, gaining her attention once more. "Jake bribed ol' Ralph to stop the wheel when you guys are up top so you'll have to kiss."

Bree looked over the group at her booth. She hadn't seen which kid had ratted him out, but guessed, by the way her pursuer slugged him in the arm, that it was the tall, skinny one.

"Don't listen to that guy. C'mon, what do you say?" He turned to hush the rowdy group while Bree thought about things like driving all night long, collecting Sophie and Carter from Dallin whether he agreed to it or not, and fleeing the country without a moment's delay. If she took off in Greyson's SUV right then, would he be able to catch a ride back with Mila?

"I think that's a no, dude."

Bree had been stuck in a daze, seeing nothing that went on before her. At last she focused on the group once more. It took all the effort she could muster to form a reply. "I'm flattered," she said through a shallow breath. "But..." What should she say? *I've got to get out of here? I'm about to get killed? Call 911?* "I'm married," she blurted.

"Ooohhh....." the guys moaned in unison.

"Shot down."

"Dissed."

"Forget about it, man."

The teens were pulling away from the booth, but the kid stayed put, looking down at her hand. Her *left* hand. A lengthened beat passed between them. Her eyes held his, an almost pleading expression coming over her. She felt trapped. Exposed. And on the verge of panic.

His gaze moved to something just behind her before

he spoke up once more. "If you were *my* wife, I'd make sure you kept your ring on that finger. Guys like me get encouraged way too easily, you know?"

Throughout the entire encounter, Bree had been dying for the bunch to just leave. Only now, as the last of them sauntered away, she felt more exposed than ever. It seemed as if a giant magnifying glass now hovered over her booth, allowing the man in the polo shirt and dark-rimmed glasses to see just where she was.

Desperation rushed through her as she spotted the man toward the front of the line he waited in. She could bolt out of there right then before he even knew it. Take the cash, head straight to Montana in Greyson's SUV, and let Greyson worry about the rest. Heck, there wasn't so much to worry about with her out of the picture.

She'd do it. She'd get out of there.

With her still-spiraling mind made up, Bree snagged the cashbox off the table and spun to make her exit.

One massive chest stopped her after two short steps.

"Whoa, whoa, hold up. Where are you going?"

CHAPTER NINETEEN

Greyson set the nachos on the table before turning his attention back to Bree. She'd nearly knocked the food right onto the ground in her hurry. Once his hands were free, he took hold of Bree at each shoulder, urging her to look him square in the eye. The trembling of her body wasn't exactly visible, but he could feel it in the grip he had on her.

Wide-eyed, the look of sheer panic on her face. "He's here. I think he's here." She gulped. "Someone who looks exactly like Carl is here and we have to leave before he sees me."

"Show me the man you saw," he said. "Do you see him now?"

Bree began pulling him along, urging him to move. "Let's just go. Let's just get in the car and then we'll talk." Anxious fingers gripped at his shirt as she hugged the cashbox to her chest with one arm.

Greyson guided her to step through the back flap of the booth where they were covered from the carnival attendees. Bree looked over her shoulder, though the white canvas blocked anything she might see.

"Listen, the chances of Carl being here right now are slim to none. With what Braden and I have set up, we've got a solid grip on his location."

"You can't be sure," Bree persisted, shifting her weight from one foot to the next. "You just. You have to look at him. If you see him I think you'll know."

Greyson straightened up. "Okay, where is he?"

"He's in line to play the game. The one by the portable toilets. He's probably playing it now. Or maybe done already, I don't know."

Greyson cursed the panic he saw in her eyes. Wanted desperately to take it away. "What is he wearing?"

"A white and blue polo shirt. Stripes. He's got glasses and his hair is brown and short."

He held onto her hand, shuffling along the outside of the booth until he came to the edge. He worried that if he let go of her tight and trembling hand, Bree might bolt toward the lot. He couldn't have that. "Promise me you'll stay put."

Bree had her gaze set back on the canvas behind her, as if she could somehow see beyond the hefty cloth. Greyson placed a gentle hand on her chin, urged her to look at him, and gulped back his pain once those brown eyes set back on him. "Promise me you won't move from this spot."

She nodded, and Greyson rushed in to kiss her lips. Short. Reassuring. And packed with a promise that she had nothing to fear. "I'll be right back."

His concern stemmed from what Bree might do while he was gone, not thoughts of Carl discovering her there; Greyson simply knew that hadn't happened. Taking only five steps away from the tent, he spotted the game Bree spoke of. There, walking away from the large, glowing display was a fairly heavy man with a thick head of hair, wearing the striped shirt and thick glasses she mentioned.

With a nod of confirmation, Greyson strode back to Bree. Her fingers were curled around the cashbox. Her foot tapping against the base of the pole. Her eyes set on Greyson.

"It's not him," he assured. "Not even close. But since we're on the topic, I have a few things to show you."

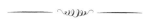

"*This* is what he looks like now?" Bree stared at the picture, shocked at just how much Carl Ronsberg had changed. The eyes were the same, she guessed, just older. Though it was hard to tell since he wasn't looking directly at whatever camera had taken the pictures. "You got these from the surveillance cameras you guys set up?"

Greyson lowered himself onto the kitchen chair across from Bree. "Yeah. This shot is from the camera set up on the property across from him. He's changed a lot. The only part that hasn't changed is the nose and the glasses."

Bree nodded. "Yeah. I didn't expect him to lose weight in prison. I don't know why, but I kind of pictured he'd just get bigger, you know?"

Beneath the golden glow of the dining room light, she flipped through three distinct photos on Greyson's laptop. He looked tall, still broad in the shoulders, but thin rather than heavy, like she remembered. And his hair – it was almost gone. Receded clear back and thinned so much it was hardly there.

She shuddered. Hating what it felt like to look at the man. Hating the man himself. Even if Carl had changed. Even if he'd gone all of those years regretting what he'd done (which, nobody said he had) Bree would be unable to muster a decent thought toward the person who'd stolen more from her than he'd ever know.

"Why didn't you show this to me before?" She glanced away from the screen to see him shrug.

He brought an elbow to the table, running a hand through his hair . "I considered it," he said. "At some point I planned to make sure you were aware of what he looks like now. But it seemed unnecessary at this point. For now we've got a pretty good pulse on him. Besides," he added, "I figured you'd maybe ask if you were curious."

"Hmm…" She took one last look at each image. Carl exiting a brown brick house, more of a head-on shot, which explained why it was blurry. Greyson had most likely zoomed into that one. The second picture was a horizontal shot — him getting into a white sedan while adjusting his glasses. Greyson was right – those looked just like the ones he'd always worn. The last image was a close up of him inside the car, depicting the other side of his profile.

That was enough, she decided, sliding the laptop until the screen faced Greyson instead of her. A residual shudder rocked her limbs. Greyson gave her a nod before closing it down and putting it back in the bag. He brought his elbows back to the table then and reached for her hands.

Bree smiled at the new, moving image that captured her attention — of Greyson's strong hands cradling hers. Gentle. Caring. The image improved even still as he lifted one of her hands to his lips, kissing the back of it with his eyes set on her. Tingling heat pooled into her chest in response. He switched hands, bringing the other to his mouth, this time closing his eyes as he kissed her there.

She tuned in to the feel of that short scruff around his lips, appreciating the way it accentuated his masculine nature. "If you ever think you spot Carl again…" he murmured against her skin. He glided his lips toward a sensitive spot at her inner wrist and kissed her there.

Mmm… Melting. She was melting inside.

"You should try to let me know before you run," he said.

Embarrassed heat warmed her face. She bit at her lip. "I didn't know where you were."

"That's my fault." A deep furrow pulled at his brow. "After getting the nachos, I snuck behind the tent so I could listen to those boys shamelessly flirt with you." He set her hands back onto the table, sunk back into his chair, and gave her an unreadable smile. "I was right, though. Those guys had their sights set on you, and they *did* come back."

Bree shrugged it off. "They were bored. I was a challenge for them."

Greyson kept his gaze on her as he folded his arms over his chest. "Just a challenge? You never can give yourself any credit, can you? Couldn't be because you're beautiful or interesting or kind. Just a challenge."

"Don't, okay?" Bree shook her head, not wanting to have this conversation again. They'd had one close enough to it not so long ago. One where Greyson had called his brother. Revealed things about himself she'd never expected. If he'd convinced her of one thing, it was that *he* found her beautiful. There was no need to go any further than that.

She looked back to him in time to see his gaze drop to the table. He ran a thumb over the smooth surface of the wood tracing the oval patterns in the grain. Bree followed the action with her eyes, feeling guilty for snapping at him.

"Sorry," she said under her breath. "I don't know why it makes me feel so uncomfortable. I think that – after the whole stalking thing – I like to think I can just go unnoticed. It's hard to want anything other than that, you know?"

Greyson's eyes moved slowly up until he looked into hers, a deep, almost pleading look in them. It seemed as if he was asking something of her. Begging. But she didn't know what it could be. At once he broke off the gaze, turned his attention to the dark window, and stood to close the blinds. He walked over to the sink then, poured himself a glass of water, and stayed in place while he tipped it back.

An old clock in the kitchen ticked. The sound of water trickling down the drain joined in. And Bree tried to think of just what Greyson was to her in that moment. A man she'd grown close to. A friend, for sure. She cared about him. Knew he cared about her. But there was more. He did things to her no other man had. He made her feel brave and powerful. Capable of initiating a kiss between them at the door. A memorable, incredible, keep-you-dreaming-of-it-in-your-sleep kiss. Warmth moved up her neck at the thought of it; that was the second way he affected her – differently than any other man had – passion.

Sure, she'd felt wanted by Dallin. But not to the same degree. With Greyson it was heightened. Intensified. Magnetic.

"What was your ex-husband like?" Greyson asked, setting his glass down on the counter. He strode back over to the table and lowered himself in the chair once more.

Bree glanced at the ticking clock, feeling as if he'd just read her thoughts. It was almost midnight. Beyond that, it had been one of the longest days she'd had since being there. But this – talking with Greyson in the dim glow of light – was just where she wanted to be.

"Kind," she answered. "I've had a lot of time to think

about why I chose a guy like him. Someone I didn't have a whole lot of chemistry with…"

Greyson raised a brow, but remained silent.

She grinned. "I think I gravitated toward him because I knew he was safe. I'd um… built up profiles in my head. People who were dangerous. People who were safe. And those who fell someplace in between." A part of Bree was surprised that she was actually sharing this. But the larger part of her said that it felt very right to open up to Greyson about it; the simple fact made her like him even more.

"I'll admit to you, I was quick to judge. I just kind of put people in their own little box with the label I felt was right, and didn't look back. Say, if you were overly quiet and withdrawn, avoided eye-contact – like Carl – you were unsafe. If you were loud and outgoing, cocky or popular, you were unsafe. If you were somewhere in between. Reserved, but polite enough to engage in conversation. Went out of your way enough to be kind even when it was uncomfortable – you were safe. Mostly only girls fell into that category."

"Wait, I get why the backwards ones weren't safe – like you say – because that was like Carl. But why were the loud and outgoing kids dangerous?"

She'd known this was coming. He was putting pieces together, realizing she'd deemed him unsafe back in high school. "I didn't say it was fair or accurate, but in my mind, those were the type of kids that bullied Carl in the first place. They were the ones who helped shape somebody who would look for a target of his own. Someone to torment and bully and make afraid: me. For that reason, I stayed away."

He gulped. "So, the dance? When I asked you... that's why?"

Bree looked down at her hands and nodded.

"I've never bullied a kid in my – "

"I know," she blurted, looking back to him. "I know and I'm sorry. I didn't know you. And I didn't think in a million years that you would have been hurt by my reply. I couldn't understand why you'd asked me in the first place. Had my dad told your dad to ask me out because he feared I wouldn't get a date? Had Braden? I made up all sorts of possibilities in my head. And if nothing else, I was certain that you'd be relieved when I turned you down. I figured you could go ask who you really wanted to go with instead."

Greyson remained very still as he seemed to process what she'd shared.

"I never did find out who you asked after that," she said.

He shrugged. "No one."

A tingling warmth spread over her limbs. "Hmm."

"So Dallin – he was safe?"

"Yes. He was kind. Polite. Talkative, but not loud. There was nothing about him that threatened me or made me uncomfortable. And I really grew to love him. Just not the way he deserved, probably." She shrugged. "It may not have worked out between us, but he's a great guy. And a good dad too." The final comment had her recalling the conversations she'd had with the kids earlier that day. She'd promised to make caramel apples with them when she went back for her visit, and was looking forward to it already.

Small pats sounded just beyond the window, causing Bree's eyes to widen. "Is that rain?"

Greyson nodded. "Sounds like it."

"Wow, it's perfect timing."

"It is?"

She nodded. "Yes. We just made it through the most beautiful, perfect day selling caramel apples; it's like the rain was waiting for us to finish up." The idea delighted her. Caused a smile to stretch over her face.

"Well a little rain never hurt anybody," Greyson said.

"I don't know," she countered, "when you have food and vendors and rides and crafts and so many things that shouldn't get wet... a little rain can spoil a whole lot of things."

"True." A smile crept over his face. "But now that all that is through, how about going for a walk with me?"

She gasped. "Are you kidding?"

"Nope."

"At night? In the rain?"

"Sure. We'll just stroll along the orchard, is all."

She laughed. "Okay. I've got some rain boots."

Greyson came to a stand. "Alright then. Meet me back here in five."

CHAPTER TWENTY

Greyson's phone buzzed as he waited for Bree to grab her boots. He was still mulling over the things she'd shared with him – about their high school years and why she'd viewed him the way she had. Just thinking about it made him shake his head. He was far from the bullying type. Of course he couldn't argue that he'd been one cocky kid back in the day. Who knew he was making such a rotten impression all that time?

His phone showed one short text from Braden. *Call me when you can.*

A stinging surge of heat shot through his veins, causing his heart to hammer within his chest. He didn't like the look of those words. To anyone else they might look innocent enough, but to Greyson they were an indication of trouble. There was something Braden wanted to tell him– something he didn't want Bree to know about.

He tore off his flannel shirt, draped it over a kitchen

chair, and snuck out the back door. Rain pelted the small awning outside the kitchen window, the fray reaching his forearms as he dialed the number. He welcomed the cool feel of it against his skin.

"Hey," Greyson said once Braden answered. "I only have a couple of minutes, but uh... what's up?"

"I think I got his car on surveillance."

Greyson gritted his teeth. "At Dallin's or her house?" He was about to tag the third option – Braden's house – onto the list but Braden spoke up before he could.

"Her place. I was fast-forwarding through tonight's footage, and as I got toward the end of the tape I spotted a white sedan. Looks a whole lot like the one he drives."

"Did you get a shot of his face?"

"No. He parked a good distance from the streetlamp. Only way I knew it was white was when he drove beneath it before parking."

"What about a license plate?"

"Nope. Another car drove by as they passed the light, blocking it. But you know that dent he's got on the passenger side? Looks kind of like a triangular gouge?"

"Mmm, hmm," Greyson mumbled with a nod.

"This car has it. Same place. Same shape."

Braden's discovery was a sock to the gut. A hard one. "Damn it," he hissed, kicking a nearby bucket. The thing sailed out into the yard, the hollow sound of it lost in the growing spread of rain. All hope for a reformed Ronsberg was officially gone; it was only a matter of time before things escalated.

"Did he park and watch the house?"

"Yep. Just shy of fifteen minutes."

Thunder erupted over the sky, adding to the mounding chaos in Greyson's head. He knew he didn't have much longer before Bree would be back down. He'd need to get ahold of himself. To put on his everything-is-just-fine face. In his line of work it was second nature. *Even if the woman he was protecting was Bree*, he assured himself. *Especially* if it was her. He needed to shield her from the worries this new development would bring.

Still, there was so much he wanted to do. So much he wanted to know. "Do you think he knows Bree doesn't live there anymore?"

A thoughtful pause followed his question.

"Only if he could see in the windows. And even then, it's hard to say. Family living there has small kids. But she doesn't look a thing like Bree. Woman's blonde, heavyset."

Greyson nodded. "That's good, I guess. As much as we don't want Ronsberg fishing for her new location, we don't want anyone else in danger."

"Exactly. Hey… about telling Bree. Since it's not quite concrete, it might be best to keep it under wraps for now."

A jagged knot formed in his gut at the thought. "Agreed. Though if he shows up on the footage again, I'll mention it to her before we come back for the kids' break."

"Yeah. Sounds good."

He heard dishes clanking beyond the window, and realized Bree was back in the kitchen.

"I better go," Greyson said. A thought occurred to him then. One that had him speaking up again before he could reconsider. "Braden?"

"Yeah?"

Greyson gulped, wondering just how to phrase the question swimming through his head. *Mind if I date your sister while we're here? No way.*

"Uh, just, thanks for the update. Sure as hell isn't good news, is it?"

"You can say that again."

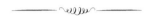

Greyson lifted his face to the sky, allowing the tiny drops to sprinkle his face. He was glad that the rain had reduced to no more than a trickle. Just enough to splatter cool drops on his skin. Too bad it couldn't reach the boiling blood inside him. The hissing, raging fire that licked at his temper, urging him to act.

"It's so nice out here, isn't it?" Bree said. "I never knew a late night walk in an orchard — in the rain, no less — could feel like this." She nuzzled deeper into him as they walked, releasing a contented sigh.

Green-leaved walls surrounded them on either side, the rows looking longer than ever in the dark night.

"You're right," he agreed. "It's beautiful." At the end

of the aisle, Greyson urged her toward the home rather than the next row, wishing he could pull his mind from thoughts of Ronsberg and the new information he'd received: Carl was still obsessing on Bree. His drive out to her old place said it all.

A stream of curse words spewed through his mind. He wanted to secure his hands around the guy's neck and choke the life out of him. He wanted to –

"What's wrong?" Bree had pulled away from him, was tilting her head to look up at his face.

He shook his head. "Nothing. Just thinking." He knew better than to think the answer would satisfy her, so he searched for something more.

"I uh, was just worrying about Todd." It was only a partial lie, since in some ways Greyson's worry for the guy never quit. "He's helping my dad run the orchard, you know? But he's still going through AA for his alcoholism, and I'm scared he's going to have one weak moment and we'll be back to square one." He shook his head, suddenly gripped by the truth of it. "I don't know if my old man could take it." Greyson pulled Bree closer as they neared the house.

"Is it hard being away?" Bree asked.

"In some ways, but I know it's for the best. Plants need air if they're going to grow. Just like all these trees. They need plenty of soil for the roots. Space to stretch their limbs." He shook his head. "I probably stifle the poor guy."

She laughed. "With good intent, I'm sure."

He didn't reply to that, only led her behind the house where he unlocked the back screen door, followed by the other. He motioned for her to step inside.

Bree looked down at the keys in his hand as she stepped past him and into the dimly lit pantry. "You locked the screen?" she asked. "That's new."

Greyson shrugged. "It's not necessary, with the main door being locked and all, but I figure there are probably a few kids from the fair wandering around, looking for mischief."

"True," Bree said with a laugh.

He locked up behind them, his mind fighting the strong and building desire to put Bree on lockdown and sit out front with a loaded gun. He blew out a deep breath, working to release some of the pressure in his chest.

Bree removed her hoodie and looped it over a hook by the microwave. She ran her hands over her bare arms. Her dark lashes were slightly wet; her brown eyes tinted with hints of gold from the dining room light. Her brows furrowed. "I'm sorry you're worried over your brother. I wish there was something I could do."

Greyson pulled off his ball cap, ran a hand through his hair, and took a step toward her. "You do?"

"Yes," she said with a giggle. Bree's gaze followed the path of his hat as he plunked it onto a notepad at the table.

He smiled at the way she glanced down at his feet, watching as he took another step closer, and then another.

"What do you have in mind?"

There went that dimple, sinking right into that rosy cheek of hers. She was helping already. She took a step back. "*I* don't have anything in mind."

"Fair enough," he said, taking one final step. Bree was against the counter now, the light above the nearby table grazing just parts of her lovely face. "I'm thinking of a way you can help right now." He slipped one hand along her delicate neck, her skin slightly cool and damp from the rain, and caught hints of her floral perfume.

She grinned, her gaze darting to the floor before settling back on him. "Hmm."

Boy did the look of those lips set his belly ablaze. Bree had been bold enough to make the first move the night before. It was only fair he return the favor. Besides, she'd offered to help. And Greyson couldn't think of a better way to take his mind off his unpleasant concerns.

Her hands reached tentatively toward him until they wrapped up over his shoulders. He could sense it took bravery to do it, as it had before; something about that thrilled him all the more. To know she'd push past what was comfortable to get what she wanted: him.

He leaned in at last, pressed his lips to hers, and relished the euphoria that pulsed through his body. He kissed her again. Soft, teasing, urging her lips to part with his own. When he tilted his head, deepening the kiss, Bree released a quiet sigh of pleasure.

He felt her fingers move up the back of his neck, rake through his hair and grip, causing a deep moan to sound in his chest. Bree was his to own in that moment, and he wanted nothing more.

His heart beating wildly, he gripped the full curve of her hips, leaning into her as he memorized each passing beat. The tempting heat of her lips. The playful touch of her tongue. He'd wanted her kiss for nearly half of his life, and it had been worth the wait.

So worth it. A small voice in the back of his mind warned him that this was a risk. Somebody wanted her dead. Somebody who was on the lookout again.

To silence the unwanted voice, Greyson hoisted Bree onto the counter at her back, moving in to close the gap. Her legs wrapped around his waist, encouraging the act, drawing him impossibly closer still. "Bree," he murmured between kisses, assuring himself it was really her. Bree's kiss. Bree's lips. Hips. Legs. It was *her* hands that moved longingly over his back.

Yes. He deepened the kiss once more, in drawn-out movements that heightened each sensation. Tilting. Touching. Tasting.

Too fast an inner voice warned. Way too fast. This was only their second kiss and already he was having thoughts of carrying her upstairs. Talk about setting himself up for heartbreak. Not to mention distrust. Bree wouldn't want a thing to do with him if he rushed things in such a way. And Braden would probably kill him.

Slowly, torturously, Greyson eased up on the kiss. He brought his hands up to her shoulders, pulled slightly away and rested his forehead on hers. "It's getting late," he said through jagged breaths.

When stating the obvious didn't cause her to stir, he tried again. "And I should let you get to sleep."

Damp strands of her dark hair clung to the side of her neck. He wanted to smooth it away and kiss her there at the delicate slope. Long and hard.

Bree blinked, shifting her gaze to the small clock behind him. "You're right."

Greyson backed up and took hold of her hands, helping her off the counter. Once she was back on the tiled floor, Bree cleared her throat, dropping her chin into her chest. Her cheeks flushed red. Her shoulders curled in. And Greyson's heart sunk as he realized his abrupt end to things had made her uncomfortable. Maybe even self-conscious.

"Goodnight," she mumbled, stepping around him and toward the stairs.

Do something! He knew he should speak up and say something but he didn't know what. He could hear her at the steps now. Rushing. Hurrying away so fast she'd be gone in a blink.

"Wait, Bree?" He followed her up the stairs, caught her at the top where she rested one hand on the banister.

She turned to face him. "Yeah?"

Greyson held her gaze while he marched up the final steps, closing the gap between them. He reached out to cradle her face with his hand, soft and warm against his palm. He pictured saying all sorts of things: *I'm trying to slow things down because I think it's the right thing to do. I think it's best if we don't rush things. I don't want to mess this up.* All of it sounded lame.

Instead he came in for one final kiss, the act making him ache with desire from the inside out. He pulled away, barely managing a regretful grin. "Goodnight."

CHAPTER TWENTY-ONE

"Mom, I can't believe there's only five beads left!" Sophie exclaimed, excitement pouring from the receiver. "That means you get to come here in just five days!"

"That's right," Bree said, "I can hardly wait!" She thrilled in the knowledge –just five more days until she got to see them. Hold them. Love on them.

Having stepped out into the backyard to call the kids, she took in the beauty of the rising sun, hoping it would lend its warmth soon. As gorgeous as the mornings were – that familiar mist floating over the orchard like a dream – they were growing increasingly chilly as the days passed.

"Oh, Wendy says it's time to eat," Carter said. "She made us a big Sunday brunch like you always do."

"She did? That's so sweet of her."

"Yep," Sophie agreed. "And Dad even got the jam you

buy with the strawberries in it."

Bree nudged a pinecone with her shoe, her view of the sparse grass becoming a blur through welling tears of gratitude. "Remember your manners and tell Wendy thanks for doing that, okay?" She made a mental note to thank Wendy herself as well; how grateful she was that Dallin's wife was so good to the kids. That she was doing what she could to help them have a good experience while they were there.

"You guys have a delicious brunch and a happy, happy Sunday and I'll talk to you tonight, okay?"

"Okay. And it's my turn to switch the marble over tonight," Carter said.

"Oh, good. I'm glad sissy is sharing."

"Mmm, hmm," Sophie hummed proudly.

"Love you guys."

"Love you too," came their sweet voices in unison.

She took a moment to bask in appreciation. She made a habit to pray daily about the kids having a smooth transition throughout everything, assuming that her own experience would be rough no matter the weather. Yet somehow she'd managed to have days – not only void of lonely tears – but filled with real joy. She sent a silent word of thanks to the man upstairs, knowing that her angel parents must be helping out from the heavens. That very thought had her thinking of Greyson, of what a gift he had been. She couldn't imagine trying to run the orchard without him. Or being in that home by herself. Forget about how frightened she might have been, she would have made herself sick over missing the kids and worrying about their adjustment. Beyond that – she would probably be obsessing over the fact that Carl Ronsberg was no longer in prison. He was out. And because of Greyson – and Braden's efforts too, of course – she felt safe.

Bree stepped into the house through the pantry, rounding the corner into the kitchen. The hickory smell of bacon permeated the room, causing her mouth to water. Yet it was the sight of the counter in the kitchen that made her yearn for something entirely different. Ever since Greyson had kissed her there, lifted her onto the counter even, Bree could not stop thinking about his incredible kiss. The way he'd made her feel. Over a week had passed since then, but she could still remember every sensual move and gentle touch.

She wasn't sure how most romantic relationships went, but things between her and Greyson seemed ideal. She had never had a man slow things down between them before, like he'd done that night. She hadn't known what to make of it at first, feeling rejected, even when he'd stopped and told her goodnight. It was the kiss he'd given her after – at the top of the stairs – that said he wasn't rejecting her at all, simply taking things slowly. And she was grateful for that too. There was a whole lot going on in her life, and she didn't want to complicate it by jumping in too deep too soon.

"How are the kids doing?" Greyson walked into the kitchen, coming up behind her, and wrapped his arms around her from behind.

"Wonderful," she said, "I can't believe it's almost time to go back for a visit." She enjoyed the warm kiss he planted on her cheek before spinning around to wrap her arms around him in return. The spicy scent of his aftershave made her inhale more deeply. "Mmm. This is nice. Lazy Sunday morning. Yummy brunch ahead of us."

He ran his freshly shaven cheek along her temple. "You're right. It *is* nice." He pressed his lips to her cheek once more. "Let's see how the bacon's doing, should we?" He creaked open the oven and reached for a hand towel. The fragrant strips sizzled and popped as he lifted the iron skillet from the heat. "Ah, yes. It's perfect."

"Here," Bree said. "I've got a hotplate set out for it." She directed him to a spot at the table. The eggs and hash browns had been warming on the stove while Bree talked to the kids. She brought them over to the table and grinned. "This looks perfect."

She and Greyson had gotten into a comfortable groove since coming to the orchard house. On weekdays, the two would grab a quick breakfast on their own. Cereal, yogurt, or fresh apples. Occasionally they ate lunch together while taking a break from the orchard duties. But dinner was something they always did together. It had become their unspoken daily date. The conversations always dug deeper than any daytime talk the two engaged in. Their courage seeming to rise with the set of the sun.

But weekend breakfasts, Bree noted, were very much like their dinners in that regard. Easy, unguarded conversation. Longer glances and bolder flirtations.

"Think we're about there," Greyson said, drawing her mind back to the moment.

She looked over the table. English muffins with strawberry jam for her, grape jelly for him. Hash browns with ketchup for her. Hot sauce for him. "The juice," she said, remembering the batch she'd made up for breakfast the day before.

Greyson slid her chair away from the table as she neared. "I thought we could talk about the trip back to Montana."

Bree gave him a nod while lowering herself into the chair. "Okay."

He sunk into his own chair and brought an elbow to the table. "I figure if we drive most of the day Thursday, catch some sleep in a hotel that night, we should arrive by the time the kids get out of school Friday."

A smile spread over her face at the thought. "Oh, my gosh. I can't wait to get my hands on those guys. I swear I'm going to smother them so much they'll be sick of me by the time we say goodbye."

Greyson gave her a thoughtful smile, the expression laced with hesitation. She reached for the eggs, lifted a portion with the spatula, and slid them onto her plate. When she glanced back up at him, the off expression remained.

"What is it?" she asked.

He shook his head. "Nothing."

"No, really," she persisted. "Something's on your mind. I can tell."

"I don't want to ruin breakfast."

A tight knot built up in her chest. "Did something happen?"

"No. I was just wondering... well Braden told me briefly about what happened over the years, with the whole stalking thing. I just wondered if it's something you ever talk about or not."

"Oh." She waited for the rapid disruption that usually roared up in her gut at the mere mention, but it didn't come. In fact, the odd jolts of anxiety that always gripped her at the thought of him alone – weren't there either. "I rarely speak of it, to be honest. But I don't mind talking about it with you."

She loved the warm smile that eased onto his face. Enjoyed the familiar sparks it caused to flitter through her veins, heating her blood in a single beat.

"Braden said it started when you befriended him at school. Was it that simple? One day you're total strangers, the next he's standing out front of your house?"

If her composure was like the sturdy tablecloth beneath their spread, the words *standing out front of your house* unraveled just one small thread. She choked it back and reached for the hash browns. "Not quite. I told you that he'd been picked on. That I spoke up to defend him. So later that day I decided to reach out to him in health class, you know? Ask how he was doing. Where he lived. Did he have any brothers or sisters?" She shook her head, recalling what she considered to be one of the biggest mistakes of her life.

"He was receptive and polite. Awkward, for sure, but nice. So we began chatting more often during class. I considered him to be a new friend, even, but then all of the sudden he freaked out on me one day. Stormed up to me out of the blue and started yelling. *'Why weren't you in health today?'* But he wasn't just asking. He was screaming. He thought that I'd transferred out so I didn't have to see or talk to him anymore. I hadn't, of course. I mean, it was just one day. I had actually just been checked out for a dentist appointment." She finished smearing jam over her English muffin and took a bite.

"Wow. That's bizarre. What did he say when you told him about your appointment?"

Bree held up a finger as she chewed. It seemed strange: the topic of Carl Ronsberg was on the table, and she hadn't even lost her appetite. She felt empowered at the realization.

"He didn't back down or apologize at all. It was crazy. It was like, once he decided I had wronged him, he was set on making me pay for it. Later, after talking to a few specialists, I learned that he was getting off on my reaction to him. I was scared when he confronted me, and that made him feel powerful. He liked that I was afraid of him."

"Braden said he threatened to rape you once, but not until years later. Do you think he had a thing for you all along?"

She shot a look at him, surprised by his bold question. "Not really. They found a whole bunch of child pornography on his computer. In fact, that's why he got such a long prison sentence. Only two years of his sentence was for stalking. The rest was for that." She took a drink of her juice. "Apparently it's typical of this type of stalker to be involved in that kind of thing, and to make threats of rape, but it has more to do with dominance. He wants to be bigger. Stronger. In control. You know?"

Greyson nodded, a look in his eyes making Bree wonder how much of this he'd heard.

"Is this stuff you already know?" she asked.

"Only some of it. I'm just trying to wrap my head around it. I've dealt with a whole lot of crazy people in my life. Had to protect clients from obsessed stalkers like him. But never someone of this unique profile. If it's the domination that makes him tick, he's going to escalate until he has an effect on you." Greyson drummed his knuckles on the table, his brows furrowed in concentration. Bree took the quiet moment to sneak in a few more bites, wishing she could read his thoughts. Had he heard all that he wanted to hear, or would he want to know more?

She finished off a crisp strip of bacon and moaned in appreciation. "I can't believe I never knew you could cook bacon in the oven like this."

It seemed Greyson didn't hear her. She took a few bites more. Hash browns with ketchup, English muffin with jam.

"So all of the sudden he just started showing up at your house after that?" he asked.

Bree finished chewing and took a swig of juice. "Sort

of. I can't remember exactly how long it was after the day he yelled at me. Could have been weeks even. He just started being really weird at school. Glaring at me in the hall. And then one day he just showed up outside my house."

"This is in your freshman year?"

"Mm, hmm," she mumbled over a bite.

A long pause elapsed as he shook his head. "I hate thinking that I might have been able to help. I wasn't too close to Braden yet," he said, "but I was very aware of you, as we've already established."

Her face warmed.

"Huh." Greyson sunk inside himself once more. Not touching his food. His brows scrunched like he was in pain. He seemed to be more disturbed at the topic than she was.

"There's nothing you could have done, anyway. By the time things got out of hand, Braden and my parents knew about it, the local officers, eventually. Nobody could help."

"Yeah, but I just … I liked you so much and I had no idea. It just really bugs me."

Bree reached over, slipped her hand over his where it rested on the table, and waited for him to meet her gaze. Stormy blue eyes. Filled with a mixture of fury and remorse. "You didn't owe me anything, Greyson. It's not like you let me down in some way." She shrugged. "Besides, it's in the past. You're here now. Helping me so much that I can talk about the guy and still eat. That's a pretty big deal."

He held her gaze. Thinking. Thinking. The look stern on his face as his wheels turned. "Go on," he finally said. "I keep interrupting. He showed up in your yard. So it was on the weekend?"

"Yes. At first I thought maybe he was coming by to say he was sorry. I went out to ask him what he was doing, but he wouldn't answer. He just stared at me with these mean eyes, arms folded over his chest. I told him if he wasn't going to talk to me he could get off the property but he refused. Braden wasn't home that day. He and my dad were off delivering furniture. So my mom, after trying to talk to him from the porch, just told me to ignore him. He couldn't stay there all day." Bree shook her head, the months that followed playing out in her mind. "We had no idea it was only the beginning.

"The next time he did that – it was just my mom and me again – she called the police. They came right out, had a talk with him, and we watched from the window as he walked away. We thought that would be the end of it, until he showed up just a few hours later. Mom didn't hesitate. She called the police again, let them know he'd come back, and got met with a blow she hadn't anticipated." Bree shook her head, recalling the disheartening look on her mother's face. "They wanted to know if he was standing in the place he'd been before, or if he'd moved outside the property line. She told the officer that he was standing on the other side of the mailbox, just along the gutter, and was told that she could call back if he moved onto our property. They couldn't do anything otherwise." She sighed. "We later found out that the police had told him that very thing."

"Yep," Greyson spat. "Punks like him learn to dance around the lines real quick." A wry expression came over his face. "Until guys like me step in, that is."

Bree had not missed the threat in his words. Or the edge that ran through his tone like a razor. She realized then that Greyson wasn't touching his food. "I'm not going to be able to go on if you don't eat." She waited for the expression on his face to shift. It happened as she grinned at him. A softening along his strong jaw. The slight ease of his massive shoulders. He reached for a piece of bacon, took a bite, and then lifted his brows.

She nodded in satisfaction. "I'm almost done with my food. You keep eating, and I'll keep talking." When it looked like he would obey, Bree continued. "That was just the first of many disappointments where the police were concerned. Due to existing laws, their hands were tied at nearly every turn. And trust me, at times they seemed as frustrated as we were.

"Anyway, it lasted for ten years – the stalking – so it's kind of hard to remember all the details. Exactly when it got worse and in what order. It's all kind of a blur. Big events in my life help pinpoint certain parts though. Like when my mom was battling cancer two years later. I had gotten a job, and he'd started showing up in front of the grocery store during my shifts. Not all, but a couple of them a week. It wasn't public property of course, but the owner kept playing the whole thing off like it was some lover's quarrel. He wasn't willing to get in the middle of it."

"Nice guy," Greyson mumbled.

"I remember trying to keep it from my mom at that point. She had enough to deal with. All of us did. I didn't want to burden my dad or Braden with it either. And since he'd kind of switched to harassing me outside of work – rather than my house – I was able to hide it for a while. Besides, the guys on duty usually made sure I got to my car safely, so that helped."

She shook her head as a particularly frightening encounter replayed in her mind. "One time I tried to appeal to him, you know? In the parking lot one night after my shift. I was already in my car, the guy who walked me there was headed back into the store, and I decided to pull back around and just... try to appeal to him, I guess. I rolled down my window and told him that we were going through enough right then. That my mom was in chemo and we were barely staying afloat. I broke down in tears even, begging him to rid me of this added burden. I didn't need it. I couldn't take it anymore." A cold chill rippled over her scalp at the memory, gripping her with that sick, eerie feeling once again. She was back there. On that day. Begging. Pleading. Hoping to see a human in that mean, heartless face with hateful eyes.

She grit her teeth. "I couldn't believe his response. It was psychotic. 'At least your mom can get treatment for *her* cancer,' he told me. He said, 'I'm *your* cancer. And I'm going to keep getting worse. Your mom's the lucky one. She might live, but you won't. One day, I'm going to kill you.'"

"Son of a..." A loud *bang* – Greyson's fist on the table – covered the rest of his words. He was on his feet in a blink, pacing around the kitchen with his hands in fists. "I could kill that guy," he growled. "I really could."

Bree put a hand over her startled heart, calming the mad thump with the warmth of her palm. Greyson was a protector, she knew that. He'd be angry hearing about the accounts no matter the victim. But even still, as Bree watched him cover his mouth with the back of his fist, the outrage she saw in those ever-telling eyes, she knew that he was *her* protector first and foremost. That his rage had less to do with *someone* being wronged, and more to do with *her* being wronged.

"This guy doesn't deserve to live."

"Greyson," she said in surprise. "It's possible he's changed, you know? He might have rehabilitated in prison. We don't know where his head's at."

A spark of something new flashed over his face, but it was gone before she could place it. He exhaled a deep breath and dropped his arms to his sides. "You're right." He nodded, breathing in deeply before letting it out in a slow, paced breath. His eyes caught hers as he lowered himself back into the chair. "It's hard for me to listen to. I hope you understand that. It's just..."

She waited as he gathered his thoughts, watching as he ran a hand over his face.

"You were a child, practically. I don't care if he was too. I just hate the control he had over you. I hate it."

Bree nodded. She hadn't even told him the worst of it. Wondered if she even dared after his unexpected reaction. She looked over the food at the table. "You're not going to eat right now, are you?"

He shook his head. "I'd like to hear this first."

"Let's go out on the porch. We can clear this up after." She knew he wouldn't argue. With his anger tensing him up, he almost looked too big for the small space. Clearly he needed the fresh air and room to breathe.

During the short walk along the side of the porch, the bright sun beaming, Greyson seemed to get ahold of himself. By the time he sunk into the largest patio swing of the bunch, he looked calm once more. He sat on it sideways, legs sprawled out over the length, and patted at the space before him.

Bree had snatched her velvet throw on the way out, having noticed the chill in the air earlier. With it wrapped around her shoulders, she sat between his legs, her back against him, and snuggled into the warm nook he created. After a few deep sighs, she glanced back at him over one shoulder. "Are you cold? I can share this blanket."

Squinting from the bright sun, Greyson shook his head and wrapped his solid arms around her. "No," he said, "this is perfect."

Bree got the impression that he needed the closeness as much as she did. The idea made her snuggle more deeply into his solid warmth before setting her mind back to the chore before her: telling Greyson the rest of her story.

"So after that I was more scared than ever. I don't know if I believed him or not. All I knew is I couldn't tell anyone in my family, there was just no way. So it continued off and on. My mom went into remission, and then my father died of the heart attack. That was probably the hardest thing I'd gone through. I almost became… desensitized to Carl during that time. It felt like nothing could hurt me more than my father's death, not even him."

She thought about that from what seemed to be an entirely new perspective. "He backed down during that time. Back then I thought it was because he felt bad for me. But I actually think – now that I consider it – that it had more to do with the fact that he wasn't getting a rise out of me. It wasn't worth doing unless he could build that fear in me."

"Hmm," Greyson mumbled behind her. She felt his arms tighten around her in preparation for what she would say next.

"Of course after a while, he started back up. I graduated the summer before my dad died. So in the fall, I decided to go to school at the community college. It was close enough to home to go back on the weekends. But far away enough for me to get some distance. I lived in a rental home with five other students, worked full time while I went to school, and during that time I hardly ever saw the guy. And, I don't know, I felt optimistic. And empowered. He hadn't stopped me from going to school. Moving on with my life. Meeting a guy, even."

"Dallin?" Greyson asked.

She nodded. "Yeah. But after finishing only half of my schooling, I learned that my mom's cancer was back." The words got choked in her throat, the subject suddenly very tender. Greyson's strong hands moved up the length of her arms. Encouraging. Comforting. Warming her skin through the blanket.

Images of her suffering mother flooded in like a heavy rain. She'd talked of her mother's passing several times since, and was usually able to keep the emotion at bay. Why now... but then it struck her. Being away from her children, away from Braden – the one person who'd suffered it all along with her – had left her barrier thin. Her emotions closer to the surface than ever.

"I decided to stay home that year. My mom, she didn't have the same kind of fight in her after my dad died. I know she wanted to beat it. I know she did. But she was ... I guess anxious is the word, for me to get married. To get settled. I wanted to give her that before she died, once I realized she wasn't going to make it." Bree sniffed. "But a lot happened before then. Carl started back up once I came back. We did a whole lot of calling the police, making complaints, at one point I finally got a protective order. One day, as things really started getting out of hand, Braden almost ran right over him in a fit of rage. He got out of his truck, punched Carl so hard it knocked him out."

The memory gave Bree a wicked chill. "I was scared that Braden – the one trying to protect his sister and provide for his dying mother – would be the one going to prison. It was awful. And the whole time Carl just danced around the law. Anyway, I got married. Had Sophie, and a few months later Mom finally lost her second battle." Bree closed her eyes against the stinging pain of welling tears. Emotion gripping hold of her anew.

Greyson smoothed a hand over the back of Bree's hair, tucking it over her shoulder, before bringing his face to the opposite side. He ran his nose along the curve of her neck, his slightly whiskered cheek along hers, and then pressed feathery kisses over her skin. "I'm sorry," he murmured against her cheek before kissing her there again. She could feel the fervor in the firmer press of his lips. "I'm so sorry."

After a moment of silence, Greyson urged her on. "So at this point, you're living with Dallin and you have Sophie, who's just a baby."

"Right. And then during my pregnancy with Carter, it all just came to a head. My fear of him was heightened after everything I had lost. It wasn't like it was after my dad's death, because now I had even more to lose. More to protect. I worried about Sophie and Dallin. I worried he'd do something to harm me and that it would hurt Carter. It was a nightmare, and it reminded me of those words he'd said to me so many years ago. He was *my* cancer, and he was going to kill me.

"He started sending threatening emails from random accounts, but he wouldn't say who they were from. And we couldn't track any of them so the police – again their hands were tied. They couldn't touch him. And Dallin –

he'd just had enough. It was such a strain on us. And even though he knew it wasn't really my fault, I think a part of him resented me for it. He regretted getting involved." She didn't elaborate on the topic, but it was the very reason she hadn't wanted a relationship with anyone since.

"So this is about the time when they finally put him away, I'm guessing." Greyson's assumptive words were laced with stifled fury. A time bomb about to explode.

"Right," she said cautiously. "So as much as the police couldn't do anything about what was happening, they knew exactly who was doing it, and they were looking for any possible way to catch him. He slipped up enough that I was finally able to get a protective order against him. That was huge. Right after that went into effect he left me alone. It was instant. No calls. No visits. No watching my home. But one night he sealed his fate with an email."

Another dark chill crept over her at the memory – the moment she realized he'd been in her home. He sent me a message with a single image attached – it was a picture of me sleeping. In my own bed."

Greyson cursed under his breath. Through the thin blanket she'd wrapped around her back, Bree could feel the growing heat and tension from his form. "So then what?" he asked through a clenched jaw.

"I flipped out. Called the police, told them about the image. They had me print it off, along with the email where he threatened to rape me. Since I already had the protective order against him for similar conduct, the police were able to get a search warrant for his home."

246

"About damn time," Greyson grumbled under his breath.

"You wouldn't believe what they found there. Videos he'd recorded of himself saying what he planned to do to me. That's when they found the child pornography, and from there they built a case to put him away for five years." She sighed, feeling lighter all at once. Like surviving the burden of saying it all out loud was a feat in itself. She knew it was time to go back inside, let Greyson finish his food while she got the kitchen cleaned up, but Bree could hardly get herself to move. It felt too nice. Solid and secure in Greyson's arms. So instead, she took another deep breath, closed her eyes, and sunk into the silence with him.

Greyson had felt the change in Bree's form once she finished sharing her account. Her warm body going limp and loose all at once, melting into him. He was glad that she felt better after getting all of that off her chest. He'd waited long enough to hear it too. Had resisted his urge to ask her about it nearly a dozen times before.

Trouble was, now Greyson felt more distraught than ever. Hearing about the torment she'd gone through — along with everything she'd suffered over those very years

— made him ill, not to mention that one detail he hadn't shared with her: That Carl Ronsberg had showed up on the surveillance footage outside her home in Montana.

He looked down to see her eyes closed as she breathed slowly in and out. Her cheeks were flushed. Her floral scent as tempting as ever.

"You know what's funny?" she said sleepily.

"No," he said. "What?"

"I always dreaded what it would feel like once he was out. I worried that, once he was no longer behind bars, I'd be a nervous wreck. Of course, I had my breakdown moment, but now... being here with you, knowing my kids are safe and Braden is secure, I feel good. Safe."

A mean trail of pain lurched down the center of his chest. He hated that she had ever felt anything but. He leaned down and pressed a kiss to her face. "You *are* safe," he promised. "You are." Once she fell asleep in his arms, the morning light shifting higher over the orchard, Greyson put his thoughts to work. They'd be going back to Montana in just a few days, and he needed to consider every possible way Carl could get at her. He made a mental note to call Braden at his soonest convenience. He'd talk with him, discuss the latest surveillance footage, and come up with the safest way to allow for this visit with her kids. Already, Greyson was dreading what it might bring.

CHAPTER TWENTY-TWO

"Have you got everything?" Greyson watched Bree tap her bottom lip as she looked over the luggage she'd heaped into the SUV.

At last she nodded. "Yep."

He closed up the back and walked around to let Bree in on the passenger side. "Guess we'll be on our way."

Though the sun hadn't hit the yard just yet, Greyson could see that the grass was peppered with golden leaves from the great oaks lining the drive. Upon backing out, he looked up at the massive branches, a spread of gold and green mostly, but a few orange leaves clung on too. He imagined what it might be like once they started to fall. "We may just want to hire someone to rake those leaves when the time comes," he said as he pulled onto the road.

"I don't know," Bree said, an unreadable grin at her lips. "I think raking leaves sounds fun. Jumping into a big pile once we're done."

He chuckled low in his throat. "Well when you put it that way... I'll play in the leaves with you any day."

She giggled, leaned over to close the gap between them, and pressed a warm kiss to his lips. A small fire roared in his belly at her touch. Boy, had he enjoyed getting closer to Bree. It seemed each day that passed only brought them closer. He'd never known his feelings for her could grow into something so strong and deep. But he was certain there was only one word for it – one he felt terribly close to saying to her right out loud.

He gripped the wheel tighter and cleared his throat. He couldn't go telling Bree he loved her already. Heck, they'd been dating only a few short weeks. In reality they'd been in the home together for closer to a month. And it was concentrated time at that. Most couples got scattered weekend dates while talking once or twice on the weeknights. A casual dinner here and a formal evening there.

Their experience had been different. He and Bree had enjoyed night by night, day by day, getting-to-know-you time for close to thirty days straight. Ups. Downs. And all that lay between. Things were going better than he could have imagined.

A sliver of fear disrupted his pleasant musings as he remembered something. He'd been keeping information about the surveillance videos from Bree since the beginning of the week. Ronsberg's appearance down the street from her Montana home. He and Braden planned to tell her if anything further came of it, but so far nothing had. The fact that Ronsberg hadn't gone back could mean one of two things: The man was doing his best to stay away but had given into a weak moment. In which case, there was no telling when he'd show up in that area again. The next option was no better. Carl may have seen for himself that Bree wasn't living in the home. In that case he'd be using other methods to hunt her down. Either way, Greyson had decided – and Braden agreed – that it was something he should tell her before they went back to Montana.

Now here they were, well on their way, and he still hadn't done the job. Bree had seemed to read his thoughts the other day at breakfast, when she'd noticed something was on his mind. But he hadn't had it in him to tell her then. And after everything she'd shared about the years she'd been stalked, he couldn't possibly break the news that Ronsberg was – after all his years in prison – still on her trail. It was like dropping a bomb. Was he rehabilitated or not? For all Bree knew the man was on a new path that didn't include so much as a thought about her.

Greyson tried telling himself that perhaps that was still the case. Maybe he'd just been having an off day. One that led him to discovering where she'd been living while he was locked away, and then parking outside her house for nearly a quarter of an hour. Didn't seem too likely.

No, chances were she was back on his radar in a big way. And showing up at a home – only to discover she no longer lived there – was just the beginning.

———— ～⁀⁀⁀‿ ————

The lighting in the warm diner put Bree on what felt like familiar ground. The comfort of the place, the warm glow of the hanging lights overhead – had her feeling right at home and ready to ease into yet another conversation that would tell her more about the man she was falling for.

"You mentioned losing someone you really cared about in your profession," she said, reaching for her ice water. "Who was it, if you don't mind my asking."

Greyson exhaled a long, slow breath, moved his napkin and utensils from one side to the other. "Naw, it was a good friend of mine. My mentor, actually. He helped train me, showed me the ropes. Introduced me to several people in the business. His name was Rex, and boy, he was larger than life."

A pensive look came over Greyson's face as he seemed to consider this guarded part of his past. "The man was, well he was untouchable. Killer instincts. Immeasurable strength and skill. A whole lot of wisdom too, having been in the profession for so many years."

He shook his head. "He was protecting a monarch somewhere in Southeast Asia. There'd been threats of a kidnapping and Rex was someone they wanted on the scene." Greyson pulled his elbows onto the table, looking at Bree before turning his gaze back to the window. Darkness stood beyond the glass, making it hard to see anything more than a reflection of the bright diner.

"From what I understand, they staged several decoys. Each guard was to secure their vehicle, make sure it was free of explosives, trackers, anything along those lines, and follow a specified route. Rex was in one of the decoy vehicles, but as he headed out on his route the thing burst into flames."

Burst into flames. The image was too much to bear. For some odd reason it made Bree worry for Greyson suddenly. For the danger his occupation posed.

"I don't know..." Greyson said, as if answering an unspoken question. "He just hadn't done a thorough enough inspection. He, uh... had a wife at home. Three kids. One brand new grandbaby."

A warm ache settled over Bree's heart as she imagined receiving such tragic, life-shattering news. "That's terrible," she managed. "How long ago was this?"

"About three and a half years ago."

She thought back on some of their prior conversations. Talks about the training center he ran. Would this new direction keep him from putting his life on the line? "So is that when you shifted gears in your career? Went from body guarding to training those in the field?"

"Yeah. I chose that route because I wanted to help prevent those types of accidents. Physically, Rex was untouchable. But with the new devices and technology out there, he'd just kind of slipped I think, on some of the latest tools we have to detect or disarm." He straightened up in his seat, a new sort of passion evident in his eyes.

"I want his life – his death – to count. Rex's death was preventable. One hundred percent. And I can't stand to think of others losing their lives when simply fine-tuning those skills could prevent it." He flicked the corner of his napkin with his thumb. "That's why we do trainings for agencies that have been up and running for years. They send a few of their agents to us each month – when they can afford to staff-wise – and we update them on new dangers and trends. Up and coming equipment and how to use it in fast and efficient ways. Yes we are there to save lives, but it doesn't have to be at the price of our own."

A deep appreciation stirred within her. A gratitude for men and women like him, who took action to help and serve and protect others. Beyond that, she felt her admiration and respect for the man before her stretch and swell and fill her chest with something that made her feel powerful and weak all at once. "I think that's great," she managed, her voice raspy, affected by the emotion rising within her. Did she dare say it to herself? Was she falling in love with Greyson?

She reached across the table where his hand rested in a loose fist. She took it in both hands, encouraging him to straighten his arm over the small table, and then lifted it to her lips. She pressed a kiss to his outer knuckle. "I love that you did that." She moved to the next knuckle and planted another firm and fervent kiss. "I love how much you care." Another kiss. "How passionate you are about it." One last kiss. She turned her eyes up to his, captured by the blue depths, the words teetering on the tip of her tongue as he held her gaze. I love you. *Say I love you next.* Only she couldn't. It was too soon. It would probably send him running in the other direction.

But that did bring up a question she'd been thinking about since they'd shared their very first kiss. What about the kids and Braden? Would she tell her family they were — what she considered — at least dating? It felt more accurate to call him her boyfriend, if the term was still used for couples her age.

She lowered his hand, feeling her face redden from the thoughts in her head.

"What's the matter?" he asked.

"Okay, you two," the waitress said as she approached the table. "Food's up, hot and ready."

Bree leaned away from the table as their waitress slid their hot bowls and plates across the table. She let the aroma of her food work to distract her, realizing, only now, just how hungry she was.

"Looks delicious," Greyson told the waitress with a nod. "Thank you."

"Yes," Bree agreed. "Thanks." She almost regretted seeing the woman go; her buffer between Greyson and the words she'd almost said.

She took hold of the spoon alongside the creamy soup she'd ordered. Aromatic steam wafted over her face as she stirred. "Mmm. My mom used to make a creamy potato soup," she said, pausing to blow on a spoonful. "I have her recipe. I'll have to make it for you sometime."

"I'd like that." Greyson had been still as she spoke, watching her as his untouched plate lay before him. But after replying, he reached for both his fork and knife and cut into the steak on his plate.

Bree sighed, grateful that they had made it beyond her declarations of things she loved about Greyson. She'd save the conversation of what they were to each other for later. For now, she'd enjoy her nice warm meal with a man who had – over the last month – entirely stolen her heart.

CHAPTER TWENTY-THREE

Greyson set Bree's suitcase on the floor before securing the locks in their hotel room.

"Man," Bree said, flopping onto one of the beds. "I am exhausted."

He eyed her while walking to the window to close the drapes.

"Aren't you?" she asked. "Aren't you so tired after that long drive and that nice big meal? I feel like I could just drift off to sleep right... now."

Greyson glanced over his shoulder in time to see her lids flutter. His heart thumped out of rhythm as he considered finally telling her. The words, *Ronsberg was spotted outside your property* ran through his mind. They hopped onto his tongue next, and Greyson opened his mouth to let them out at last.

But Bree spoke up first. "Do you see yourself getting

married one day?"

Whoa. He was not expecting that question. The air in his head got thick and crowded. His legs felt as flimsy as the swaying drapes. He lowered himself onto the opposite bed and cleared his throat.

"Sorry," she whispered. "You don't have to answer that if you don't want to. I'm just curious."

"No," he said, "I don't mind answering. Just caught me off guard." He took a moment to scrub a hand over his face, trying to think of where to start. "To answer your question, yes. I do see myself getting married one day. It just ... hasn't been easy in my profession. It didn't happen when I'd have liked it to, but I still picture being a husband. Being a dad."

He let out a deep exhale. "I'd have to say that whole incident with Rex... I don't know, part of that made me wonder what I was doing with my life. In fact, I chose to build the second facility in Montana because it would give me a chance to settle down. The property is massive. It has an old, restored cabin. That's usually where I stay when I'm in town. It's got four bedrooms and a giant loft. There's also a pond and several trails. It's the perfect place to raise a family." He didn't speak his next thoughts aloud, but Greyson mused it'd be the perfect place to raise a family *with her.*

"Sounds nice. I'd love to see it."

He nodded. "I can take you and the kids there if you'd like. I've got paddleboats, canoes, and lifejackets for both kids and adults. And it's all tucked up against the mountainside. Guarded by a long stretch of trees. Most folks would never know it was there."

A thoughtful expression came over Bree's face. "I would love that." She left it there, but something about the look in her eyes told Greyson she had more to say. His pulse sped as he watched her shift position, sitting up at the foot of the bed with her gaze fixed on him.

Greyson gulped, everything he knew and loved about Bree seeming to sway and pulse in his mind, urging him to get closer. He moved toward her, closing the small gap between them in two short strides until he stood before her.

His palm grazed the warm curve of her neck as he bathed in whatever current flooded the room. Sweet. Warm. Intoxicating. Greyson leaned down and planted a kiss to her forehead. Soft. Gentle. Loving. He pulled back, tilted his head until their eyes met. Gravity had no stronger grip on him than Bree Fox did in that moment.

"Bree," he murmured, running a thumb along her cheek. "I'm in love with you." He came in for a kiss then, encouraged by the firm press of that bottom pout. Her arms circled his neck, and Greyson gave into the pull. The invitation to join her on the bed for a time, to celebrate the love they had found.

Gently he lowered himself over her, enjoying the sweet taste of her kiss all the while. He sensed there was something she wanted to say, but could hardly bear the thought of their lips parting for even a breath. She released the soft sound of a whimper as he deepened the kiss, his hand moving up the length of her back. Even through the blouse she wore, he could feel the heat of her skin. The sensation caused a low groan to rumble in his chest.

The rhythm of their kiss changed, slower, more drawn-out movements that reminded Greyson he should not take things any further just yet.

Bree backed away slightly, ran her parted lips over his for a breath. "I love you too, Greyson," she said before kissing him again.

If words could be flammable, those words – spoken in Bree's smooth and certain voice – were like a blowtorch. They nearly lit his belly ablaze. He relished the feel of her mouth on his once more, the magnitude of what she'd shared flowing through him like a life source. Bree Fox – mother of two, friend to few, and lover to only one in her life – loved him.

Each push and pull of his kiss was a promise. He would be patient. Take things slowly. And not rush something so sweet. So right. Soon he would withdraw, shift back to his quarters of the room, and say goodnight. But for now, he'd revel in the new knowledge she'd shared.

CHAPTER TWENTY-FOUR

Greyson scanned over the recorded surveillance footage for the last day and a half, baffled by what he'd found. *Hadn't* found was more like it. Since securing a job, Ronsberg had left the house each morning like clockwork, at a quarter to six. Evenings weren't too different. Anywhere between 5:15 and 6:30 Carl would pull into the driveway in his white, beat-up sedan. It wasn't often the routine varied.

Only last night, the guy never came home. Braden had been the first to notice, what with Bree and Greyson driving back from Oregon and all. Greyson was sure the guy would show up at some point today, but that still hadn't happened. And it was nearly midnight.

"Damn it," he grumbled under his breath. "Where the hell are you?" Greyson scratched at his arms and legs, something about the guy's unknown whereabouts making him feel like checking the floor for roaches. He stretched an arm overhead before reaching to shut off a nearby lamp. His laptop screen seemed to glow brighter once the lamp was off, causing him to squint while his eyes adjusted.

He shifted through the surveillance out front Dallin and Braden's homes, scrutinizing the footage more than ever before. He only wished he had something set up out front of the home Bree and the kids were staying that night.

Braden's wife, Allie, had volunteered her parent's place out on Emerson Ranch. And while Greyson agreed that it'd be a safe place – one far beyond Ronsberg's radar – Greyson couldn't stand being separated from her at a time like this. A flashback of the moments they'd spent the night before played through his mind like a dream. *Damn, he loved that woman.* And he'd be damned if he was going to let anything happen to her or those kids. A part of him wanted to drive out to the property and sit out front with a gun aimed at the shadows.

Cool it, he grumbled to himself. Bree was fine. Heck, he'd just gotten off the phone with her a few minutes ago. He glanced at his watch to see that only three minutes had passed since they'd spoken. Three minutes that felt more like an eternity.

Forget it. He came to a stand and walked to his closet in the laptop's glow. He wasn't about to get any sleep tonight. He may as well drive by the Emerson's place and make sure there was no one lurking around the home.

Tomorrow Bree and the kids would spend the day with him. He looked forward to that. Liked the idea of having them safely within his reach. Especially since he and Braden had lost their pulse on Ronsberg. If they weren't able to locate Carl before nightfall, he'd see that they stayed there at his place instead of the Emerson's.

Greyson shrugged on his holster as the idea took root. He'd drive past Ronsberg's house and see if Carl had found a new place to park. Somewhere down the street, perhaps. Maybe he'd entered the home through the back door somehow. Greyson wasn't sure he'd discover anything new. He only knew that sleep wouldn't find him that night. Best to see if he could find Carl Ronsberg instead.

Bree sighed with contentment as her two children slept next to her. One snuggled at either side. The soft, even sound of their breathing, the warm, silky feel of their skin – oh, how she'd missed it. Sophie, having just showered before bed, smelled like the cupcake-scented shampoo Bree had given her for her birthday. Carter smelled like a combination of hair gel and maple syrup. She smiled, figuring she'd make sure he bathed in the morning.

Bree loved it here on Emerson Ranch, such kind and wonderful people. Braden, Allie, and their kids had joined them for a family gathering. Allie's brother had come too, bringing his wife and their darling baby. The welcoming family treated them to a wonderful night of food, fun, and enough distractions that Bree hadn't thought much of Carl. Simply enjoyed the time with her kids. What a gift it had been.

There *was* a man however, who'd captured more of her thoughts than she wanted to admit: Greyson. Bree smiled, missing him already. She could hardly believe he'd uttered the words he had at the hotel. *I'm in love with you, Bree.* Her heart swelled at the sheer memory. And boy was she in love with him. So in love. She mused back on the kisses they'd shared, the tender moments of passion before they'd said goodnight, and thanked the heavens they hadn't moved any further. The last thing she wanted to do was wake up with a world of doubts or regrets nagging at her. Greyson seemed very aware of that – of the need to let things progress at a slower rate. She appreciated him for that.

Already Bree was looking forward to spending time with Greyson and the kids. He'd invited them to go to his property to spend the day on his pond. Fishing, canoeing, heading out on the paddleboats. It sounded like a dream.

With that thought, and the hope to dream of that very thing, Bree let her eyes close, ready to welcome a pleasant night's sleep with her kids by her side.

*

The moonlight pooling through the bedroom window guided Bree as she made her way to the hall. She hated sneaking away from the kids to make for the kitchen, but she couldn't sleep another minute without quenching her thirst.

Long strides took her through the quiet hallway, her feet looking bony and white against the darkness.

The kitchen was as still as a graveyard. She could hardly believe it was the same place that hosted the lively bunch just hours before. The once-warm glow of overhead light had been replaced by a pale, ghostly glow of gray. Where loved ones had stood scattered throughout the dining area, shadows loomed. Tall, broad, and menacing. She shivered, noticing the drop in temperature too. The cold chill that seemed to sneak right under her skin.

Bree reached for the cupboard, secured a glass, and twisted the knob on the faucet. She placed the glass beneath the small stream and set her gaze on a sight out the window. An odd cluster in the yard that caught her eye. It seemed as if someone had been raking leaves out there, but that's not what had gained her attention. It was the arrangement of the piles. Long lines, like letters. Letters made from leaves.

A gasp pulled from her throat as she leaned toward the window, squinting her eyes for a better look. The first letter came into view.

I

She leaned further still, making out the shape of the next letter.

C

And then the next.

U

"I see you," she said in a whisper. Her body went stiff. The water from the faucet continued to pour, flooding the cup in her hand as she stood there, stunned. Too terrified to move.

It was too much. *Too much.* The conscious thought took over, waking her mind in layers, rescuing her from the wretched dream.

It's a dream.

It's only a dream, Bree.

Wake up!

A deep gasp of air broke her from sleep at last. She sat up, searching the space around her while fear rocked her limbs. She was in the room. Still in bed with the kids. She hadn't left the room.

She gulped, attempting to soothe the dryness from her throat. It had only been a dream. There was nothing to fear. No messages in the leaves. No visitors in the dark. No stalker beyond the house. She was safe. The kids were safe. They were well.

CHAPTER TWENTY-FIVE

The warm afternoon sun reflected off the water in a bright glow, nearly blinding Greyson as he helped Carter into the paddleboat. Sure, Ronsberg hadn't shown up on the surveillance just yet, but that hadn't stopped Greyson from enjoying the day. Here, on his own property, he knew they were safe. And he'd made his mind up; this is just where he'd keep them until it was time to leave.

"I bet we're going to win," Carter whispered as he climbed into the seat.

Greyson settled in next to him. "Heck yeah, we will," he agreed, glancing over at Sophie and Bree. The two were already secured in their paddleboat. By the looks of it, they were doing some conspiring of their own. Suddenly Bree looked up, set her eyes on Greyson, and eased into a slow, alluring grin.

His belly burned in response, causing his pulse to start

up a race of its own.

"You boys are going down," Sophie hollered, tucking a black lock of hair behind one ear.

Greyson's eyes widened. "Oh yeah?" He took in the little girl's face, caught the spark of determination in her brown eyes, and smiled. She looked a whole lot like her mom right then. "We'll just have to see about that."

"Yeah," Carter hollered. "We'll see about that."

Greyson chuckled, turning back to the little guy and lowered his voice. "Okay, what's the plan, Stan, my man?"

Carter's eyes were slightly lighter than his sisters, more hazel than brown. His face scrunched for a beat. "We paddle super, super fast and then we just do it faster until we win."

"Good plan," he replied with a laugh. "Do you really think we can go faster than them?"

"Yeah because first we caught the biggest fish," Carter said. "And then we won at the canoes, so now we're going to win at this too."

"Sounds right to me," Greyson said, raising his fist to meet the kid's in a fist bump. But then he looked over his shoulder at the girls' boat once more, and motioned for Carter to huddle in. "You know I played a whole lot of sports growing up," he said.

"You did?"

He nodded. "Yep. Mostly football. But I played some basketball too."

"That's awesome," Carter said through a small-tooth grin.

Greyson smiled back. "One time – when our team was really slaughtering the other guys – I saw this sad look in one of the player's eyes toward the end of the game. I noticed he kept glancing at the bleachers. I figured maybe his dad sat there and he wanted to impress him. Anyway, it was toward the end of the game, their ball, and I was the one blocking that kid during the final countdown. I had this feeling that – if someone went to pass it to him – I shouldn't get in the way. I could let him catch it and shoot."

"So did he? Did someone want to pass the ball to him?"

"Yep," Greyson said. "I pretended to block him, stood guard so no one thought I was slacking, but I didn't get in the way of his shot. And you know what? He scored a three pointer right during the last second."

"That's awesome!"

Greyson nodded, remembering the joy like it was his own. "It was. They didn't win the game or anything, but I'm sure the kid was glad he made that shot in front of his old man. Or whoever was there to watch him. Made me feel good too."

Carter nodded. "Hmm."

Greyson let the news simmer for a bit. "It's only that..." he looked over his shoulder once again, "I think Sophie was pretty down after catching just one fish, and a kind of small one at that."

This time Carter's face changed. "Yeah, it was sorta small."

"And she was talking a whole lot of smack before the canoe race, and they lost that one pretty bad."

"That's true." His thin lips twisted as he peeked around Greyson. And then went the brows, puckering with concentration. "Maybe we should do what you did in basketball. Like, kinda let them win one."

Greyson straightened up. "You think?"

Carter nodded, cute little guy. Not only was this kid smart, he was kind-hearted too. "I don't want her to feel sad about losing *everything*."

"Me neither," Greyson said. "And to be honest, I think your mom wants to win too."

A giggle slipped through Carter's lips. "You do?"

"Oh, yeah. I played a few games with her while we were away and when she'd lose, her face would get all mad, and her eyes would get this look in them, and all of the sudden she'd start throwing things at me."

"She *would?*" Carter's eyes went wide.

Greyson chuckled. "Naw, I'm just teasing." Carter joined in on the laughter. "But she did throw a few things at me. That part's true."

"Hey," Sophie blurted. "Are you guys coming up with a plan?"

Carter and Greyson stared at each other. "Oh, no," Carter whispered. "Do you think they heard us?"

Greyson shook his head. "No." He spun back to the other boat. "You better believe we're making a plan," he said, winking at Carter.

The little guy nodded, squinting against the reflecting

sunlight. "Yep," he said. "We've got a plan to win."

"Well we do too," Sophie said, "so you better watch out."

Bree's gaze was set on him, her grin glued in place. Greyson liked knowing that she was enjoying herself. Loved the idea of making her happy. He'd welcome doing that for the rest of his life.

"You guys ready?" Greyson asked.

"Ready," Bree hollered back. "On your mark... set... go!"

Streams of sunlight caught the splashing water as Greyson and Carter paddled away, but not at full strength. Just as Greyson was holding back, he could sense that little Carter was too. Soon Bree and Sophie passed the half-way mark a good ten feet ahead of them.

"Let's go harder now," Carter mumbled. "We don't want them to win too much."

"Good idea," Greyson agreed. The two paddled harder, instantly picking up speed, but the girls kept a surprisingly good distance ahead. Greyson had to wonder if the two would have beat them even if they hadn't held back. They were fast.

With Greyson and Carter still several yards behind, the girls reached the other side of the pond, an explosion of triumphant cheers at their lips.

"Oh, man," Greyson said once they'd drifted to a stop. "We almost gained on you, too."

Bree gave him a knowing grin. "Better luck next time, boys."

He chuckled, musing today had been a perfect day. It was often that Greyson had dreamt of having a family of his own. How he would love being a part of this one.

That thought stayed with him as he tied up the paddleboats and led the small crew inside. While cooking the fresh fish for dinner, Bree at his side, Greyson couldn't help but wonder if she was musing on similar thoughts.

Nightfall came on quick. It wasn't until the bunch was settled in the large den that Greyson realized just how late it had gotten. "I've got plenty of space here if you guys want to stay the night," he told Bree, not bothering to mention the this-is-not-optional part.

The kids lay zonked out on blankets before the crackling flames, the reflection dancing off their little cheeks.

Bree hid a yawn with the back of her hand. "That's actually kind of tempting," she said. "I'm exhausted."

Greyson nodded, glad she'd agreed so easily. "Why don't you give the Emerson family a call, and I'll head up to the loft and pull down the sleeping bags. I've got half a dozen beds up there. You can stay with the kids. I'll be right down here."

Bree's eyes widened. "Half a dozen?"

He grinned. "Large family used to own this. Had lots of grandkids." With that he stood, strode over to where she sat on the couch beside her kids and leaned down for a kiss. Bree lifted her chin just in time, teasing him with the most gentle touch of that pretty pout. He stifled a groan. "I'll be back to help you move the kids."

Mismatch fitted sheets covered the mattress on each bed in the loft. Sure, they might be a bit dusty, but the sleeping bags would make for a good night's sleep. He creaked open the cupboard, pulled down several pillows along with the sleeping bags, and set up three beds. With Ronsberg on the loose, there wasn't a place better suited for Bree and the kids.

It was that very thought that had Greyson's mind turning over a new idea. Thoughts of the surveillance video and something he might not have considered: Carl's job. More specifically – the vehicle he drove on that job. This whole time the guy had had access to an entirely different vehicle. One he might have been using all along. Using to track down Bree. A jagged knot began to build in his chest, jabbing his ribs as he pulled in a breath.

Sure, they hadn't spotted Ronsberg surfing the monitored streets in *his* car... But what if?

What if the man had been back in his stalking patterns and they hadn't even noticed? Perhaps they'd misidentified his work vehicle as that of a neighbor's.

The idea terrified him. Had him getting Bree and the kids settled into bed in record time. Greyson had just said his goodnights and was headed toward the loft stairs when Bree spoke up.

"Rushing off so soon?"

He could sense there was something more to her

tone, but couldn't quite put his finger on it. Was it suspicious or playful? Accusing or flirtatious?

He spun back to look her way. A sliver of moonlight spilled in through the window. It grazed the foot of her bed, but left her expression a mystery.

"I've got a few things to take care of," he explained. "Maybe I'll sneak back up here in a bit and see if you're still awake."

He could think of nothing more to say. He had a mission on his mind and was anxious to get to it. The knot in his chest grew bigger and sharper with each thought and breath, propelled by a fierce sense of urgency. He needed to look at the surveillance footage with new eyes, and be ready to deal with whatever he might find.

Bree couldn't help but sense Greyson's anxious manner. The purpose that seemed to pull him back down the stairs of the loft. Her eyes wandered over the moonlit space. A high peaked ceiling bearing wood beams and copper hanging lights. Of course, they didn't look copper now. The definition was barely visible against the surrounding darkness. The sweet sound of her kids breathing filled the room. Peaceful, steady, and even. She took a moment to thank the heavens above for them. For the fact that they were safe. Well. Healthy. She had so much to be grateful for. Forget about the situation that tore them apart for a time, she would take her problems over another's any day.

The idea led her to thoughts of Greyson. Seeing him with her kids had been... well it had been better than she could have imagined. He was playful and kind. Silly, yet sensitive. It brought something to mind. Something Bree hadn't realized she'd been secretly worried over as she and Greyson had become close. Would he hit it off with the kids? Was he even open to a serious relationship with a single mom? Sure, the two of them got along very well when it was just him and her. But how would he handle the day-to-day stress of raising children?

After their time spent today, she was more hopeful than ever. The kids had done a fair amount of quarreling. And Carter had thrown an ill-timed tantrum as they were heading out to catch some fish. One that resulted in Dallin driving out to the property to bring his lucky fishing pole.

Still, Greyson hadn't seemed fazed a bit. A warm dose of hope rose within her, a dose that turned cold the moment she recalled the rushed manner he'd said goodnight. She'd expected him to invite her back down to the fire where the two might get cozy after the kids were down. But he seemed to have something else on his mind.

With that thought urging her forward, Bree pushed back the top of her sleeping bag and climbed off the bed. Scents of pine and burning logs wafted through the air as she climbed down the narrow, wooden staircase. The spacious great room was dark and still, lit only by a dim glow of yellowed light coming from the hallway. She followed the fray, let it lead her to him while flutters of nervous energy flocked to her chest.

She stopped at an open doorway, the second room on the right, and calmed her breath as she took in the sight. Greyson's back was to her, a laptop open before him. She remained motionless as he leaned back, releasing a heavy sounding breath. The shift in his position gave view to the screen before him. An image. She squinted, realizing it was surveillance footage of some sort.

Greyson tapped a button on the keyboard, flipping the pictures from one still shot to the next. To Bree they all looked the same. She brought her hand up to the doorframe, ready to ask if there was anything wrong, when suddenly Greyson shot up from the chair. A curse flew from his lips as he reached out and knocked something off the edge of the desk. A spray of pencils and pens scattered toward the corner of the room. The container that held them rolled to a stop.

A flare of startled heat burned beneath her ribs. "Greyson?"

He spun around, looking as stunned as she felt.

"What's going on?"

Tension seemed to tighten his every limb, the angles of his muscular build sharp in the lamplight. He ran a hand through his hair, clenching his jaw with a tortured look in his eye.

An unseen clock ticked the seconds away.

At last he blew out a breath. "That scumbag has been watching Dallin's place for the last two weeks."

Bree's heart pounded in protest. "He has? How can you tell?" A frenzied whirl of denial and doubt spiraled in her mind as she waited for his reply.

Greyson shook his head and began to pace. "I can't believe I missed that," he grumbled.

"Missed what?" She tilted her head, attempting to catch his gaze, but failed to even slow him down. Back and forth he went, fury etched on his face.

"We never watched for any car but his. The one we saw him come and go in all this time. Never once did I consider that he might be driving by in his work truck."

"Work..." she mumbled. "You mean like the towing truck?"

Greyson stopped walking and nodded. "Yep." He motioned for her to join him at the desk.

Bree shuffled closer as a sweat broke out over the bottoms of her feet. Her palms were damp too, something that used to happen every time Carl would disrupt her life. Soon the heat would come. Building in her chest, racing over her skin like a fever.

Greyson flicked back through some of the digital images on his laptop. "Here's the car we've been watching for all along," he said, pointing to a white sedan. "It's the only vehicle he's been spotted in at home. But it occurred to me — just this evening — that with him operating a tow truck and all, he could have been stalking neighborhoods in an entirely different vehicle all this time."

And there it was, the uncomfortable burning in her chest. "Okay." It came out shaky and weak. Numbly, Bree lowered herself onto the empty desk chair.

"After researching tow trucks and how they vary, I checked out the website of the place he works. Most likely he's driving one of these." Greyson hunched down beside the laptop and clicked on the tab of a webpage. "They probably own multiple tow trucks, and they might not all have the logo on it, but at least it gave me an idea of what to look out for, assuming he might have been looking for you between jobs."

Looking for you. It was enough to make that volcano erupt. Already the back of her neck was on fire. She pressed a clammy hand to her forehead. "And?"

"And if this right here is what I think it is," he said, hovering the cursor over a spot on the image before them, "he's been watching the activity at both Braden's and Dallin's for the last two weeks." His hand was rubbing her back, she knew that much, but her skin could barely feel it.

"He's been watching Carter and Sophie?" More heat. More ache.

"To see if you'd be picking them up sometime, no doubt."

Vomit. She was certain it was creeping up her throat. "What are we going to do?"

"We're going to change the course, that's what."

She glanced back at him. "What do you mean?"

A stern look of resolution formed on his face. "I mean we take the kids back to Oregon with us."

CHAPTER TWENTY-SIX

Of all the ridiculous, bone-headed mistakes. Greyson could hardly breathe through his frustration. What the hell was wrong with him that he hadn't thought of this sooner? Of *course* the guy was going to drive by in his work truck between jobs. Park and watch for signs of Bree outside the home she grew up in. As well as the home where her kids were staying.

An explosion of anger raged through his chest at the thought. "Too busy making out with the woman to see straight," he mumbled, shoving a loaded gun into his holster. Followed by another. He was in full work mode now. On high alert and ready to fight. Bree and her kids would come to no harm under his watch. He'd make damn sure of that.

"The kids are ready to go," Bree said, her voice coming from somewhere beyond the room.

"Alright," he said. "Are they still half asleep?"

She let out a nervous sounding laugh. "Pretty much. They're snuggled into their sleeping bags on the couch."

"You can come in, you know. I'm decent." He set his gaze on the doorway, his chest aching at the sight of her delicate frame and timid grin. Man, he loved this woman.

Bree's gaze ran over the length of him, as if she was seeing him for the first time. Greyson looked down, wondering if the holster made her uncomfortable.

"I decided to suit up. It's just a precaution until we get out of here."

She shook her head. "No, that makes sense." She gulped, her face flushing with warmth.

He extended an arm toward her. "Come here. I'm going to get you guys out of here safely, you understand?"

Bree shuffled closer before wrapping her arms around him. Soft strands of her dark hair grazed his neck as she nuzzled her head against his chest. Smells of her sweet floral scent filled his next breath. It almost distracted him from the details on his mind. The things he wanted to share.

After a few quiet moments, he forced himself to speak. "You know that we haven't spotted Ronsberg in a while," he said. "I've started to worry that maybe he somehow found out we're in Oregon. It's possible he headed out the same time we left."

Bree's body went rigid. She pulled away from him, her eyes wide and questioning. "You think that's what happened? You think he's in Oregon now?"

Greyson shrugged. "It's probably more likely that he decided to take a weekend someplace. Maybe he took off to Vegas with a friend, decided to test his luck there." He reached up, smoothed a static-drawn lock of hair behind Bree's ear. "I can't say it's *likely* that he's in Oregon by any means. But I *can* say there's a chance, as slim as it might be, that he's discovered where you've been all this time."

A pain-ridden grimace pinched her face. She pressed a hand to her chest and blew out a breath through pursed lips. "I don't know what to do," she said in a whisper. "It's like there isn't a place to just get away from him."

"I think we should head out to a hotel tonight. Stay there for a couple of nights. Meanwhile, I'll see if Amelio would mind setting up a few surveillance cameras outside the orchard home. We could easily set a few up to watch the street — as quiet as it is — for any signs of action. Any vehicle frequenting that route or spending time outside the area. During that time, we keep an eye on things here. If Ronsberg comes pulling into his driveway in the next few days, you and I take the kids to the orchard house and get them enrolled in the school there for the rest of the year."

The ache that radiated off Bree's body made Greyson cringe. The defeated curl of her shoulders. The flushed appearance of her skin. "Hey," he said, taking both of her hands in his. They weren't smooth like they normally were. Instead her palms felt cool and clammy.

"Listen, I'm not going to let that guy touch a hair on your head. And that goes for Carter and Sophie too. I'm being cautious, is all. Taking every precaution I can to keep you guys safe."

Bree pulled her hands away, pressed them over her face, and shook her head. "I just…" Only she didn't get any further than that, her words being replaced with a small whimper. And then another. A series of sobs came next, the sound like liquid fire to his heart.

Greyson wrapped his arms solidly around her frame, pulling her in as she wept. "I'm sorry," he said. "I'm so sorry you've had to deal with this. That I can't take it all away from you now." He stroked the back of her head. The delicate curve of her shoulders. And pulled himself more tightly against her. Without a conscious thought, he was pressing kisses to the ridge of her shoulder. And then her neck, where he buried his face into the warm nook. "We're going to get this guy out of your life," he whispered against her skin. He pressed a firm kiss of conviction there, inwardly swearing to make it so. "He'll be out of your life soon" he added, "I promise you that."

It was in that moment that a thought came to him. One that felt more like a hunch. *Here. Carl Ronsberg could be here. On this very property.*

The mere idea made him tense up in a blink. He glanced at his watch, glad daylight wouldn't hit for another few hours. Greyson had backed the SUV out of the garage last night so Sophie and Carter could kick at the punching bag hanging there. He'd pull it back in before even loading the kids.

"I'm going to go get the car ready," Greyson said, giving Bree's shoulders one final squeeze. "Then we can load up the kids."

She gave him a subtle nod, sniffing while reaching for a tissue. "Sounds good."

Bolts of anxious energy prodded at Greyson as he strode down the hall, through the dining area, and into the garage. He was just about to press the lever when he thought better of it. No need to announce himself just yet. Not if his new suspicion held any merit.

At the back of the garage, a single door led to the backyard. Of course it wasn't much of a yard at all. More of a mountainside, really. Greyson secured his gun and turned the old knob as slowly as he could. The door creaked as it opened, the sound louder than he'd anticipated. The rhythmic beat of crickets chirping echoed in the vacant garage.

Greyson checked behind the open door before stepping into the shadows, his eyes scanning the scene. A large trash can and recycle bin stood side by side on the small pad of cement off the garage. To his left, a near-forest of trees stood close and tall, shielding the home and most of the pond from sight. On the other side of those trees – acres back – lay the digging ground for his new center. But that area didn't concern him then.

What he cared about in that moment was getting Bree and the kids out of town safely. With key in hand, he locked up the door to the garage and closed it behind him.

If he circled the right side of the home, heading toward the mountain, he'd come to the driveway. There, Greyson would check the surrounding area, start up the SUV, and pull it into the garage. The glass in his vehicle was bulletproof, which offered a level of comfort as he pictured tearing out of the drive.

With slow precision, Greyson scanned the base of the mountain, moving toward the driveway one methodical step at a time. He cast his eyes up, into the shadows, listening for a break in the crickets' song. A rustle in the nearby trees. The snap of a hidden branch.

He hadn't considered putting cameras up on this property. He'd never had a reason to. Only now, as he moved slowly toward the drive, the sneaking suspicion that Carl was near, he wished that he had.

With his gaze still set on the mountainside, his ears perked for any crackle or crunch, Greyson took backward steps onto the cement of his driveway. Once satisfied that nobody hid in the surrounding shades of black and grey, he spun around to inspect the SUV.

Only it wasn't there.

"Wait a minute," he mumbled, scanning the area with wide eyes. Just where the hell was his car? He'd just walked through the garage, and it definitely wasn't there.

His pulse bolted into a speeding, chilling race. Pushing ice through his veins as he tore down the drive.

One long stride after the next.

Inspecting the narrow dirt road that led to the main street off his property. He was sure he hadn't parked on the road, but still his feet carried him numbly down the dark drive. Doubt and shock warred in his head. Could Carl Ronsberg have actually stolen his car? Surely Greyson had just parked it someplace else. Maybe left it by the pond...

A few slower paces carried him further down the way until he stopped short. *No.* Greyson had backed the SUV out of the drive, parked it just outside the garage, and locked it up.

A beat of angry heat flared in his chest, prodded by thoughts of Ronsberg and his stupid tow truck. The man could have stolen that thing in a million different ways. Greyson's mind raced as realization settled into his head at last, settled like a massive crack in foundation: Carl had linked Bree to him. Figured out where they were. And declared war.

Visions of a large chessboard played out in his mind. Pawns, key players, kings and queens. Carl Ronsberg may have taken out a few key players with this move, weakening them to a degree, but Greyson was on to him. Thoughts of revenge wove through his mind. Ways he could torment the guy in return, make him suffer as he had Bree for so many years. But Greyson had learned to bury those urges over time. He had one purpose and one alone: keep his queen safe no matter the cost.

Check, he could almost hear Ronsberg say. *Your move.*

Yes, Greyson agreed as he stormed back inside. It was his move, indeed.

CHAPTER TWENTY-SEVEN

Bree held tightly to her sleeping kids as she watched Greyson pace. Back and forth he went with the phone up to his ear, his voice rising as he picked up speed. "The police are coming to file a report now," he grumbled, "but I don't want to be stuck here shooting the breeze with the cops while Ronsberg is out there scheming his way in. I need to get these guys out of here. Now."

He nodded a few moments later, and Bree could hear Braden's voice coming through the line from across the room. "Uh, huh." Greyson stopped walking, tucked a hand into his pocket, and huffed out a deep breath. His eyes narrowed as he stared across the room. "That might work. Bring out Allie's minivan. Leave Allie and the kids at home. You and Logan help fill out the report while we take off in the minivan."

The minivan? Hmm. Bree hadn't fully digested what Greyson had revealed. She'd heard the words just fine, was aware that Greyson's SUV had been stolen, but she couldn't exactly let it all sink in. Not until she, the kids, and Greyson were safely on their way. Still, she could feel the panic bubbling and brewing beneath the surface. Threatening to undo her entirely.

"Sounds good," she heard Greyson say. Bree wasn't sure how much more had been said, could only tell that his conversation with her brother was coming to an end.

"Okay," he said. "See you in a bit." Greyson hit a few buttons on his phone before bringing it back up to his ear once more.

"Who are you calling now?" she asked.

"The police. If they could send an extra officer, we can have one of them escort us off the property while Braden files the report. If Ronsberg is anywhere near, we'll want all the security we can get."

Bree liked that idea. She felt a level of tension drain from her shoulders. She appreciated that Greyson wasn't above relying on local officers for help.

"So Logan and Braden are both headed out here now. Since we're going to take off in Allie's minivan as soon as he's here, Logan will take Braden home." A new flash of interest flared in Greyson's eyes. "The good news is that this puts Ronsberg on their radar. If he's the one who did this, and I'm positive he is, we'll be able to press charges no matter where we are."

He walked back toward the dining area before

spinning around once more. "And it also means the guy's not onto our other location. He's obviously desperate to stop us from leaving again."

Bree took a moment to let that sink in. "Hmm."

Greyson nodded as he moved toward her. She watched as he sat at the edge of the couch. "We'll still stay at a hotel for a few nights and monitor the street and drive. We'll wait and see what turns up there."

He was back on his feet then, striding toward the window where he peered through a crack at the edge of the drapes. With the shake of his head, Greyson mumbled a few short words. Words Bree felt with each pull of her breath. "We've just got to get you out of here."

Never had Greyson felt so torn. There was no better place for him to be than by Bree's side, assuring that her and the kids were safe. Yet a part of him longed to stay behind and scour his property. He wanted nothing more than to come face-to-face with that scum-sucking lowlife and make him regret the day he ever spoke Bree's name. Heaven help him, he wanted that man out of their lives once and for all.

Braden showed up before the officer. Logan arrived just after that. Once Greyson was told that no second officer could be spared, he loaded the kids into the minivan Braden had brought out for them.

While Braden and Logan talked with the officer on the front porch, Greyson backed out of the driveway. As he neared the end of the long stretch, a distinct thought came to mind. *Go the back route.* There were two entrances onto his lot – one on the south end where the training center would go, and one closer to the house and pond.

At the base of the driveway, Greyson made his choice, steering the minivan onto the narrow dirt road.

"Where are we going?" Bree asked from the passenger seat.

"Just have a hunch we should go this back route. Not sure why." In the work field, Greyson's hunches had often led him to the very source of danger he was working against. In most circumstances, that was exactly what he wanted – to gain access to the root of his problem so he could eliminate it one way or another.

But was this one of those times? After all, he wasn't alone. He had Bree and her small children. In a minivan that did not have bulletproof glass.

Tall, dry grass stood in the fray of the headlights' beam, dirt from the pathway clouding at the base. Rocks and twigs crunched beneath the tires as they moved, his mind working to predict Ronsberg's next play. Just how in the world would that man have found Greyson's property? How could he have linked the two together? They'd been extremely careful. To the point it was nearly... but then it hit him: the extra trip. Dallin had driven out to the property to bring Carter his lucky fishing pole yesterday. Was it possible he'd led the guy right to them? Dallin hadn't come straight from home, rather his father's house, where the pole was kept. That alone had kept Greyson from worrying. But Ronsberg had been following Dallin all along.

Greyson gripped the steering wheel tighter, a low growl at his throat. He sunk his foot further into the pedal, kicking up speed. He had to get Bree and her kids off the property. As much as he wanted to get this guy out of Bree's life for good, he couldn't afford a run-in with him now. He rounded a large cluster of maples, slowing to make the sharp curve, and squinted as a strange sight unfolded before him.

"What in the hell?" Greyson slammed his foot on the brake, clenching the wheel as the van skidded to a stop.

There, a few yards off, a large tow truck blocked the dirt road, making it impossible to get by. His eyes followed the length of the massive vehicle to find that something was hitched onto the back. Shiny. Black. And familiar: Greyson's SUV.

Bree gasped. "Greyson? What are we going to do? Should I call Braden? The police?"

"We don't have time for that," he grumbled. "Whatever his game is, we don't have time to play it." The trees to his left made the way clear. Greyson cranked the wheel hard to the right, pushing the van to its limit as he sped toward the tall, dry grass. His pulse raced, working to make up for the gutless response of the minivan.

"Where are we?" Sophie asked from the backseat. The sound of her tiny voice, barely heard over the rustle, planted a new level of determination in him.

"Just heading to the hotel," Bree assured. "Go back to sleep, sweetie. We still have a long way to go."

Her final words were swallowed up by the commotion of long blades whipping at the base of the van as they plowed over the neglected land. Heaven knew what loomed in the tall, woven growth. Hidden rocks and branches. Rusty, abandoned tools. An obsessed stalker hoping to get his hands on Bree?

The thought had him gripping the steering wheel harder, a rush of savagery surging through him. It was a side of himself he didn't like, but in the moment there was no squelching it. He welcomed the thought of running the guy over.

Once he rounded the SUV – hitched to the back of the massive tow truck – Greyson steered the minivan back toward the dirt road. From the corner of his eye, he saw Bree glance back at the kids, a hand pressed hard against her chest. Only a few yards more and they'd be out of the grass and back on the road.

The bumpy ground seemed to propel them forward, ever closer to the dirt road. Yet suddenly the van lurched and slowed. A loud hiss filled the space of the vehicle.

Greyson revved the engine for a blink, but stopped once he realized what had happened. The lurching, stopping, hissing – all of it meant the tires were flat. Gone. Shredded.

Damn it. "Either we ran over one hell of a plow," Greyson said, "or Ronsberg set up a tire shredder."

A line of curses spilled through his mind. He scanned the sight within the headlight's glow. "Call Braden," he said. "Tell him we're on the property. Have him send the cop out and call for back up." With that, he shrugged out of his seatbelt and pushed open the car door. Already, a plan was forming in his mind — an idea that would allow him to watch over the area from a place of advantage.

"Greyson, no," Bree cried, "stay in here." She pulled the phone from her purse with one hand, the other stretched out toward him.

He couldn't get into all the reasons he could not do as she asked. Instead, he simply muttered three small words while stepping out to lock up the van. "Sorry. I can't."

CHAPTER TWENTY-EIGHT

Bree held tight to her cellphone, her palms damp as she watched Greyson secure his gun and walk toward the back of the minivan. She'd never seen him in action like this, had hoped she'd never have to. As frightened as she was for her and the kids, Bree couldn't help but worry for him the most.

He was an obstacle after all, a barrier in Ronsberg's pursuit.

Third ring, and Braden hadn't answered. Her skin was an eruption of fevered heat and rippling panic. A living force that nearly paralyzed her.

"This is Braden," came the voice from the speaker, "sorry I missed your call..." Bree clicked the button, hands shaking so hard it took effort to tap out the next call. 911.

After two short rings, a young, male operator picked up the line.

Between jagged breaths, Bree quickly explained their

predicament. She didn't have the address to the property, but told them they already had an officer out there. "You can see where Greyson Law called earlier, can't you? And reported the stolen car? We need the officer to come to the south end of the property along the dirt road. And anyone else you can send. Please, this guy wants to kill me." She panted there for a breath. "We're all in danger out here."

Bree tried very hard to listen to the operator's response, but her mind was a million places at once. She tuned into the gist of it. He'd told her to stay on the line; that he'd see what he could do. He sounded young. Too young. Was the kid really capable of sending help in time?

A growing desperation pricked at Bree from the inside. She wanted to help. To somehow figure out what Carl had in store for them. Had he known that she and Greyson would exit the property this way, or had the staged roadblock and tire shredders been meant for someone else? Perhaps law enforcement. Too bad the officer at the house hadn't come this way.

The thought made her heart sink with guilt. She hated the idea of anyone coming to harm. There was no telling how dangerous Carl Ronsberg really was. Drawing attention to himself by taking Greyson's car – the action seemed to say that all bets were off. It hinted to some desperate state. A final card one might reserve for the end of a game, knowing they had nothing left to lose. Greyson was right – he must have figured that Bree would leave soon, go back to wherever she'd been hiding the last month.

Was Carl so certain he'd get his hands on her that he'd risk exposing himself? It seemed he didn't care whether he was discovered after the fact, he only wanted to finish what he'd started with her, and she knew just what that meant.

With his back to the van, his gun drawn and aimed at the shadows, Greyson headed toward the great cluster of trees.

"Mom, Mom," came a little voice from the backseat. Carter's. His tone was laced with fear, and Bree could sense that if she didn't act fast, his panic would escalate.

In a rush, she set the phone on speaker and rested it in the car's drink holder. "It's okay," she shushed, tearing off her seatbelt. A large gap between the bucket seats allowed Bree to step toward the back part of the van, where two more bucket seats held Sophie and Carter. She moved to kneel in front of him, running a shaky hand over his forehead. It was flushed hot and damp with sweat. "It's okay," she said again.

His body jerked in response to her touch, his lids squinting tight.

"Shh...." she lulled gently, comforting him as best she could. She pressed a kiss to his head. "It's okay. I'm right here." Bree leaned back to look out the windshield, unable to see where Greyson had gone. *Please, please keep him safe,* she pled, clenching her eyes shut for a breath. *Oh, please protect that wonderful man who's come into our lives.*

Her heart was a bundle of dynamite – wick lit, spark speeding toward the base. She gulped hard, nodding as Carter's lids softened; he was falling asleep once more. For a moment, all was quiet and still. Yet just as she moved to get back into the front, a rustle sounded from the back of the van.

Not the part where Sophie and Carter sat.

The part farther back.

A small bench seat that lay hidden in black.

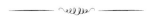

Greyson shook his head as he kept watch. The police should arrive any minute. He shifted his weight from one foot to the next, grateful he'd thought to climb onto the massive boulder beside the trees. It was the perfect spot. While the shadows kept him hidden from sight, Greyson had a clear view of the van and its surroundings.

Crickets chirped in the night. A ghostly spill of moonlight reflected off the hood of the van.

His heart pounded like a jack hammer as he secured his grip on the gun, eyes sharp. Ears perked. Senses heightened to the point it hurt.

Any minute now the police would show. They'd discuss their next course of action once Bree and the kids were off the property and far away from Ronsberg.

His eyes narrowed at the thought of the man. If only he'd make himself known – approach the van or the tow truck – Greyson could finally get his hands on him. He reminded himself he'd have to stick within the limits of the law. Heaven help him, that wouldn't be easy.

A breeze picked up then, rattling the surrounding leaves like dry, brittle bones. It stirred at his insides somehow, had him shifting his weight again. Keying into the sounds of the night once more, he tightened the grip on his gun. *Just where the hell are you, Ronsberg?*

I'll never get in a vehicle. Those familiar words – words Greyson had made her swear to while teaching her self defense – cycled through Bree's mind. Along with the warning that accompanied it. Something about being as good as dead once you're in.

Too late.

I'm already here.

She kept her eyes pasted on the darkness at the back of the van. Had she just been hearing things, or... That thought was interrupted by another noise. A small one.

Subtle.

Human.

Like knuckles popping.

That bundle of dynamite – the one in her heart – exploded, shooting fractured shards through her chest like a million stabbing, pounding beats.

"You weren't supposed to drive over the tire strips," came a voice from the darkness.

Bree gasped, thrusting a hand over her aching heart. Strange how time and distance had not stripped her recollection of his voice. Nasal-like and whiney.

Sophie stirred in her seat, snagging Bree's attention in a blink. She gulped the massive lump of fear rising in her chest while watching Sophie's little form shuffle awkwardly. Seconds ago she'd been facing the window, but now she faced Bree. Her eyes still closed for the moment.

"You guys kept making it harder," Carl mumbled from the shadows. "Gaining access to another car, having extra people at the house." A suppressed laugh slithered from his lips. "You really had me scrambling. Luckily I managed to sneak into this thing while Mr. Star Quarterback loaded your kids in the car. Some help he was."

Jagged, aching breaths forced their way through Bree's lungs as she glanced over her shoulder once more, peering into the night for any sign of Greyson.

None.

She shot a glance at the phone in the cup holder, no sound coming from the line. Had it gone dead? Was she still on hold?

"They're getting older now, aren't they? Your kids." A

white arm protruded from the darkness toward the back of Sophie's chair. Though Sophie's head was tucked much lower than the top of the bucket seat, Carl stroked a hand gingerly along the rounded edge of leather as if it was the small child's head. "This one's starting to look like you."

"Carl," Bree pled, desperate to put a barrier between him and the kids. She moved on her knees between the seats until there was no more than two feet between her and Carl. Dark, open space. "Please, let's get out of the van. I'll go with you if you'd like. We can get in your tow truck or whatever you want, but let's just…" The words fell weakly off her tongue, desperation clinging to her tone as she reached for the sliding door. She unlocked it with a shaky hand, the short, clicking sound interrupted by Carl's reply.

"You'd like that, I'm sure. But that's not how this is going to play out."

"What do you mean?" Though she knelt between Sophie and Carter, Bree kept her eyes pasted only on him. The two had often wished they could teleport. Magically move from one place to another like heroes from their favorite show. Oh, how she wished for that very thing in that moment. She needed them to be somewhere – anywhere else but here. In the same vehicle as Carl Ronsberg.

Her eyes were adjusting, an outline of Carl's head coming into view. She lowered her gaze to look over the rest of him, desperate to make out the details. What was he holding in his hands? A knife? A gun? A homemade bomb?

"Well," he said, an odd laugh strangling the word. "If I step outside, Mr. Quarterback could get me before I get you. Can't let that happen."

Get her? Just what did that mean? Carl had been in the car while she spoke to the operator; he knew an officer was headed toward them as they spoke. And that Greyson stood right outside. His game was up, wasn't it?

No, she realized. How could it be when she was there with him, face-to-face? It wasn't over. In fact, it had only begun.

Carl Ronsberg had gotten her alone.

Worse.

He'd managed to get her and her children alone – trapped in a hidden space. Locked away from the world beyond. A world where Greyson stood, poised and ready, watching for any sign of him. A world where police would soon arrive and search the area on foot. The area surrounding the vehicle. Not within it.

She gulped, her eyes pasted on the grayed area before her. If Carl had a gun or some sort of device, he could take her out before anyone could do a thing. The kids too.

Distant sirens sounded, and Sophie stirred once more. "Mom," she whined, "mom." Her small arms reached out toward Bree, but the seatbelt held her in place. Bree shushed her as she had Carter, hoping the sound would be enough to calm her.

The siren's sound grew louder as a blaze of red and blue light flashed beyond the glass. Carl would have to act soon if...

As if reading her thoughts, he lunged toward her.

Bree caught sight of his speeding shadow in time to flinch, but nothing more.

A wall of fabric and flesh slammed into her face and chest, knocking her back, hard against the floorboard.

Pain thundered up the back of her head as she worked to orient herself. The moment seeming anything but real. Desperate, she squirmed to press his smothering weight off of her, but she was trapped – pinned beneath his panting chest and sweating limbs. Everything from her bent knees down was stuck beneath her, causing the front of her thighs to cramp and burn.

Suddenly Carl's weight lifted the slightest bit.

Bree scrambled to take advantage, her next breath seeming to hinge on her ability to break free, but he came back down fast and hard before she could budge. His mass seeming to multiply.

She groaned beneath the crushing blow, trying to assess the reality of her new predicament. Trying to believe it was actually real.

Carl rammed his forearm against her neck, forcing her cheek against the floorboard. The action assured her that this was no mere dream; it was a living nightmare. She managed a thwarted gulp, the coarse, wiry hairs on his sticky arm crumpled against her skin.

There was no getting out from under him. No shaking him off. Her legs were restrained, her arms smashed against her chest, and her senses fading fast as she fought for breath. The last realization took a little longer to hit, but it struck her mind like a cold blade. It was the feel of something digging into the side of her head. A metal ring – the barrel of a gun.

Eyes clinched tight, she begged the heavens above for a way out.

Sophie was screaming now. Carter too. How long had they been screaming? Bree inwardly begged them to stop. If they made too much noise, Carl might shoot them.

"Did you think about me while I was in prison?" His hot, sour breath coated her face. "Did you?" he demanded.

Bree uttered a silent prayer. *Please soothe the kids somehow.* "Sometimes," she admitted.

Carl shifted his weight the slightest bit, his arm against her shoulder rather than her neck. Bree found that she was able to pull in the next breath with less resistance.

"Were you afraid of me, even when I was locked up?" There was triumph in his tone. He wanted her to say yes. Wanted it very badly.

"Why would I have been?" she asked, lifting her head slightly off the floorboard. Anything to buy time. She just had to buy some time.

Heightened bolts of energy surged from his frame, the frantic puffs of his breath dampening her cheek. "Because I terrorized the *hell* out of you for half your life, that's why."

Yes, she admitted inwardly. He had. He'd caused her and her family immeasurable grief over the years. He'd nearly destroyed her. But she hadn't allowed him to do that. She'd moved on with her life. Finally gotten him put away. He hadn't won back then, and she wasn't about to let him win now. Not after everything she had endured. Not after everything she stood to gain.

Carl Ronsberg would not win.

A thought came to her mind like the voice of an unseen angel. *The gun. It's not against your head anymore.*

So where was it?

She searched the space in her limited view.

Black and gray tones, lit by splashes of white and blue light. The sound of the sirens had died down, which meant the officers were doing just as Bree had feared – searching the grounds for Carl while neglecting the one place he'd be found.

"You're right," she said, a spark of bravery rising from the depths of her core. "You're good at scaring me, Carl. You're very good at that." The flashing lights continued to spin a pattern over the van floor, highlighting spots at a time. A box of tissues under the seat. A sippy cup from baby Jacob. A pistol in Carl's hand, flush against the floorboard before her.

She wiggled her arm the slightest bit, realizing it was free from Carl's weight. Free to move as she wished. If she could only move quickly, she might be able to snatch the gun from him.

"I want to know how scared you are now," he spat, his nauseating breath making her cringe. "Tell me. Are you more terrified than you've ever been? Ever in your whole life?"

She opened her mouth, let a few labored breaths proceed her answer. With her kids in danger at either side, Greyson nearby as well, the answer was clear. "Yes," she spat, and moved into action.

One fast jerk of her arm.

A reach for the gun in his hand.

A solid grip on the barrel.

It was all she could do. With her other arm pinned beneath her, Carl flush against her chest, she could only grab on for dear life, hope to control the aim of that gun. Prevent it from going off in her direction.

But what about the kids? She couldn't have it go off at all. Not with the two of them close, their cries quieting a bit as more sirens neared.

Carl's weight shifted as he wrestled for a stronger grip on the gun. She could feel his other hand now too, working to tear her hand from the barrel.

She pulled harder, sensing defeat as he pried it from her fingers. Slipping. Aching. Trembling.

Bree grunted, her elbow burning as she ground it into the stiff carpet, working to free her other arm. Inches at a time.

Just as she managed to wrench it from beneath his weight, a silence fell over the space, followed by the sound of one sharp click.

Cartridge loaded.

Bree's hands shot toward the pistol as Carl

repositioned his grip.

The barrel was no longer cool against her skin. It was warm from the struggle. And slick too, the smooth metal slipping beneath her hands as she fought the aim he had on her – an arm's length from her face.

Muscles burning, arms trembling, she tilted it back toward him. Red light bounced off his horn-rimmed glasses, revealing a deep snarl at his lips. His hands tensed, squeezing as he gritted his teeth. Something was about to happen, Bree knew it. She flinched in preparation just as a loud commotion rocked the van.

Carl froze in place. Bree did too. The sound wasn't that of a gunshot, as she'd anticipated, rather the shrieking, clanking sound of the sliding van door.

At once Carl's body was ripped off of her. His upper half first, followed by the rest of him. She shot up to see Greyson dragging him out of the vehicle, Carl's legs flailing like fish on the shore.

With a tight grip on Carl's shirt – two strong hands at either shoulder, Greyson shoved him onto the ground. Bree squinted against the interior light as she fought to see.

"He's got a gun," she warned, eyes adjusting in time to see Carl roll from his stomach to his back in the tall grass. One arm straightened toward Greyson, the dark pistol in his grasp.

And then came the sound.

The piercing blast of a gunshot.

A deep gasp tore from her throat as she lunged

toward the open door, praying Greyson would survive the blow. Her eyes darted over the length of him, from bottom to top, and then back again, no hint of the wound in sight. She puzzled there as her eyes settled on the gun in his hands. In Greyson's hands.

Her gaze fell to Carl as relief flooded her body. It wasn't *his* gun that had gone off. It was Greyson's.

And from the looks of the dark crimson stain on the man's chest, the lifeless expression on his frozen face, he wouldn't be raising that pistol again.

"Mommy," Sophie's high-pitched whine barely sounded over the deafening hum. Carter's sniffling cries joined the chaotic chorus.

"It's okay, Soph. Carter boo," she assured, barely able to breathe out the words. "We're fine."

Officers joined Greyson, the group hunching by Carl's side. Bree freed the kids from their belts and carted them to the front seat, away from the scene by the door.

"Are you guys okay?" Greyson asked.

She looked up to see him leaning into the van, his face tight with concern. *Thank heavens.* Thank heavens they'd made it through.

"Yes," she assured. "We're fine." A wave of gratitude spilled over her as she realized the truth of it.

It's done, she assured herself. *It's finally done.*

CHAPTER TWENTY-NINE

"I like this house almost as much as yours, Greyson." Sophie spun herself in the hanging hammock, the way her mother had done so many times before.

"Me too," Greyson agreed. Dang, that girl's grin was contagious. "Did your mom and Carter already head out to the orchard?"

"Yep. But I told them I wanted to wait for you."

Greyson's smile broadened. "You don't say?" He grinned. "Well what are we waiting for?"

Sophie set her feet back onto the porch once the spinning slowed. "Can I get on your back for a piggy ride?"

"You betcha." He chuckled, hunching down so she could climb up.

Sophie's little arms tightened around him as they neared the orchard. "Oh, it's so pretty," she exclaimed. "How long do we get to stay here?"

Greyson smiled. "A week. And you get to miss school

the whole time," he added.

"And eat lots of apples?" she asked.

"Yep."

"With caramel and toppings?"

Greyson chuckled. "Heck yeah!"

He was glad they were able to spend a bit more time at the orchard home before leaving it behind. They would help in hiring out replacements and get the things settled before heading back. But for now, the kids and Bree could make up for lost time. Enjoy the week off together after all they'd been through.

It would take time for them to get past the events from that dark night, but healing was well on its way. With the worst locked firmly behind them, they could focus on the here and now, unhindered by the grip of fear.

"What took you guys so long?" Carter asked, his little feet speeding over the grass. "We got here like... fifty minutes ago!"

"More like five," Bree said with a laugh. She stepped up beside Greyson, helped Sophie climb back to the ground, and then wrapped her arms around him as the kids played.

"It feels like I've been handed a new life," she said, her smile causing that dimple in her cheek. And there it was – that look of contentment on her face. The spark of confidence in her eyes.

"Me too," he admitted, bringing his lips to hers.

Giggles sounded in the distance as the kids tore through the aisles of the orchard. "Tag," he heard Sophie holler. "You're it." He wondered if they'd enjoy playing the innocent game in his father's orchard one day. Perhaps with Uncle Todd and Grandpa Lloyd. The thought was a pleasant one. He liked the idea of having Bree and the kids with him forever. Only hoped he could put the idea into action.

He slipped his hand through hers, walked with her along the rows as the kids played. Yep. One day, Greyson mused as he pulled in a deep breath, one day he'd like to make Bree his own.

CHAPTER THIRTY

Bree kicked the snow off her shoes against the stairs on Braden's front porch, the porch of the very home she grew up in. Sparkling lights lit up the area, their glow adding to the magic of the day. Christmas Eve, one of her favorite days in all the year.

"It looks beautiful out there," she said to Braden as she entered the house. The delicious aroma of ham and pie filled the home, and Bree took a moment to breathe it in, picturing Mom at the stove fussing over the glaze while Dad toyed with the train set circling the tree. "The lights remind me of the way Dad used to do them," she said.

Braden took the stack of gifts from her hands and walked them over to the decorated tree. "I cheated," he said with a grin. "Found Pop's old map. He'd drawn out every detail down to the wreaths lining the woodshop windows."

"I'd like to see that." Bree smiled wistfully. "I have a feeling those wreaths were Mom's touch."

Braden gave her a nod. "Me too."

Allie bustled into the room, baby Jacob in her arms.

She shifted him to her hip before leaning in for a hug. "Merry Christmas."

"Merry Christmas to you, too," Bree said, returning her sister-in-law's embrace. She reached her hands out for the baby, pleased when the smiley little guy reached out in return. "That's right," she cooed. "Come see Auntie Bree."

"Where are the kids?" Allie asked, eyes scanning over the room.

"They're out front with your girls," Bree said with a laugh. Oh, how Bree loved Jillian and Paige. The two had taken to Sophie and Carter right from the start. And it was a good thing too, considering how much those kids loved them in return. "Greyson taught them how to build a snow shark. My guess is that they're showing off what they learned."

Allie tipped her head back with a laugh. "Ah, I see," she said, gaze veering toward the clock on the wall. "And are Greyson and his family on their way?"

Bree pressed her forehead against baby Jacob's warm little head, smiling as his eyes twinkled. "He should be."

"I was so happy to hear that his dad and Ms. Carson are hitting it off," Allie said, arranging a holiday throw along the back of the couch.

"Me too." A burst of warmth and satisfaction washed through her at the thought. "He's such a great man. I wonder if Todd's ready to find someone yet." She bounced Jacob on her hip. "He's been clean for about a year now. And Greyson said he's doing a great job of running the orchard."

The doorbell rang, the loud chime echoing in the room as all went still. Bree glanced up to see Allie and Braden look at one another across the room.

"You guys going to answer that?" she asked.

"Yeah." Braden cleared his throat and motioned for Allie to join him at the front. "Just uh... stay there for a few seconds, and then you can come out."

Allie rushed to get the baby from her arms, snagging a small blanky off the couch as she went. Bree scrunched her face as the couple closed the door behind them, leaving her alone in the house. *Come out? Why?*

"Weird," she muttered, walking slowly toward the front door.

She pulled the thing open before pressing the lever on the screen door.

Whoa, where did all of these people come from?

There, on the snow-covered ground, stood two rows of people, each holding a light of some sort. Candles, Bree realized as she climbed down the salt-rock covered steps. She let go of the railing at the base, followed a small, dotted trail leading toward the group. It took her a moment to realize the dark dots creating the trail were rose petals, crimson against the white snow.

Ice crunched beneath her shoes as she made her way to the opening of the aisle they'd created. Bree took time to glance at each beautiful face lit by the flame they held. Braden, Paige, and Jillian. Allie and baby Jacob, who looked mesmerized by the glowing sight.

It was warmer here, the gathered flames fighting the

chill of the night.

Greyson's dad, Lloyd, stood next to Ms. Carson, the two seeming to sneak a meaningful glance at one another in the candlelight. Todd was there too, giving Bree a warm grin as their eyes met. Bree was pleased to see Allie's brother there too. Logan and Candice, each carting a baby at one hip.

A warm burst of emotion flooded her chest as she caught sight of Lilly and Earl next. Oh, how Bree loved them. When Braden married Allie, her loving parents had embraced him as one of their own. Even more, they'd wrapped their affectionate arms around Bree and her children, giving Sophie and Carter the grandparents they never had. It was fitting that they'd be here in a moment like this.

With the Christmas lights glowing behind her, illuminating the very house she grew up in, Bree sensed the presence of her parents, sensed that they were smiling down on them in the moment – alongside Greyson's dear mother too – and oh, what a gift that was.

A feeling of reverence filled the small space, swelling in her chest as she wiped moisture from her eyes. Bree had, of course, been very aware of the man standing at the other end of the aisle, Sophie and Carter at either side. She just hadn't let her gaze settle on him. Yet.

She started at the half-circle of candles at his feet. Let her gaze travel up the length of him. No man looked better in a suit than Greyson Law. She'd seen magazine articles featuring him in that attire, and it was no wonder the camera loved him. He straightened his suit coat as she neared, his gaze on her, the look of determination on his face.

She felt the warmth of each flame as she passed, her eyes shifting from Greyson to the loved ones surrounding her. Carter shuffled his candle from one hand to the next before waving at her. Sophie began hopping up and down. Bree wondered if they'd ever worn such big smiles.

Her gaze settled back on Greyson as she came to a stop.

He cleared his throat, straightened his suit coat once more, and dropped to one knee right there in the snow. Her heart jumped, sputtered, and sped into action.

The group shifted, creating a circle around them as Greyson took her hand in his. "Bree Elizabeth Fox," he said, rubbing a warm thumb over her cold knuckles. "I've loved you since we were in grade school. While you were busy reading books and ignoring my very existence, I was writing poems about you for class. Arranging secret kisses at parties. And finding ways to ask you out. Not that any of that worked," he muttered under his breath.

She chuckled, wiping at the cold tip of her nose.

"I finally got a chance to get close to you. Some might say the circumstances weren't great, being undercover and all, but it gave me a chance to know you. To really know the woman who'd caught my attention all those years ago. I came to find that... that I had dang good taste even back then."

The crowd chuckled. A small breeze picked up, causing

the circle of flames to tilt and sway.

"I came to know a woman who has a passion for life, even when tough times worked to snuff that out. A woman who's strong and resilient and beautiful in every way. A woman I want to spend the rest of my life with."

He dug into his pocket, pulled out a small box.

Sophie, still hopping in place, let out a squeal, earning chuckles from the group once more. Cameras flashed, and Bree was grateful for whoever had thought to take pictures of the moment. A moment she'd never forget.

"I love you, Bree. And I'm going to love you for the rest of my days. Days I want to spend with you and the kids." He cracked open the box, revealing a diamond that glistened like magic in the candlelight. "Will you marry me?"

Now it was Bree's smile that couldn't get any wider. She let her gaze drift from him, and circle the group surrounding her. People she loved. Family. Sophie nodded her head at her. Carter bounced up and down now too. Greyson bit at his lip.

"Yes," she assured, reaching out as he stood. "Of course I will."

At once she was wrapped in Greyson's strong embrace as he lifted her off the ground. The crowd whistled and cheered.

After setting her back on her feet, Greyson turned to the group and threw a triumphant hand in the air. "We're getting married!"

EPILOGUE

It was often described as butterflies — the tingling, fluttering sensation of nerves and excitement in one's belly. Bree pictured a mass of monarchs taking flight in hers as they neared the orchard home, the setting sun lighting their way.

With window paint announcing their *Just Married* status, Greyson and Bree had driven straight to the airport. Still in their wedding clothes, they'd hopped a plane from Montana to Oregon for their honeymoon. Braden and Allie agreed it was the perfect place for such a celebration, and Bree was sure they were right. Especially in springtime.

With that thought, the orchard came into view, causing a gasp to pull from Bree's throat. "Wow," she breathed.

"Ditto," Greyson mumbled.

Gold light from the sunset poured over the long lines of fruit trees, adding to their whimsical beauty. Who knew the lush rows could possibly look better than they did at harvest, with the juicy, colorful fruit filling the limbs?

But in that moment, Bree was sure that the fall sight paled in comparison to what spring had done. Puffy blossoms of bright white and pale pink stood in great contrast to the deep green. Like rows of cotton candy growing in some magical land.

She rolled down the window as Greyson slowed alongside the property. There was distance between the orchard and roadside, but that didn't stop the sweet balmy scent from filling the air. Bree pulled in a deep breath, absorbing the joy it lent. It was just one of the many gifts offered to her in that day, and she wanted to take time to enjoy it.

"Wait," she said, reaching into her purse. "Let me get a few pictures." Sunlight bounced off the screen of her phone as she snapped. "Let's get one with us in it now. I'll send it to the kids." She motioned for him to lean into her. Once he did, Bree straightened her arm and snapped a picture. Newlyweds with their honeymoon destination in the background. Greyson turned and kissed her on the cheek, the coarse feel of his trimmed facial hair grazing her skin. She snapped a picture of that too and grinned. "This is perfect."

Greyson slipped a hand around her neck, his sea-colored eyes burning with desire. He tilted his head, pressed his lips to hers, a sudden intensity behind his kiss. She'd been anticipating this night for a long time now. They both had. And as his velvet tongue grazed hers, as he moaned low in his chest, Bree wondered if they'd make it into the house at all.

She pulled away, gulped, and smiled as Greyson subtly shook his head.

"My patience is up," he mumbled. "I'm ready to take you here and now."

She laughed. "Let's just get inside. From there, you name the place."

After a moment of contemplation, Greyson complied and set his gaze back on the road while pressing the gas.

Beneath the arc of oak branches they went, only this time the leaves were shades of luscious green. He tore off his seatbelt once the car was parked. "Be right back," he muttered.

She watched as he wrestled with the keys. First the screen door. The main door next. And then a soft, yellow glow lit the giant window through the drapes. He'd tossed his tuxedo jacket during the long drive, but his white shirt remained. Bow untied and dangling at either side of his loosened buttons. Bree had never seen a finer specimen in all her life. Doubted one could exist.

He pulled open her car door. "Mrs. Law," he said, stooping low beside her. He scooped her from the seat with ease and kicked the car door closed. "Anywhere I want?" he murmured, his warm breath teasing her neck.

"Mmm, hmm," she managed, though it sounded more like a sigh. Once inside, Greyson kicked the door to a near close. With her solidly in his arms, he backed against it, closing it completely before setting her to her feet. He gave her the questioning lift of his brow, and Bree realized the significance of where they were. Their first kiss. Well, first *adult* kiss.

Barely had the thought come to her when Greyson brought his mouth to hers in a teasing, playful kiss.

Bree moved her hands up his chest as he kissed her again. Slow and alluring. One masterful kiss after the next. He'd only just said his patience was up; she wouldn't know it by his measured cadence. The seductive way he lingered in each blissful touch, taste, and pleasure.

His strong hands wrapped around her hips, pulling her closer as he moved to her neck. *Mmm, yes.* Planting a near desperation with each spellbinding kiss. Her fingers slid into his hair where she gripped at fistfuls, a soft whine escaping her lips.

"I'm the luckiest man alive," he murmured against her skin. "I can finally say that you're mine, Mrs. Law."

Yes, she was. And as Greyson's hands moved to the back of her dress, began working at the zipper there, she agreed with the fullness of her heart. Finally free from her past, Bree could give herself to her future. And better yet, she mused as her dress fell to the floor, she could give her whole self to Greyson, the man who – after all this time – had finally managed to win her heart.

And oh, how wonderful it was!

Dear Reader,

Thank you for taking the time to read Fresh Starts. As a reader myself, I dive into novels seeking an enjoyable getaway from the daily grind – I hope this story provided that for you! If you enjoyed the book, I could really use (and would sincerely appreciate) your rating and or review on Amazon or Goodreads.

If you'd like to contact me or sign up to hear about my latest releases, join my mailing list by visiting kimberlykrey.com and clicking "get on my mailing list". Also follow me on Facebook, Bookbub, and Amazon for info about my other novels, sales, and giveaways. Simply search Kimberly Krey on each site.

Also by Kimberly Krey:

The Sweet Montana Bride Series
Witness Protection – Rancher Style

by KIMBERLY KREY

(Complete collection on Amazon now)

Reese's Cowboy Kiss

Blake's Story
(Sample chapter included)

Jade's Cowboy Crush

Gavin's Story

Cassie's Cowboy Crave

Shane's Story

Sample Chapter from Reese's Cowboy Kiss. When Reese shows up at Emerson Ranch, Blake is left with just one question: Did he just add to his troubles, or find the girl of his dreams?

CHAPTER ONE

Reese glanced over the large crowd of dancing bodies as she caught her breath. It hadn't been easy to keep up with the fast-paced line dance in a gown and high heels, but she'd be lying if she said it hadn't been fun. Still, it was almost time to pass off her crown to this year's winner, and she needed to freshen up.

With a shallow sigh, she searched the crowd once more, glad when she failed to see the man with the unyielding gaze. The gawking stranger had set her on edge since she'd arrived. Perhaps he'd gone home, she decided, feeling hopeful at the mere thought.

The rowdy song came to an end while she moved along the outskirts of the dance floor. A warm Texas breeze wafted over her skin just as the band started a new tune – a slow and easy number. The kind that had her picturing warm days at the lake. Or romantic strolls on a moonlit night. She smiled as a young couple among the group caught her attention. Their intimate contact seeming to reach into that longing place in her heart.

Reese's glance shifted to the man's hand, clenched around the woman's waist as he kissed her, passion oozing from his every move. Never had she been kissed in such a manner. Or even known a man she wished would kiss her that way.

"Some folks just don't know when to get a room," a familiar voice spoke.

Reese spun around to see her younger brother, CJ, standing close by. Her face flushed with heat as her gaze fell back to the couple. "Yeah," she agreed with a sigh. "I guess you're right."

"Why ain't you dancin' with nobody?" CJ asked. "Too big of a snob?"

She slapped his arm. "You know I'd never turn anyone down. I'm just looking for Mama, is all. She's got my makeup bag."

"Well, wish I could help ya, but I'm off to find a pretty little thing to dance with." He flashed her a mischievous grin, rolling his shoulders back.

"You enjoy yourself," she said. "And don't you go makin' out on the dance floor."

Her brother cocked one eyebrow, gave her a wink, and then disappeared into the crowd. Reese's gaze wandered to the auction tables along the stage. And there was her mom, frantically scribbling on a tattered notepad.

The lights on the stage were bright against the night, causing Reese to squint as she moved. She'd made it only part-way up the steps when a wiry hand clamped around her wrist.

"Would you like to dance?"

Reese spun around, knowing who'd asked before even seeing the man. She forced a polite smile as her fears were confirmed. It was him – the man who'd burned holes straight through her body with his steely glare alone. He was fairly thin, but his features were soft and round; from the outline of his clean-shaven jaw, to his small nose and bulbous cheeks. He blinked a few times, his bright green eyes watering from the blaring stage lights.

"I'd love to," she lied, guessing the makeup would have to wait. Her peace of mind would be put on hold too, but it was just one dance. She could get through it.

His clammy fingers skidded down her wrist to where he took hold of her hand, pulling her deep into the crowd before settling on a spot. Reese grimaced, suddenly feeling like a giant. With the help of her three-inch heels, she was half-a-head taller than the guy.

He glanced up at her, the intensity she'd seen in his eyes replaced by something entirely different. Reese tilted her head; she'd made a habit of looking for the inner light in folks – that unique spark that made each person shine. She could usually sense it quickly enough. A humble kindness or confident gleam. A determined spirit or forgiving heart. Surely this guy was no exception.

Or was he? She furrowed her brows as she looked at him further, unable to get past the odd shifting of his eyes. The strange way he evaded her gaze.

He was simply shy, Reese decided, as he stepped closer and wrapped his arms around her back. She rested her hands on his shoulders in return, unnerved by his tense and rigid form. Her skin objected to him too. The very feel of him against her was all wrong.

There was an obvious rhythm to the slow song playing, but the guy barely lifted a foot. Reese had danced with several men that evening. Everything from true Texas gentlemen to cocky, bull riding brutes. But none of them had made her feel the way this guy did. On edge. Almost ... afraid. She pulled in a deep breath, counting down the seconds, dying for the song to end. She felt guilty for being so turned off by the man; he was obviously nervous. Most likely he'd simply been working up the nerve to ask her to dance as he'd stared throughout the evening. Why couldn't she be endeared to him instead?

The answer stood in the energy surrounding him; it felt off. Eager. Intense. And as much as she wanted to make polite conversation to ease the discomfort of it all, she couldn't think of a word to say. He'd just have to be the one to speak up first.

Yet as the band played on, the odd stranger never uttered a word. And as ugly as it felt, staying silent as they danced, Reese did just that.

At last the music began to fade as a deep voice blared from the stage – Corbin Carmichael, the host of the annual event. "One last song, folks," he announced, "and then our Pearland Rose and our new title holder will take the stage for the passing of the crown." Hoots, hollers, and cat calls sounded from the crowd. "Now let's hear one more round of applause for our rip roaring band for the night, the Texan Blasters. I wanna see all y'all on the dance floor for this one. Time to get those boots a stompin'!"

Reese cleared her throat and backed away from the awkward man, causing him to drop his arms at last. "Thanks for the dance," she said, turning away from him. She was anxious to be free from the man, to find her mom, and to get freshened up before passing on her crown.

It was that tight and sudden grip around her wrist that stopped her short, a repeat of what he'd done the first time. His palm felt cool and wet. "Guess it's time to finally give up your title," the young man said. "I'm really going to miss seeing you in that crown."

Reese's gaze had been set on the grip he had on her. She glanced over to the bodies stepping to the line dance before looking into the man's face. Beads of sweat coated his forehead and upper lip. The surface of his cheeks looked red and swollen. "I hardly ever wore the thing," she said.

"You wore it to all your public appearances." His fingers loosened the slightest bit. The corner of his lip twitched.

Reese nodded, his intrusive gaze causing her to shift; the striking green of his eyes becoming oddly familiar. "Do I know you from somewhere?" she asked.

"High school," he explained. "I'm Donald Turnsbro. We were in Mr. Li's biology class together."

"That's right," she said. Only she couldn't actually place him. It'd been five years since high school after all. The crowd started to move in on them, forcing their bodies close once more. "Well, thanks again for the dance," Reese said. "I better go freshen up." She darted toward the stage, barely dodging a collision with the dancers on the floor. She folded her arms over her chest as she sped up the stairs, recalling the way he'd reached for her wrist; the recollection making her shiver.

She spotted her mom next to the auction table, arranging paper slips next to each item sold. "Mama?"

A large smile spread over her face as she spun around. "Hi, darlin'. You're going to be up in just a bit."

Reese remained motionless as she adjusted the hair around her crown. "Is it a mess?" she asked.

"Nah, I've seen worse. But here, you'll be wanting this." She spun around and began scrounging under the picnic table at the edge of the stage, the curtain barely covering the mess of tote bags, Tupperware, and boxes. "Here." She handed over her makeup bag. "Doesn't look like there's a line to the ladies room. Why don't you sneak on in there."

A deep sigh made its way through Reese's chest as she tucked the small bag under her arm. "Thank you."

"What's a matter, baby? Sad about giving up your crown?"

Reese shrugged, looking over the crowd for the strange man. "Maybe a little."

Her mom placed her hands on Reese's cheeks, waited until her gaze settled back on her. "Well there's a bright side to it, ya know? Close your eyes and take a whiff."

Reese looked back at her warily.

"Trust me, baby. Just do it."

While releasing another sigh, Reese closed her eyes. Her mom's hands moved to Reese's upper arms.

"Now," she said, "inhale a nice, deep breath."

Reese inhaled until her chest rose.

"What do you smell?" she asked her.

"I don't know."

A chuckle escaped her mom's lips. "Boy, you *have* been dieting for a while. Haven't ya? Try again."

Reese focused as she breathed in, noting the incredible aroma, thick on the evening air. Rich and smoky, tangy and sweet. "Barbeque," she said. "Smells just like Grandma Dee's."

"That's right. And you don't have to worry about fitting into these gowns or keeping trim for any special events. Soon as you hand over that crown, let the new girl count calories and you go get some *real* food."

Reese gasped. "Mama," she said with a chuckle. "I can't believe my ears."

"What? I ain't suggesting you let yourself go completely. But you need to take advantage of the perks of *not* being Miss Pearland's Rose."

Reese smiled. "Yeah, maybe you're right." Her mouth watered at the thought.

"That-a girl. Now skedaddle on outta here and go freshen up." Her mom had managed to distract her from the disturbing encounter with the strange man; Reese was grateful for it. She always did know how to make things right.

Feeling a bit more at ease, Reese sped toward the restrooms behind the stage. She gripped hold of the thick, black curtain along the sidewall, knowing the bathroom doors were entirely hidden by the thing, and spotted a man among the hefty cloth.

Her heart jumped.

She tilted her head, anxious to get a better look at his face, when he disappeared into the fabric folds. With renewed force, Reese shoved the curtain aside once more, wondering if her mind was playing tricks on her. She might not have gotten a solid look at him, but the man she'd seen looked just like Donald Turnsbro; she was sure of it.

Her hands trembled slightly as she tugged the curtain back one last time, knowing she was in the right place. And there it was, the sign she'd been looking for, the letters carved right into the bathroom door: *Senoritas.*

Anxious thumps pressed their way through her chest as she pried open the heavy oak door, desperate to get into the quiet space and grip hold of her rampant thoughts.

The music died down as the door closed behind her, the soft glow of light a welcoming change. She skipped the mirror altogether and sped straight for the only stall. Reese had the door partway closed before she noticed a young woman standing at the sink. She tilted her head to catch eye contact with her through the mirror. Blonde hair, a sash over her shoulder, and a dress that matched the color of Reese's gown.

"Howdy," Reese offered with a shaky voice.

The girl blinked her lashes through a wand of mascara before glancing at her. "Can't wait to get my hands on that crown," she said. "Are you sad about giving it up?"

Reese shook her head. "Only a little. I mean, it's

been a great year, and you're going to enjoy every minute of it I'm sure, but I think I'm about ready to be done with it and move on. You know?"

The girl reached into her makeup bag before twisting a small lid off a tube of lip gloss. She smothered it over her top lip as she spoke. "I don't know," she said, moving to the bottom lip. "I'm not gonna stop here. I plan to go onto Brazoria County, Miss Texas, Miss America. I want it all."

Reese smiled, charmed by the young woman's ambition. There was quite a difference in their ages. Pearland's new rose had won at the young age of eighteen, while Reese had taken the crown at the maximum age of twenty-three. "Well, good for you. I'll be cheering ya on from the sidelines," she said before closing the stall door. The latch to lock the metal door was old and rusty. Nearly impossible to slide. She tightened her grip around the dull knob and shoved, the loud 'pop' filling the quiet space. "Sorry," Reese said. "Stubborn lock."

Her gaze fell to the small tiles on the floor as she folded her arms over her chest, wishing she could skip the ceremony altogether, slip out the back door and go home. Her interaction with the man on the dance floor had her feeling nervous. Afraid, though she knew it was foolish. The guy couldn't possibly mean her harm. He'd only been awkward was all. Not dangerous. She nodded to herself, convinced to shake it off.

With a wave of assurance urging her forward, Reese reached for the latch to unlock the stall. Just as she shoved the stubborn thing into place, an earsplitting explosion rocked the room. Reese pressed her hands to her ears and ducked down, cringing as the deafening blast echoed throughout the small space.

A gunshot? Had somebody just shot a gun? Her heart thudded against her chest, the pressing rhythm making it hard to breathe. A sharp ringing pierced her ears as she lifted her chin, and then straightened to a stand altogether. Through the crack of the stall frame, a view of the mirror came into sight. Only she didn't see the girl. Instead Reese saw a man reflected there – his green eyes wild. And then he was gone, lost in the black fabric folds.

The door creaked to a close. The shrill ringing only intensified as she yanked open the flimsy stall door. Blood. A dark, oozing pool of it soaked the satin banner across the young girl's chest. A hand flew to Reese's mouth as she screamed, a horrid realization coming to mind: The man in the mirror – it had been him. The one who'd sent her rushing to the restroom in fear. He was dangerous after all. And though it hurt to think it, Reese was certain the bullet in the girl's chest had been meant for her.

FRESH STARTS

ABOUT THE AUTHOR

Writing Romance That's Clean Without Losing the Steam!

Kimberly Krey lives in the Salt Lake Valley with her husband, four children, and two dogs. She has a great love for literature, family, and food.

Made in the USA
Charleston, SC
27 September 2016